Also by Anita Brookner

Altered
States

Altered
States

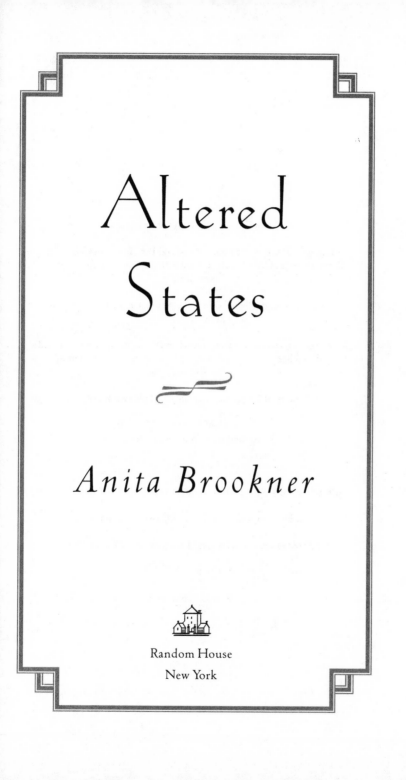

Anita Brookner

Random House
New York

This work was originally published in Great Britain by Jonathan Cape,
Ltd., London, in 1996.

Altered States is a work of fiction. The characters in it have been invented
by the author. Any resemblance to people living or dead is purely
coincidental.

Library of Congress Cataloging-in-Publication Data

Brookner, Anita.
Altered states/Anita Brookner.
p.   cm.
ISBN 0-679-44973-6
I. Title.
PR6052.R5816A77   1996   823'.941—dc20   96–17268

Random House website address: http://www.randomhouse.com/

Printed in the United States of America on acid-free paper

2 4 6 8 9 7 5 3

First U.S. Edition

Book design by Caroline Cunningham

Altered States

1

The woman on the station platform had her back to me. If she had turned round I would have been able to satisfy myself that she was not someone I had once known. Even at this distance of time and place I should have known that other woman anywhere. As it was I could only contemplate this particular back view and once again return my memories to the oubliette to which I had consigned them. I was in any case reluctant to proceed to an identification. The woman on the station platform was smartly but not fashionably dressed in a sober chestnut-coloured suit and the sort of brown felt hat still favoured by certain middle-aged middle-class women in Germany. I doubted whether this woman was German, although she certainly looked European. This much was attested by her shoes, which again were smart without being fashionable: narrow brown brogues, with a medium heel. I noticed that they were brilliantly polished.

That I was able to contemplate this woman at such length no doubt says something about myself, but I am averse to falsely intelligent summaries, such as seem to be prevalent nowadays, and prefer long moments of reverie and speculation, which seem to me more conducive to satisfactory conclusions. We were the only two people on this particular platform, and I was only there because I had come down to the station to buy the English papers, which usually arrived at about four o'clock. The light was already going: it was a misty dusky afternoon, still quite mild, but with that particular stillness that speaks so eloquently of the decline of the year, and with it all hopes one had had in the spring, season of false promises. Behind me, in the town, I had left the subdued comfort of the English Tea Rooms: beyond, at the end of the main street, at the foot of the steep path leading up to the hilly suburbs where all the more prosperous villas stood, was the Hotel Eden, and my small and dreadfully quiet room. This was too like a monastic cell to convey any prospect other than that of austere rest, such as might be appreciated by those who had spent the day walking, as I was supposed to have done. Sometimes I managed to coax some whispery music out of the bedside radio; that, if I were particularly tired, was generally distraction enough. But on this quiet afternoon I was bored, and had felt the need of some human presence, or at least of newsprint. If I lingered on this station platform it was because it seemed an appropriate place to be at the end of an uneventful afternoon. And because, for one shocking moment, I had thought the woman with her back to me, with her sensible hat and shoes, might be Sarah Miller, or Sarah de Leuze, as she now presumably was, who had the gift of turning up when least expected. It was part of her ravaging charm to disarm one with her presence when one had thought her lost for ever, only to disappear again when one's need had turned to the most intense and hopeless longing.

I felt that longing now. That was why I lingered, in the misty half light, in my bulky English clothes: Burberry and tweed cap, woollen socks and walking shoes. I tend to wear everything when I travel, so as not to carry much. With my small bag I can pick up and disappear quite easily. I had nothing much to do with my time, and no one was expecting me, which was why I lingered, a substantial English ghost, haunting the woman in the German hat, until it became borne in on me that she was not at all like Sarah, was older (though Sarah would now be nearly my age), was more settled, with a fantastic air of capability conveyed by her back.

A housewife, I concluded, although that term is anachronistic these days, or perhaps just a wife, married to one of those silent substantial peaceable men in whom this region abounds. The woman too had an air of peaceable worth about her, and in my fantasy I endowed her not only with an excellent digestion but a good conscience, the one usually contingent upon the other, in no particular order. Then the woman shifted her weight from one ankle to the other, and the way her knees came together reminded me again of Sarah, and her habit of swaying from one foot to the other, a mocking smile on her face, as if enjoying one's too fervent gaze. If this woman were Sarah I would fold my arms around her, as I had always tried to do, and sometimes succeeded in doing, before she escaped. There was of course no question of my touching this utterly respectable woman, whose face I still had not seen. It was simply that the combination of dull weather and grave silence, the thin white mist that so often descends without warning here and seems to lay delicate fingers on the skin of one's face, and the benign emptiness of this quiet little town might have emboldened me, not to embark on any crude adventure, but to remember the woman for whom I had been searching, and not only metaphorically but in pursuit of a mission. That was the fruitless task which I had undertaken in order to pacify a poor sick woman, not quite a relative, on what was too obviously her deathbed.

I felt that this person on the platform might hold the key to the mystery, might in some extraordinary way enlighten me as to where Sarah might be, for although I tended to see her everywhere I had not yet laid eyes on her in ways that might be construed as physical, verifiable, even disappointing, as the end of certain stories sometimes turns out to be. This woman in the brown hat, this very real woman, would no doubt have a settled existence and many friends: she could ask questions, might already know a certain amount. The fact that her presence, or rather what I could intuit from her back view, was so compelling, awoke in me the suspicious feeling that if she were not Sarah herself, restored to me in this strange manner after an absence of fifteen years, then she might possibly know where Sarah might be. My desire to address her, so that she would turn and show me her face, was negated by my immobility, my inability to move, and by the weight of memory that I allowed to overwhelm me for a brief moment. I felt that even if I managed to open my mouth no sound would come. Besides, the silence of that still afternoon laid a kind of enchantment on the scene which was not unpleasant to me: to break it would have seemed unmannerly. I felt that the woman and I were contained in this enchantment, and that the station of this little town was the setting for some drama that would eventually unfold, and in which we would both be bidden to speak, although our lines had not yet been written.

Then the guard came out and posted the sign for the Geneva train, and within seconds people arrived from nowhere, some of them dragging suitcases on wheels, and I lost sight of the woman who was probably—undoubtedly—not Sarah. When the train disappeared and silence was restored she was nowhere to be seen. In an hour's time she would be in Geneva, perhaps in an apartment in the rue des Bains—the last address I had for Sarah—drinking a cup of coffee, raising a forkful of cake to her mouth. I stood for a few minutes, feeling heavy in my raincoat, feeling too a regret that nevertheless had something anticipatory about it, a very small dawning of excitement that was less like an ending than a beginning. Then I turned, and with my papers under my arm, began the long and by now chilly walk back to my hotel.

I usually take my holiday late in the year, leaving current matters in the capable hands of my partner, Brian Smith. I am, as ever, beguiled by the prospect of a golden October, trees still full but changing colour, thoughts of the vintage occupying one's mind. In my politically incorrect way I like to think of smiling inhabitants ready to welcome me. These people would once have been described as peasants, though if peasants still exist they are mostly indoors watching television. What I invariably encounter is this curious sense of withdrawal, this intermittent mist, and trees a sullen but darkening green. I do not altogether dislike this, although sometimes I straighten up from unpacking my bag with a sigh, knowing that long walks and the English papers are to be my only distractions. There is no one who expects me, no one to whom I might telephone, but I have always been reasonably content with my own company. My mother always commended me for this, taking it to be a sign of character. Her values were old-fashioned, somewhat austere. I can hardly blame her for her reticence over my choice of the woman I was to marry, although she was very kind to my wife. As it turned out her kindness was needed.

I now feel that this interval, which I describe to others as a holiday, is peculiarly suited to one of my temperament, which is stolid, and my history, which is not. I accept the solitude, the routines, as old people do, and although not technically old—fifty-five is not old these days—I begin to anticipate a time when small landmarks, such as my mid-morning coffee at the Grand Café de la Place, and my walk to the station to pick up the English papers, will be appreciated. My old age will come as no surprise to me, and something tells me that I might spend it here, in this little town of Vif—a misnomer, for no place could be more somnolent—on the Franco-Swiss border. I come here every other year in October; it is healthy, and monumentally dull. In the spring I spend a week or ten days at a small cottage I own at Shoreham, on the south coast. I am always glad to get back to London and the office, which casts my plans for later life in a rather illusory light.

It is just that when I am here, with nothing at all likely to happen, I feel incapable of leaving, as if under some sort of sedative. And although the place has little to offer except tranquillity, this tranquillity has become fraught with consequences, owing to the burden placed on me, and which I was only half minded to discharge. Old Mrs Miller, with her strangely changing name and identity, had been lying on the sofa when I had last been to see her, her ugly feet protruding from under the shawl she had taken to wearing in the house. 'Find Sarah for me,' she had said, and her eyes were still trustful. I assured her that I would try, knowing that the whole thing was an impossibility. I had nothing to go on apart from two addresses on a piece of squared paper: the pencil was faded and the paper limp from much folding. One address, the one in Paris, I already knew about; the other, in the rue des Bains, in Geneva, is almost certainly unreliable.

I have my own reasons for searching for Sarah, reasons I

am careful not to admit to, even to myself. Grand passions are no longer the order of the day; divorce has replaced fidelity in the gardens of the West. I am not even sure that my memory of her is exact, for I frequently winced at her cruelty until I learned to laugh at it. What is needed, I tell myself, is a certain pragmatism. I shall not find her, but I shall have been in her vicinity, and the impression I shall take away from my quest will be precisely this dullness, this inconclusiveness, the peace of this little town, an apt comment on my inadequacy, but not a harsh one. Maybe all life-long searches end like this, I tell myself, as I begin the steep climb back to my hotel, and the only verdict on all my activities, on my life, in fact, contained in the withheld kindliness of the slowly and inexorably descending night.

2

My name is Alan Sherwood and I am a solicitor, as were my father and grandfather before me. By a pleasing coincidence my partner, Brian Smith, is the grandson of the original Smith: we are thus the true inheritors of the firm of Sherwood Smith, founded nearly one hundred years ago. We have our offices in Gloucester Place and we pride ourselves on our effectiveness, although the premises are not imposing and by no means extensive. There is one office apiece for each of us, while our clerk, Telfer, who is into Eastern religions, has to share a rather pleasant room overlooking the back garden with Mrs Roche, who is more of a hostess than a secretary and who knows more about the business than any of us (or so we tell her). Mrs Roche in her turn commands—and that is the right word—the services of Amanda, Julie and Anne and their computers; they share an adjacent room, also overlooking the garden, and have charge of the coffee machine. Brian and I, soberly dressed in dark suits and white shirts, look out on to Gloucester Place and its curiously bleak Georgian façades. In all the years afforded me for study of this particular architectural style I cannot view it as anything better than town planning of the cheapest kind, guaranteed to confer a deadly conformity on the urban landscape. Gower Street is another example. I am a Victorian myself, or better still an Edwardian. In my opinion Lutyens should be our national architect and afforded all the respect normally given to Christopher Wren. He too has his boring moments.

Brian is my oldest friend. We have known each other all our lives, were at school and university together, although our paths diverged for a time after we came down. Brian went to Hong Kong to stay with an uncle, a prominent lawyer there, while I spent three guilty but hedonistic years in Paris, supposedly studying international law but in fact doing very little. My memories of Paris in those years are not of Sartre and Camus but of the nightclubs to which I took my French girl-friend Simone. We went to the *Rose Rouge*, the *Vieux Colombier*, the *Cabane Cubaine*, and believed for a time that we need never grow up. But family pressure extended itself imperceptibly, and when I received news from home that my father was ill I said goodbye to Simone and left Paris, never willingly to return. I had been happy there, but I knew that this particular form of happiness could not be sustained. I also knew that once I reached home—and it was always home—I should become what I was always meant to be, a respectable member of the middle class, affectionate towards my mother, reliable in an emergency, but unsentimental. Emotional clients think me too severe; I tend to say nothing and watch them impassively while they reach for their handkerchiefs. Oddly enough this does not put them off. The women tend to come to me, the men to Brian. 'You appeal to the masochists,' Brian says. 'The sadists know I am one of them.' Actually he has a kind heart, as he has shown me over the years.

Brian is a livelier character than I am, and is unfaithful to his wife Felicity with a variety of women, usually in the lunch hour. I have had to cover for him several times, particularly when Felicity telephones. She supposes me to have her interests at heart, since I was best man at their wedding: in fact I like her enormously, though I have come to dread her voice on the telephone. For decency's sake I have to make conversation with her, while expressing surprise that she does not know that Brian will be out of the office for a good part of the day. Surely you remember him mentioning it, I say. In that way I avoid telling a direct lie, justifying my squeamishness on the grounds that Brian has the stronger claim on my friendship. I do not approve of his behaviour but I tolerate it. Brian has proved a powerful ally in the past. I have to remember that it was Brian who broke the news to me of my daughter's death. One does not forget these things.

We both hold the treacherous view that men are superior to women in the areas of love and work, since we appear to derive more pleasure from these activities than we are supposed to. Although our natures and temperaments are quite different, Brian and I share moments of levity in the office at the expense of plaintive women suing for alimony and other hard luck cases. We also derive enormous pleasure from the appearance of our secretaries, all of whom are nevertheless protected by us: we view their innocence as part of our responsibility, and even Brian respects this. He would not dream of offering them more than an appreciative compliment. They in their turn are devoted to him, and are more at ease with him than they are with me. They seem to sense something not quite straightforward in my sternness, and they are not wrong. The even landscape of my life became quite jagged for a time, and my equilibrium suffered for some time after that. It is not that they are frightened of me, rather that they are more at home with Brian and his affectionate and meaningless compliments. It is as if they sense that a compliment from me might have an undesirable weight. They are right. My conduct towards them is entirely proper, and I am not particularly interested in any one of them beyond their performance in the office. This confers on them a degree of immunity which they welcome. In this and other ways they negate my threat as a man, although they are clever enough to perceive this threat. It is as if they know that, left to myself, I could become a lonely fanatic. I believe that, apart from my mother, these excellent girls are the only ones to penetrate my disguise.

But is it a disguise? I neither parade nor deny the fact that I suffered a grievous blow while still fairly young, and that I do not appear to be taking any steps to restoring my life to any sort of normality. This is what disconcerts me. They know that my wife died after only eleven months of marriage, and that our baby was stillborn. They know that I live alone in my flat in Wigmore Street and am quite kind to elderly acquaintances. They suppose my heart to be broken, although I give no sign of this, and they must surely be disarmed by the occasional bark of laughter that has been heard to issue from my office. This worries them, as well it might. They are more comfortable with my Robespierre-like impassivity as I wait patiently but without indulgence for female clients to put away their handkerchiefs. They have no access to my secret life, which is not one of licence, or sexual excess (would that it were!), but rather of emotional aberration. I have been in love, and was once in love for a very long time, but I claim no indulgence for these facts. I persuade myself that nobody knows about my love for Sarah, not even

Brian, but this is unlikely. Brian has always been supremely tactful; even at the height of my madness he had the grace to keep his comments to a minimum. Men are better at this than women. Perhaps it is an example of the sort of affection between men that women rarely understand.

Although solitary by nature I should welcome a large family, the sort of panoply of odd relatives that surrounded me in childhood. Mad old ladies have never frightened me, although I have not had much success with younger ones. The first love of my life was my mother, a delightful woman by any standards, not merely my own. She was my father's second wife, the first, always referred to as 'poor Mary', having died abruptly of a wasp sting to which she proved allergic. My mother was a friend of her daughter's; her subsequent marriage to their father, many years older, was regarded as a scandal by the daughters, Sybil and Marjorie, and my mother was never truly forgiven, though relations of a kind were resumed some years later. The girls, as they were invariably known, seemed mysteriously older than my mother, although only a few years separated them, a consequence perhaps of the dreadful dignity they assumed whenever my mother tried to revive the friendship. But as they were incompetent they often had recourse to her counsel, particularly in later life, when my mother was a widow, a fact which seemed to mollify them.

The girls were devoted to each other. Marjorie, who was lame and walked with a stick when I knew her, was presumably unrecognisable as the once dashing redhead she had been as a girl, when she owned and ran a dress shop in Dover Street. The day when she could no longer afford the overheads, and when 'Marjorie' ceased to exist, was the saddest day of her life. She declined slowly after that; her limp became more pronounced and she spent lonely days at home, earning a living from her now somewhat dated skills as a dressmaker. Gradually she became more and more dependent on her sister Sybil. When I knew her she already looked old: her make-up was craggy and her hair dyed the colour of Mansion Polish. I rather liked her, as did my mother.

The chief eccentricity of these two sisters was the fact that barely into middle life they made active plans for their old age. These plans were quite concrete: they were to take a flat, on which they had already put down a deposit, in one of those converted country houses that turn themselves into retirement homes for old people with money. They frequently visited this place, which was near the Dorset Coast, not far from Bournemouth, to see that their investment was in order. This despite the fact that Sybil was a married woman with a small daughter, Sarah. Somehow married life was expected to take second place to this plan of a lifetime, a fact apparently accepted by Sybil's husband, Bertram Miller. 'I expect you'll go first, anyway,' Sybil frequently assured her husband. Obligingly he did, slipping down silently behind the counter of the old-established jeweller's shop in High Holborn which he ran with his brother Humphrey.

Sybil was not much put out by this: she saw it as divine confirmation of her plans. With the demise of her husband she was able to make a home for her sister in their house in Parsons Green. As time went on the two women became closer to each other, viewing my mother with suspicion, although frequently telephoning her to ask her to mediate in some quarrel or other, or to go with them to Sarah's school to ask why Sarah was doing so badly and was so disruptive, hurling other girl's hats to the ground and stamping on them before the morning bell had stopped ringing. My mother's calm and authority worked wonders on more than one of these occasions, but she had her reservations about Sarah, whom she thought privately even more odd than her mother and aunt put together.

The connection did not stop with Bertram Miller's death. His brother Humphrey, a melancholy bachelor in his late fifties, was inconsolable: tears often misted his eyes as he sold engagement rings to young couples in High Holborn. The young couples, thinking the tears were for them, pronounced him terribly sweet as they left with their purchases, whereas in fact he was simply lonely. For years the two brothers had run a successful business in wordless harmony. When Bertram married, Humphrey moved out of the family home and bought himself a flat behind Marble Arch, in a fusty, somnolent solid building which suited him very well. He saw his brother every day, so felt that nothing had really happened to alter their relationship. When Bertram died he aged considerably. His heart was no longer in the business, which was itself in decline, owing to extensive building works on either side, old-established premises like their own being knocked down to make way for smart new offices. He would have declined with it, had it not been for the sisters, his sisters-in-law, who came driving in every Sunday from Parsons Green, the back of the car packed with casseroles, pies, roast chickens, Marjorie's special cake, and various other provisions which they calculated would take him through the week until their next visit. The girl Sarah occasionally accompanied them. Humphrey Miller was fond of her, as only a childless man of outstanding simplicity could be. She was always richer by a ten pound note when they left.

I arrived home from a friend's house one Saturday afternoon to find some kind of conclave taking place in my mother's drawing-room. That the occasion was significant was advertised by the fact that although Sybil was formally dressed, as she always was, in her heather mixture coat and skirt and trilby hat, her face and neck were deeply flushed. Both she and Marjorie were silent, though clearly longing to impart something of moment.

'Have you eaten?' asked my mother, her usual greeting.

I assured her that I had.

'I think we should like some more tea,' she went on. 'The girls are rather upset.'

'What do you think of this, then, Alan?' said Sybil, who could wait no longer. 'Humphrey's getting married!'

I thought nothing of it. Indeed I could hardly bring Humphrey to mind, although he had been present, along with the girls, at various Christmas gatherings, mainly the drinks parties my parents used to give on Boxing Day when my father was alive. If I thought of him at all it was with a mixture of amusement and distaste. The amusement was caused by Humphrey's solemn and often lachrymose unworldliness. Although young at the time of these encounters, I recognised and appreciated true blamelessness, which nevertheless disturbed me. My distaste, also occasioned by my youth, was for his collapsed appearance, the narrow chest, the burgeoning stomach, the trousers which nearly reached his armpits. I felt sympathy for his prospective wife, forced to contemplate this disgrace every day, and—but this was unimaginable—every night as well.

'A foreigner,' said Marjorie bitterly. It now occurred to me that she had had hopes in this direction herself.

'It was the holiday that brought it on,' said Sybil. 'That was your idea, Alice.' Your bright idea was what she meant.

'It wasn't a bad idea,' my mother observed. 'Humphrey's not old but he's developed elderly ways. He sits in that flat all day with nothing to do when he could be enjoying the sun somewhere. He's comfortably off, he's reasonably healthy.

But he's becoming morbid. And timid. I suggested Hyères, if you remember. He'd have been perfectly safe there. I can't think why he went to Paris . . .'

'If he wanted a holiday he could have come on the *Sea Princess* with us,' said Sybil, flushing more deeply. This project for a winter cruise, discussed many times, was never likely to be realised; indeed its main attraction was that it need never be undertaken. All three of them, Humphrey, Sybil and Marjorie, were disinclined to move. Should an uncharacteristic fit of restlessness seize them, and the booking actually be made, they would no doubt stay on board the ship as it travelled round the world and never get off it, leaving the world to take care of itself.

'Of course we shan't stay around to meet her.' This was Marjorie.

'You must, dear. What can you possibly have against the poor woman? As far as I can see this sets you free. You've both been so good to him, but it must have seemed a bit of a tie, sometimes, giving up every Sunday. And all that cooking . . .'

At this they both bridled. 'I hope we've never counted the cost, Alice, if that's what you're implying.'

'No, of course not. Oh dear, I didn't mean to offend you, please don't think that. You've both been quite marvellous, perfect friends to a lonely man. But now he's lonely no longer. That leaves you free. Or freer,' she added, surveying their faces in vain for a response.

'There'll be changes certainly,' said Sybil. 'For one thing we'll be moving down to the Hall.'

'That place in Dorset? But you're both too young to go into retirement. And what will you do with the house?'

'Sarah will live there. It can be her home until she gets married. If she ever does.' This was accompanied by a sigh of a different order, a careworn spontaneous sigh.

'How can you say that? Sarah's young, she hasn't started her life yet. When does she leave Oxford?'

'She's left. What she got up to as a student I don't know. I'm glad Alan was there to keep an eye on her. Not that she mentioned you, Alan. But then she never tells me about her friends.'

It was useless to remind them that four years had passed since I was up at Oxford. The details of my life were hazy to them, and they expressed no more than a conventional interest, which was usually compromised by incorrect information. There was no point in enlightening them. I think they were frightened of young men, if not of all men. This attitude must have deepened during the period of Sybil's widowhood. Nowadays the girls looked to each other for reassurance, and would continue to do so once both they and Humphrey were off the map. They were a married couple, in all but sex. I could not see that they would be much of a help to Sarah, whom I vaguely remembered throwing a tantrum at a children's party I had once attended. When she had found out that the beautiful yellow birthday cake was to be eaten politely by all the six-year-olds present she had appropriated several portions and would not relinquish them. Attempts to bring her to order had been countered with looks of scorn. A lot of cake ended up on the floor, I remembered. No doubt the same scorn was now levelled at her parent.

'I can't do anything with her,' Sybil went on, in a ruminative voice. 'She's not like us at all. We're peaceful people; we please ourselves, we're quite contented with our own company. I know she can't wait to see the back of us.'

'Looks down her nose,' Marjorie put in. It was clear that she disliked the girl.

'Anyway, I owe it to Marjorie,' Sybil went on. 'She doesn't complain, although I know her leg's getting worse. Sarah will have to learn to look after herself.'

'Well, of course she will,' said my mother. 'She's young, she's impulsive, she's very pretty. Young people should enjoy themselves. That's what youth is for.'

She sighed. I knew that she was thinking of her dead husband, than whom she had been so much younger.

'I'm sure we can count on you, Alice.' This, again, was Marjorie, now clearly anxious to relinquish Sarah and any responsibilities she might have incurred. If she could not have Humphrey she would have Sybil. It occurred to me, as it no doubt occurred to my mother, that the two were perfectly suited, and that their old age, so eagerly anticipated, would probably be benign. That, however, was in the future, and at this distance it seemed unlikely that they could be dissuaded from their project, even by my mother, whose attitude to them had been exemplary. She knew that they distrusted her; she also knew that they relied on her superior intelligence, a fact which they resented. Their visits were onerous but dramatic occasions, since there was so much repressed fury in the air. My mother felt an obligation towards them, though they felt none towards her. 'Ignore them,' I had once told her. 'Or tell them to get lost. They've got each other, after all. You've only got me, you poor old thing.' And yet a curious connection persisted, as if they had all issued from the same family, as in a sense they had.

My mother smiled at me lovingly. 'Are you sure you're not hungry?' she said, and I knew that she was grateful for my unspoken support. Being a tactful woman, and mindful of my own youth, she did not present her frequently bruised feelings time after time in order to hear my reassuring words, but I knew that she would not be altogether sorry when the girls departed for Dorset. Indeed, I did not see why they should enter our lives again.

'You're not going!' protested my mother, trying to keep the relief out of her voice. 'Alan, Marjorie's stick.'

'We don't want to get caught in the rush-hour, do we?' It sounded like a reproach, as perhaps it was. 'Where are my gloves?'

'Down the side of your chair,' I said. 'And it's Saturday.'

'All right, Alan, thank you very much. You'll be glad to see the back of us, I dare say.'

'You must come to see us again very soon,' my mother put in swiftly. 'Are you planning any sort of reception for Humphrey and his, well, his bride?'

'Certainly not.'

'Then perhaps I will invite them to a little party. You too, of course. Do we know anything about her?'

'Not a thing,' said Marjorie triumphantly.

'I see,' said my mother. 'A foreigner, you said. And he met her in Paris. Is she French?'

'She may be,' said Sybil. She was prepared to go no further.

'And has she got a name?' asked my mother, her patience beginning to wear thin.

'Edwige.' This was offered reluctantly.

'But that is French. She must be French.'

'Not quite, Alice,' put in Marjorie. 'Edwige is not her real name. Her real name is Jadwiga. Polish, you see.' She pronounced this as if it were the ultimate proof of the bride's unworthiness. 'Not quite what we're used to, Humphrey least of all. Still, we shan't wait around to see them make a mess of things. You'll be in touch, Alice?'

They always said this, as if anxious for my mother's company. Maybe they were. She was a sensitive and friendly woman, and she was always kind. I understood the sisters' desire to keep in contact, though I was in no doubt that they voiced pointed and enjoyable criticisms once they were alone. But my mother's other friends loved and trusted her, as I did. Although widowed young, she had given me a pain-free childhood and had never visited her sadness on to me. I suspected that her gift of the flat in Wigmore Street on my twenty-first birthday had been in the nature of a bribe, although I did not resent this. She wanted me to go into the firm and follow in my father's footsteps: that was her way of keeping faith with him. I am sure she never looked at another man. Such simple attitudes were my inheritance. It was to be some time before I betrayed them.

3

I first encountered Jadwiga/Edwige at the small party my mother gave at her Cadogan Gate flat to celebrate my return to normality, that is to say my joining the firm after my *années de pèlerinage* in Paris. The occasion took place on a misty Sunday in November, at midday. At first sight I knew no one in the room, although after about fifteen minutes I recognised the girls, Sybil and Marjorie, and of course Brian and Mrs Roche from the office. Brian was with his then fiancée Felicity, and Mrs Roche was with a short tubby man who was presumably Mr Roche, as he turned out to be. My mother was very animated, though she seemed to me much older. She broke away from an elderly couple to greet me, saw that I had a drink, and then took my arm and led me round the room to introduce me to various neighbours of hers, some of whom I had met at previous parties, some of whom I had never seen before.

I detest these gatherings, mainly because I sense that they are makeshift. We have no family, nor warm loving circle which would automatically respond to our needs and on which we could call in an emergency, should one arise. I detested London and its Sunday silence which was now to be my portion. Not that I rebelled against my inheritance: rather I sensed my mother's loneliness, and knew that she would soon be my sole responsibility, at least until I married, as I supposed I should have to. Indeed I saw marriage as a way of ensuring my mother's safety, although I knew that she loved me as I was, without entanglements. My line of conduct was to be dictated by two conflicting duties, getting married in order to supply my mother and myself with something resembling a family, and staying unattached in order to remain my mother's confidant. For the time being all was well. My mother was not old (I consigned my fleeting impression of age down to the strain of the occasion) and she was in good health. I had to remember that she was shy, unprotected by a man, and quite undemanding. When the time came I would enquire more deeply into the circumstances of her life, which I supposed to be quite comfortable, and arrange my own life as well as I could to answer her longings without sacrificing my own.

'And you remember Sarah?' she said.

'Hi,' said a red-haired girl in a very short skirt, and immediately drifted away.

That was to be the pattern of our relationship. As soon as I saw her I knew that I should be eternally seeking to attract her attention. I watched her for as long as I could: she seemed to be attended by two acolytes or bridesmaids.

'Who are those girls?' I asked my mother.

'Friends of Sarah's. She asked if she could bring them, and

I thought it would be nice for you to see some young faces. You can talk to them later. Now I want you to meet Jenny.'

'Jenny?'

'Humphrey's wife, dear.'

'I thought she was called something else?'

'We call her Jenny. That's what Humphrey calls her. Such a darling, Alan. We've become firm friends.'

I was prepared to embrace anyone who would be a firm friend to my mother, and shook hands warmly with a small trim woman of about my mother's age who had her arm linked through that of the sagging Humphrey, his marital status thus advertised. He appeared to be as vague as ever, but now wore an innocent smile of something approaching happiness.

'Well, Alan,' he said. 'Nice to see you again. This is my wife, Jenny,' and he patted the hand that was passed through his arm.

When I greeted his wife I could see what had attracted him to her in the first place, although to me, then, they seemed of an age so canonical that attraction was hardly in order. It was not her small rounded figure, nor her fair and largely unmarked face, so much as the timid smile of delight which she manifested whenever a favour came her way. I was apparently, at this moment, just such a favour, as would be any man who treated her with a level of respect. It occurred to me, at that moment of meeting, that such respect was something of a novelty to her, that marriage, even to Humphrey, was an unexpected bonus, and that she was pre- pared to discharge her domestic duties with a fervour per- haps denied to more settled, spoilt women, women who had married young and grown used to their status and attributes, and had learned to look outside their marriage for any excitement that they had decided was currently being denied to them. No wonder Humphrey wore a smile, albeit an uncertain one. His uncertainty was of no account. His wife was certain enough for both of them.

In the midst of this crowd—and by now there were about fifty people in the room—they looked archaic, ill-matched, perhaps, but welded together. They were each other's last chance, or so it seemed to me. They even made me feel a little wistful. I think all men long secretly to find the woman whom they can trust to look after them, with whom they can regress in the intervals of making love. This was now clearly Humphrey's good fortune, and I longed to know what benevolent providence had brought the two of them together, in Paris, of all places, a city which I thought favoured only the young and the assured. She looked at him fondly, while he stood there, with his unfocused smile, an embarrassed but happy man, one unprepared for happiness after years of silent familial closeness, the nearest he had ever come to personal fulfilment. As if unconscious of itself, his hand stole out to pat hers from time to time, and when it did her face lit up, as if they had been married that very morning.

She was a pretty woman, with that peculiar air of expectation that made her seem younger than her age. In a crowd such as this she did not attract much attention; it was only near the source of her security that she seemed to bloom, and more, to give out rays of benevolence. There was nothing in her appearance that singled her out; her figure, in her rather severe high-necked blue dress, was unremarkable, but her feet, I noticed, were frankly ugly, larger than one might have expected, and with an odd broken look, as if her shoes had had to be beaten out of shape in an effort to accommodate them. Her hands, by contrast, were small and pretty, and if she kept her left hand so constantly through Humphrey's arm it was perhaps to keep her wedding ring in evidence. She beamed at me with such affection that I felt obscurely flattered, though I had never set eyes on her before that moment.

'Congratulations,' I said, although it felt odd and inappropriate for the young man I was then to offer congratulations to an elderly woman on her marriage to a much older man. The young man I was then was also more intent on tracking down Sarah, whose red head could be seen in a distant corner, and who, momentarily detached from her two friends, seemed to be talking animatedly to a man I vaguely remembered as my mother's regular escort to the theatre.

A hand posed on my hand brought me back to order and to Jenny who was smiling at me fondly.

'I have so wanted to meet you, Alan. My dear Alice talks of you all the time. Has she told you about me?'

'Yes indeed. Forgive me for mentioning this, but your accent is quite French. Mother told me you were Polish.'

She laughed delightedly. 'But my dear, I lived in Paris for over thirty years. I went there as a young girl. I think of myself as a Parisienne.' This last remark stirred Humphrey into some kind of protest. 'But now of course I am English, an English wife with an English husband and an English family.' She laughed again.

I decided that there was no irony in this remark, although I could not distinguish the family to which she alluded. In brief there was no family: I had myself, only half an hour earlier, been regretting the fact. Certainly there was Humphrey, who took on some kind of importance now as a latter-day paterfamilias; certainly there were Sybil and Marjorie, who occupied a distant part of the room and seemed to be radiating awkwardness and isolation. They had come up from the country for this affair; despite their reluctant acceptance of my mother they never missed one of her parties. It gave them deep satisfaction to note that professional caterers had been hired to prepare the canapés and vol-au-vents. 'I see you decided to have it catered, Alice,' was usually their parting remark, thus leaving my mother with a reproachful vision of their former culinary munificence, or so they thought. I could not see that Sybil and Marjorie would be likely to extend the hand of friendship to the woman who had so effectively taken over their former charge. Of course there was Sarah, but Sarah did not seem to be part of anyone's family. Sarah, at that moment, had summoned her two friends, who seemed to act as pilot fish, and was making for the table which had been set up as a bar.

'Sarah,' called Humphrey. 'Come and say hello. We've seen nothing of you.'

She turned her back to the table and surveyed them for a moment before deciding to come over. To myself she paid no attention at all. Then she strolled languorously to Humphrey's side and linked her arm through his, so that he stood with a woman on each arm. Despite the fact that this seemed to enchant him—for even a man as old as Humphrey was susceptible to flattery—I could see that Sarah's intention was to point up the stunning contrast between herself, taut as a whipcord in her minute black suit and her low-cut silk shirt, and her uncle's elderly wife with her broken feet. In this she succeeded. Jenny detached her arm from that of her husband and moved nearer to Sarah. I registered the fact that Sarah was the family to which she now wished to lay claim. As if to reinforce this impression, Jenny put out a tentative hand and stroked Sarah's cheek. I hope that she turned away before she saw the girl's slight moue of distaste. Or was it a grimace? Whatever it was, we all decided not to have noticed. Sarah was to be allowed to behave badly on account of her youth, although she was not that young. I reckoned that she must have been twenty-three or -four, old enough to know better. At the same time I decided that she was unrepentant, perhaps because she had no fear of censure. She was certainly rather alarming. I felt my pulse rate increase, as it always did in the presence of danger. Humphrey too was a little abashed. The only person who did not seem put out was Jenny, who continued to smile fondly.

'Doesn't she look lovely?' she said, and there was a longing in her voice and in her eyes that would have told anyone attentive enough that her idea of family was perhaps no more than a lovingly cherished fantasy. In that moment, a moment of intense embarrassment, I saw that Parisian background as lonely, an affair of stratagems. I had lived there, I knew how hard it was to exist on a small amount of money, to live in a cheap hotel, never quite warm enough, never quite clean enough, to look forward to one meal a day for the relief of sitting in a restaurant and not in one's room eating a baguette out of a twist of tissue paper and perhaps a slice of ham or a piece of cheese, calculating that if one did not stop for coffee one would have nearly enough for the cinema that evening, and forgetting the discomfort of all these calculations for the sheer joy of being free to walk the streets of the beautiful city at any hour of the day or night. That was what I had felt, but I was young, and I was not a woman. To a woman of Jenny's age (and what exactly had she been doing there? How had she been living?), the reality must have seemed quite different. I resolved to get the story out of my mother, in whom everyone confided. If I could recognise anything I could recognise poverty. Perhaps that was why I was so reluctant to go back there, to the cheap hotel that I had thought so romantic at the time. Even the innocuous hardships I had suffered had left their mark. I had been happy there, but perhaps, finally, I was more at home here, in my mother's drawing-room, in London, on a misty Sunday in November.

Jenny leaned forward confidentially and took my hand. 'Your mother and I have become great friends,' she said. 'We

have such lovely long talks. And we go out! We have afternoons out! Humphrey likes to rest in the afternoon, so dear
Alice and I set out together for a couple of hours.'

'Where do you go?' I asked. I was distracted once more by
Sarah's red hair, her black figure sauntering across the room,
the calculating way in which she put olives into her small
pursed mouth. She had resumed her preferred stance, near
the bar, so that every man in search of a drink, either for
himself or for his wife, would have to confront her. 'What do
you do?' I said to Jenny, with an effort at enthusiasm.

'We go to the Royal Academy, if there's anything on. Or
we go round the stores. That's what we really enjoy. And we
have tea out, in a hotel. And then I put Alice into a taxi and
go home to cook Humphrey's meal.'

And my mother goes home to an empty flat, I thought. I
resolved to spend more time with her, as I had resolved on
many previous occasions. But she was a self-reliant woman,
grown used to her own company, and had never burdened
me with expectations I could not honour. I was glad she had
found distraction in the company of this touching little
woman, though how much pleasure she really derived from
an afternoon spent window-shopping or taking tea in a hotel
was a mystery to me. In fact the idea was vaguely monstrous. My dignified mother . . . But perhaps she had been
lonely, had been glad just precisely of this sort of undemanding contact so unexpectedly provided for her. I would do
more for her, I decided; I would make a point of eating
Sunday lunch with her. Maybe I could take her out to lunch
in one of those hotels she now favoured. This seemed a
recipe for old age. I already had the restrictions of the office
to cope with, after my years of freedom; now it appeared that
I was to take on the burden of a family weekend, I who had
just decided that I had no family. The family I would eventu-

ally want was situated in the future, had no shape, but was radiant with promise. My mother had already belonged to someone else's family. Much as I loved her—and I did love her very deeply—I did not want her to spoil my chances.

'Alan,' called my mother warningly, and with a nod of her head indicated Brian, who was surrounded by Sarah and her friends and thus effectively separated from Felicity. Felicity, I could see, would not be gracious in such a situation.

'Will you excuse me?' I said to Jenny. 'I think Mother . . .'

She smiled and patted my hand again. 'You go, dear. Go and find the young people. Go and find Sarah.'

The young people, once I had detached them from Brian, closed in on me with the vaguely menacing jollity of nymphs or maenads. Their scents conflicted; hair was tossed carelessly over shoulders, without regard for the plates of food being circulated.

'Sarah I know,' I began ponderously. 'But I don't believe I've met . . .'

'Berthe,' said the dark one. 'Berthe Rigaud. Sarah and I were pen friends. She used to come and stay with us in the holidays.' She spoke with the near cockney accent of the upper-class English girl, only the faintest of intonations giving her away as French. She seemed a cut above the other two socially; that English, I guessed, had been learned at her nanny's knee. She too was in black, a black suit, with a low-cut black camisole, which she filled abundantly. The other girl, in contrast, although doing her best and parading the same insouciance, seemed out of place, as though she had willed herself into animation and had even had a little too much to drink for that very purpose. In her prim blouse, with its piecrust collar, she was obviously self-conscious. 'Angela Milsom,' she confided. 'We're actually staying with Sarah this weekend. Your mother very kindly invited us.' She

seemed grateful for my presence, as if only a man could save
her from other women. I believe I must have subconsciously
noted this fact at the time.

'That house!' shrieked Berthe. 'In the middle of nowhere!
You have to get rid of it, Sarah. No wonder you preferred to
come to Paris. The invitation's still open, by the way.'

'I fully intend to get rid of it,' said Sarah, feeding in another olive.

'You want to sell the house?' I sounded fatuous, even to
myself. 'I can help you with the conveyancing, if you like.
I'm a solicitor.'

'We know,' said Berthe. 'Your mother told us.' She seemed
to find this amusing. In retrospect I can see that it was.

'Have you got a card?' asked Sarah. The very question
seemed to turn me into a terminal bore.

'I'll send you my address,' I said. 'I presume you're still at
Parsons Green?'

'Not for long.'

'But Sarah,' protested Angela. 'It's a lovely house. And the
garden is, well, lovely. And anyway doesn't it belong to your
mother?' A legal mind, I noted.

'It actually belonged to my *father*,' said Sarah. 'So it's come
to me, right? My mother doesn't live there any more. I'm
looking for a flat in town. Maybe you can help me with that
too.' She had obviously inherited her mother's vagueness
about my functions, although in this case annexing them for
personal use.

For the first time she seemed to look at me, drawn perhaps by the intensity of my gaze. I had been looking at her,
or perhaps looking for her, for a good while now. My higher
faculties noted the symmetry of her features, her pre-
Raphaelite shock of hair, her icy blue eyes, and registered her
as not exactly a beautiful woman but certainly an arresting
one. I also registered the fact that she was both vague and

unaccommodating, with the sort of insistent presence that made no concession to others. I blushed, in my usual deplorable fashion, and felt ridiculous, so much so that under the pretext of finding another drink I was obliged to move away. A wave of laughter followed my no doubt scarlet back, though when I was brave enough, and angry enough, to return to the group with the last of the champagne I noticed that I was not the only one to blush: the girl called Angela was a deep and unhappy red.

'You're not going?' I heard my mother protest, in the slightly carrying voice she used in these circumstances. The protest was to disguise the fact that she had had enough, and was longing for a quiet cup of tea and a rest in the silence of her bedroom.

'Alice, it's been lovely,' various people concurred, as they moved towards the door.

'Very nice, Alice,' said Sybil, whom I was reluctantly obliged to join. 'Your usual caterers? Marjorie quite enjoyed the little pizzas. Unusual, she thought them.'

'If you're ever down our way, Alice,' said Marjorie. She did not consider this an unfinished sentence, and so did not bother to finish it.

'Goodbye, Alice. Goodbye, Alan,' said Humphrey. 'Come and see us. Like old clocks, do you?' he asked me. I had not the slightest interest in old clocks. 'Got one or two fine examples, part of my father's collection. Be happy to show them to you, if you're interested.' I expressed appreciation.

'Alan,' said Brian, waylaying me on my much impeded passage to a bedroom to collect people's coats. 'A word.'

'Can't it wait?'

'I want to get one thing straight. That girl, Sarah, she, well . . . I mean she would have . . .'

'What are you talking about?'

'She made a dead set, if you catch my drift. I had nothing to do with it. Not too tactful, with Felicity standing there.'

'Are you drunk?'

'Probably. Anyway I want to assure you that I had nothing to do with it.'

'You are drunk.'

'What a stunner, though,' he said regretfully, as Felicity closed in and led him away to be punished.

My mother and I were eventually left alone with the crumb-strewn plates and the dirty glasses. My mother wore the defeated look that even the most successful parties can bestow when they finally come to an end. With the departure of the guests a sadness seemed to have settled on the room. The hired waitresses and the barman moved about swiftly, anxious now to be gone, all amiability in abeyance. A cheque was handed over. The door at last shut behind them.

'Have a rest,' I said, patting my now fragile-seeming mother on the shoulder.

'I'm all right, dear. Yes, I will have a rest, though I'm not tired. What will you do?'

'I'll walk back to the flat and read the papers. But I'll tell you what, Mother. I'll walk back again and take you out to dinner tonight. That way you won't have to do a thing.'

Her face brightened. 'Are you sure, dear? That would be lovely. Just the two of us? You're sure you don't want to bring a friend?'

My mother, it was clear, thought along conservative lines. 'A friend' meant a girl-friend, a connection she thought none of her business. But I had no girl-friend at the time, and besides, was not particularly interested in the sort of girl who would have been delighted to spend a quiet evening with my mother. If I wanted anything from a woman it was not docility, though that was what I eventually settled for. I knew myself to be fairly dull, fairly unremarkable, but I wanted my interlude of licence, irresponsibility. Simone and I had been too alike, too close in age and outlook, for our affair to have been anything but sunny, and slightly banal. A certain light-ness of touch had been in order: we had never quarrelled, and we had parted without rancour on either side. In retro-spect it seemed depthless. I did not exactly want to suffer; I simply wanted to have experienced something significant before I became middle-aged. At the back of my mind, of course, was the image of Sarah's red hair, her scornful laugh, her small pursed mouth.

'There's no one,' I told my mother. 'Besides, I want to hear all your news.'

She laughed. 'You'll think me quite silly, I know.'

I kissed her, and promised to come back at seven.

'How you've grown,' she marvelled, and looked at me fondly as I shrugged into my coat. It seemed to take me a long time to get out of the building and into the street.

Although it was only about two-thirty, London appeared to have settled into a pre-twilight calm. Sloane Street was deserted as I headed towards the park, my usual route back to Wigmore Street when I left my mother's flat. I had drunk just enough to make me depressed, and I viewed the oddly silent city without indulgence. I saw myself surrounded by old people, my mother, Humphrey, Jenny, and at the same time realised that I would outlive them all. It seemed to me then, as it seems to me now, that there is too short an inter-val for enjoyment in our lives, and that even mistakes are preferable to a prudent calculation of advantages, a return on our initial investment, such as Brian was about to make. I could have told him that he was acting out of character, but I guessed that he already knew that.

There is no combination so disastrous as that of a sus-pectible man and a dysfunctional woman, or of course of such a woman and just such a man. Walking back through the misty park I already knew that Sarah was vain, unreliable, and feckless. In this I was correct. What I did not know—and this was something I never entirely managed to fathom—was the extent of her insouciance, her literal inability to take any matter seriously. I knew that if I fell in love with her I should be embarking on a long and hopeless odyssey of missed appointments, of telephone calls that were never returned, of explanations for absence that were infinitely more mystifying than the truth would have been, of sheer infuriating disappointment. But at the beginning of an affair one does not count the cost. Already I knew that there would be an affair, and that it would not lead to possession. This did not deter me: I had confidence in the strength of my own desires. If I felt anything in the nature of a warning I was brave enough to ignore it, stupid enough to castigate myself for just those dull virtues that turn men imperceptibly into good husbands. If I were to fail with Sarah it could only be because I was not good enough for her.

My calculations displeased me. I should use this dinner with my mother to find out more about Sarah. A certain amount of bad faith was inevitable until Sarah and I were established on an equal footing. I also needed telephone numbers. I needed to know about Berthe Rigaud and Angela Milsom, in case they should be required for further information. I was a lawyer, after all, or so I flattered myself; I needed case notes. The man I was to become could have told the man I was then that these preparations are not truly necessary. If they are to become necessary then an obsession is almost certainly lying in wait. I was foolish enough to think that I was strong enough, and cheerful enough by nature, to avoid unhappiness. I was not yet old enough to see that I was in error.

The flat seemed silent and abandoned, although I had left

it only that morning. I picked up the papers and settled down to read, my mind agreeably stimulated by the prospect of a new love affair. In retrospect I can say that I never felt more of a man than I did at that moment, on that silent afternoon, before I was put to the test, before my life began and ended.

4

I took Mother to the Berkeley and we had a surprisingly con-
vivial evening. I had not realised how enormously pleased
she had been by my invitation. When I saw her in her black
dress and the cameo ear-rings my father had given her I
resolved to put my intrusive questions out of my mind and to
concentrate on her comfort and enjoyment. Her cheeks were
a delicate shade of pink; although she normally had a small
appetite she finished her sole and drank a glass of wine. A
man at a table for one, perhaps a guest in the hotel, glanced
at her appreciatively. She did not notice, though I did. Even
at my young age I liked women to be cherished. I liked to
think of them as needing a modicum of protection, encouragement. I liked them to be modest, grateful for flattery,
expert at soliciting kindness. Brought up by such a mother I
had not quite learned the crude manners of the age, although

I was aware of them. 'Patronage!' had snapped the prettiest of our secretaries when I had complimented her on her long shining hair—and this on my first day in the office. She had relented, and even smiled apologetically, and the matter was allowed to drop. I thought that a confident male and a reasonable woman could work things out to their mutual advantage. Even today I do not see why this should not be possible.

'I understand you have a new friend,' I said to my mother.

'A dear,' she replied. 'She has made Humphrey very happy.'

'And they met in Paris? That seems out of character for Humphrey.'

'Apparently she rescued him. He had lost his way and couldn't remember how to get back to his hotel, so he went into this café, the Deux Magots, I think . . .'

'Everybody knows it. Even Humphrey must have known it.'

' . . . and Jenny was sitting at the next table. He took a chance and asked her if she knew the Hotel Lutetia.'

'She must have thought it was a proposition.'

'Hardly. It would have been quite clear that Humphrey was not the sort of man to invite a woman to a hotel.'

I could see poor Humphrey, marooned in the brilliant city, aghast at its ferocious conviviality, and missing his clocks and his dusky flat. I could see him, out of sheer desperation, plucking up his courage to ask for directions from this inoffensive-seeming woman at the next table. He would have been emboldened by her smile, as timid as his own, and when she had offered to show him the way, would have eagerly paid for both their coffees and escorted her out into the street.

'But that's what he did,' said my mother. 'He invited her to dinner at the Lutetia, and to lunch the following day. And he told her that if she were ever in London to be sure to let him know.'

'Which she did.'

'Oh, very correctly, dear. She wrote to the address he had given her and mentioned that she would be spending a week-end in London, visiting friends.'

'A good touch.'

'And they met, and he took her to tea at the Ritz, and when she said she'd like to see where he lived he showed her the flat, which I think is quite dreadful. But he's fond of it, and she said she loved it.'

'Also a good touch.'

'But you see, dear, and this is the beauty of the thing, she does love it. You should see how she looks after it, dusting and polishing all the morning. She even cleans behind the radiators.' My mother looked amazed, as if such a manoeuvre had never occurred to her. 'All quite understandable, because, you see, she'd been living in a small hotel.'

'Ah! Now I understand. Where you and I would see only beige carpet and brown velvet curtains she saw central heating and constant hot water.'

'Exactly! And it is all quite innocent. She's not an adventuress, you know.'

'I don't think they still exist, Mother.'

'I think they may be called something else now.'

'But what do we know of her before the advent of Humphrey? If she was living in a hotel she must have been fairly poor.'

'Very poor, I understand. She told me about this quite naturally, without self-pity. Apparently she was an orphan, brought up by an uncle and aunt, who resented her.'

'Where was this?'

'In Warsaw. She was a pretty girl, and talented, whereas her cousins were stupid and spiteful. She could play the piano, and she was good at languages, but the uncle tried to get her a job as a machinist in a clothing factory. So when a friend suggested running away and trying their luck in Paris she didn't hesitate.'

'A friend?'

'A young man. Janek. I don't blame her. I'd have done the same thing myself.'

'So that's where the poverty came from. And living in a hotel. What did they do?'

'They were enterprising. They got jobs in one of the big cafés. He played the piano and she was a waitress. Then he got tired of it and said he wanted to see the Riviera, so they both went to Nice for a bit and did the same thing there. Then they parted company and she returned to Paris.'

'And were there other friends along the way?'

'Perhaps. Again I don't blame her. And she doesn't blame herself. I admire her for that. She makes no apologies for her past, but she doesn't turn it into a fairy story either. And latterly she was completely respectable. She got a job as an assistant at the Librairie Polonaise, in the Boulevard Saint-Germain, and that's where she met Humphrey, you see; she was treating herself to a coffee after work at the Deux Magots, and there he was. That's how they met.'

'Why are her feet so ugly?'

'Oh, that *is* sad. When she was first in Paris she was very impressed by the glamour of the women, and she saved up for ages for something new to wear. She wanted high-heeled shoes, and one evening Janek presented her with a pair. Only they were too small. She wore them anyway, so as not to hurt him, with the result that her poor feet were pushed out of shape. She may even have broken a couple of bones, with the result that you see. But now at least she can rest: she doesn't have to be on her feet all the time.'

'And you really enjoy these afternoons out?'

'I do, although I can see that you don't quite believe me. She's a very good companion; she's cheerful and affectionate and undemanding. A very loving person. I can see it's a novelty for her to have a bit of money to spend. She adores going round the shops, particularly Selfridges, and you know, Alan, it quite amuses me. I rather like being frivolous with her. It's quite a salutary lesson for me to see her appreciating the good things in life. I'm afraid I've taken them too much for granted.'

'And you have afternoon tea.'

'She always insists on treating me, though I'd rather be at home by that time. She enjoys being waited on, you see.'

What I could see was Jenny's face shining with pleasure as she contemplated a plate of hotel cakes. I assumed she was greedy, but this may not have been the case. As my mother said, she may simply have enjoyed being waited on, a legitimate pleasure after those early years of waiting on others.

'And are they happy? After all, Humphrey's a respectable sort of bloke, very little experience of women . . .'

'They are very happy—you saw that for yourself. She's grateful to him, she respects him, in fact she idolizes him, and why not? He rescued her from the Librairie Polonaise and the Hôtel du Départ . . .'

'I've passed it. Yes, he rescued her from that all right, though it's a perfectly reasonable place.' I forbore to tell my mother that I had once gone there with a girl, between trains. Only an accident of our respective histories had prevented Jenny and myself from coinciding there.

' . . . and she says he's given her a family.'

'What, Sybil and Marjorie? I can't see those two striking up a friendship.'

'Well, no, not Sybil and Marjorie, though they've behaved better than might have been expected. No, she means Sarah.'

Carefully I balanced the last of my cheese on a corner of biscuit. 'What about Sarah?' I said.

'She loves the girl. She told me that Sarah was the daughter she never had. And the worst of it is that Sarah can't stand her. Humphrey is quite a wealthy man, you know, and Sarah is his favourite niece, his only niece, in fact. Before his marriage Sarah stood to inherit a decent sum of money. Not that she's a poor girl; she has her own father's share from the sale of the business. Humphrey has been more than fair. And I'm sure he's made provision for her, even now.'

'Is it just the money?'

'No.' My mother sighed. 'She's an odd girl, irresponsible, quite spiteful sometimes. Of course Sybil was always odd. But Sarah seems unconcerned about hurting others. She was rude to Jenny when they first met, and she never returns her telephone calls. And poor Jenny telephones her all the time. She asked for your number, by the way.'

'Jenny?'

'No, Sarah.'

'You gave it to her?'

'I gave her the office number. I hope that was all right?'

I swallowed my disappointment. 'Of course. She may want my advice. She said she was thinking of selling the house.'

'The house is not hers to sell. But perhaps she's discussed this with Sybil. Although I'm sure Sybil would have consulted me—you know how she is.'

'As far as you know she's still in Parsons Green?'

I could not bring myself to ask my mother further questions. If there were to be anything between Sarah and myself it would be better if my mother knew nothing about it. Again, this stealth should have been a warning to me.

'As far as I know, though I believe she spends a lot of time with that friend of hers in Paris. Berthe. You met her.'

'She doesn't work, then, Sarah?'

'She sometimes cooks for private dinner parties. She's quite a good cook, I understand. But no, I don't think she has a regular job. Not like you, dear, not now. How are you enjoying it?'

We discussed the office, as I knew she wanted to, until, with a happy sigh, she said, 'This has been a lovely evening. Thank you so much, Alan. You're a good son. I've always wanted to tell you that, and now I have. I must be tipsy.' She laughed, she who had never been tipsy in her life.

'I'll take you home,' I said.

'Are you going to walk back?'

'Yes, I rather like the park at night. It's only just after ten-thirty, not late.'

'Be careful dear.' If her look was particularly searching I was unaware of it, for I had already turned away.

In those days I would walk across the park quite late, sometimes just before it shut, at midnight. On this particular evening I strode out as if I were being pursued, although it was a fine evening, clearer than the day had been, all those hours ago, before my decision had been revealed to me. I am ashamed to say that I allowed myself this romantic thought, though I am hardly romantic by nature, being of a philo-sophical and, I like to think, stoical disposition. I had per-suaded myself that the time for levity was past: in this I was right. Having acquired something of a hereditary position I thought it incumbent on me to behave in a fairly grave man-ner. Yet on this particular evening I could hardly wait to get home to make that crucial telephone call, the one needed to set things in train. Everything depended on it. Once the con-nection was made I could take care of the rest.

In the flat I threw my coat onto a chair and looked up Bertram Miller in the directory. When I dialled my fingers were actually shaking. 'The number you require is no longer available,' sang a voice. 'The number you require is no longer . . .' I dialled Directory Enquiries. 'Bertram Miller,' I said firmly. 'Fifty-eight Bredwardine Road.' There was silence. I was about to replace the receiver and try again when another voice said, 'That number is now ex-Directory.'

'I'm an old friend,' I pleaded. 'I've just got back from abroad.'

'I'm sorry. I'm not allowed to give out ex-Directory numbers. Do you require another service?'

'No. Thank you.'

I went to bed, but not to sleep. By the morning I had that somewhat haggard brightness that is the legacy of a sleepless night. In the office I told the girls that if a Miss Miller telephoned she was to be put straight through. After all, she had my number, I reasoned: she must have wanted it for a purpose. Then, unable to work, I told the girls that I was going out for half an hour, that I would ring back anyone who left a number, but that I had to have a number. They must have thought I was behaving oddly: they always took messages correctly, and never failed to note down contact numbers. I walked back to Wigmore Street and to a coffee bar where I sometimes had breakfast. I remembered that I had eaten nothing that morning. After tea and toast I suddenly felt tired, as if I might pass out. I roused myself and ran back to the office. There were no messages.

Oddly enough this did not depress me. Nor was I depressed throughout the whole of the next two weeks. I waited expectantly, but in a sort of dream; if nothing happened it simply meant that the delicious moment of contact was still in the future, something to look forward to. By the third week my mood changed, became more bleak. If nothing happened it was because nothing would happen. There was no contact. There never would be.

On the Wednesday of the fourth week I got back from

lunching with a client to find Sarah in the room shared by Telfer and Mrs Roche. There was a pungent smell of nail polish in the air: she was painting her nails. Avoiding Mrs Roche's eye I invited her into my office. She picked up her bottle, and with her fingers spread wide wriggled past me through the door. I smelt a heavy scent, something by Guerlain, I thought, and the waxy, more aromatic odour of her hair. I was worried that I might be too confused to speak. However, when I did I was entirely in character.

'How can I be of help?' I said.

Even then I could probably see that it was hopeless. I seemed to have to exert phenomenal psychological pressure, along the order of mesmerism, to induce her to meet my eye, since she was intent on her nails, testing them to see if they were dry, and when they were, examining them carefully, turning her hands this way and that. I wondered why she could not have completed this task at home, before she came out, but that was to misunderstand Sarah from the start. I had known her intermittently, as a distant relative, all my life, but not in the intuitive fashion to which I now had access. I could see that time and occasion would mean nothing to her: whatever she wanted to do she would do, regardless of where she was, or who was with her. And she would be so intent on what she did that reproaches would either be useless or out of order. This was one of her versions of her mother's fabled oddness, though in contrast to Sybil's eager anticipation of old age and decrepitude Sarah would live entirely in an eternal present. Her main characteristic was the kind of primal innocence enjoyed by children, except that allied to this innocence—of time, of her effect on others—was an extremely alert sense of her own importance. The psychopathology of this combination was unusual. Since that meeting in my office I have seen her enter a room full of people and fail to greet any of them, secure in the knowledge that sooner or later they would drift over to her and greet her of their own volition, drawn by her infinitely magnetic presence. By the same token she would sometimes laugh in solemn company, for example if an extremely serious matter were under discussion, simply because too little attention was being paid to her. She was not stupid, not by any means. She knew herself to be unusual and desirable, and most of the time she would be restless and bored. She probably expected the world to attend to her needs, which would not fail to be quite specific. And, more important, she would be deficient in the ability to link cause and effect, or to think in any but the most immediate terms.

Naturally I could confirm nothing of this at the time, though I think I sensed it. While Sarah was examining her nails I felt that intimation of longing and frustration that results from an inability, almost an incapacity, to capture the attention of someone who has suddenly assumed a vital and overwhelming importance. I waited patiently, my gaze no doubt beamed on her like a searchlight, until she finally decided that her nails were in a satisfactory condition. Then she rearranged her heavy mane of hair, opened her bag, and removed a piece of paper.

'I need a lease,' she explained, or failed to explain, handing over the paper, on which was scrawled the name of another solicitor, one whom I had met in the course of business. 'I've sold the house and bought this flat.'

'Your mother was agreeable to this?'

She shrugged. 'Haven't the faintest. I couldn't go on living out there, could I? Anyway, I need to be in town. This'll do for the time being.'

'And where is this flat? I presume you've already exchanged contracts? And sold the house?'

'Of course. I don't waste time. I never waste time.'

This statement, coming from one who thought it acceptable to waste others' time, should also have given me pause, yet at that moment, and indeed afterwards, I had to admire the sheer consistency of her extremely inconsistent nature. She was unpredictable, yet she could also be relied upon to be unpredictable. In this way she need never take the blame, particularly for those unexplained absences which were her stock in trade. The effect was of an endlessly delayed climax, and I use the image advisedly, for it was this particular characteristic that made her so fascinating to men. This too I could see at the time; time was also to prove me correct. When bored, as she obviously was now, her looks would fade, as if a light had gone out. One would then be on one's mettle to amuse her, to spoil her, and, yes, I must repeat this, to capture her attention. She was a woman destined to beguile men, yet most of them would leave her indifferent. She had the imperviousness of an alien, while all the time trailing evidence of her powers of seduction, which were considerable. I was not in the least surprised when the door of my office opened and Brian came in, intrigued no doubt by Mrs Roche's indignant comments.

'Hello!' he said. 'How nice to see you again! Alan looking after you, is he?'

To my despair she brightened, but, I reasoned, only because something was happening, as opposed to the nothing signified by my steady attention.

'I've bought this flat,' she said, turning to him. 'Paddington Street.'

'That's quite near where I live,' I said. 'In Wigmore Street. We shall almost be neighbours.' I wanted to ask her out to dinner, but I was not going to do so with Brian in the room. What a pity we had all had lunch, I reflected, otherwise Brian would certainly have extended his usual invitation.

'If you could just take care of it for me,' she said, suddenly switching her gaze to mine. I watched her, fascinated, as she warmed into luminous life, having decided that she had ignored me sufficiently for my own good. She moistened her lips, and seemed to will brightness into her eyes and colour into her cheeks. The effect was dazzling, and also unsettling, indications of a volatility which she nevertheless had under perfect control. She was like the weather in a mountain region, like the weather in this little town of Vif, a heavy mist descending out of nowhere, a fitful sun giving way to soaking rain.

'I'll take care of it, of course,' I said. 'Was there anything else? I'll need a telephone number.'

'Oh, sure.' She searched in her large handbag for her diary, found the number and read it out. I wrote it down. Brian, I could see, was committing it to memory.

'And I'll be giving a little house-warming party,' she said. 'Some weekend or other. If you'd like to come?'

'I'd be delighted,' I said. 'I'll telephone you.'

'Am I invited too?' asked Brian. I had never seen him so clumsy.

'Of course. Bring Pamela.'

'Pamela?'

'Your girl-friend.'

'You mean Felicity.'

'Sure. Felicity.'

At the mention of Felicity's name Brian looked unhappy, as well he might, I reflected. On Fridays and Saturdays Brian and Felicity were usually out of London, staying with one or other set of parents, or, in season, shooting on one of the estates of Felicity's many uncles. There was no possibility that he could get out of these arrangements: he was making an advantageous marriage, and he had to think of the conse- quences. And yet I knew that at some point he would con- trive to have an affair with Sarah, of which he would say nothing. It would be one of those brief affairs of which he had the secret, and she would amuse herself with him, until she decided to turn her attention to somebody else. And then, if he were lucky, and if she had left him intact, he would do the same.

My own domestic economy was simplicity itself compared with Brian's. I had only my mother, at this moment no doubt making her way to Selfridges with Jenny, and my own empty flat. I was therefore in a position to give all my attention to Sarah, which is what I did. I do not blame myself for this, nor do I blame Sarah for her part in the affair. She was not completely indifferent to me, nor was she completely untrustworthy. Perhaps what I saw from the outset was simply incompatibility. I tell myself that there have been worse cases. And yet, although my own case was so unremarkable, I very nearly did not survive it.

5

I never read love stories. If I read modern fiction at all I tend to go for thrillers of the most traditional kind, perhaps because they satisfy my sense of justice. Angela, my wife, read a lot, but in the same selective fashion, preferring up-market sagas of village life in which every mild imbroglio is satisfactorily sorted out. These novels, I suppose, flattered her somewhat exaggerated sense of her own gentility. Like Lady Stavely, in *Orley Farm*, my mother's favourite novel, 'She liked to see nice-dressed and nice-mannered people about her, preferring those whose fathers and mothers were nice before them.' On these grounds alone my mother and I qualified, though I flatter myself that Angela never knew how distant I was in my mind and feelings from that niceness she so treasured. Poor girl, she was moderate in all things, except one. In that way she ensured that she would never be forgotten.

Had I read literature, steeped myself in fantasy instead of the law, I should have been better prepared for the condition in which I found myself after Sarah's visit to the office. I should have known that being in love means knowing no respite. I should have viewed my daily telephone calls to Paddington Street with resignation, or even with indulgence. They were never answered, except at one remove. 'Hi, this is Sarah and I'm not here right now. Leave a message after the tone and I'll get back to you.' Strange how many people affect an American accent and locution on these machines. Soon I took to strolling up to Paddington Street after work; it was not far from the office after all. I was extremely lonely at this time, yet found it impossible to contact any of my friends. If they were trying to contact me I was unaware of the fact, since I was out of the flat most of the time. My evenings had come to take on a strange pattern. After a hasty meal I would walk up Baker Street to Paddington Street, to see if there were a light in any of the windows. Since I did not at that stage know which of the flats was Sarah's this was a particularly pointless exercise. Yet I came to rely on that furtive evening walk as part of the day's activities. If it did nothing else it prepared me for sleep.

The invitation to the house-warming had not materialised, and my fruitless telephone calls did nothing to elucidate the matter. I could of course simply turn up at her door in the course of one of my evening patrols, but I shrank from so obvious a solution to the problem. Three years at Oxford and nearly four in Paris should have alerted me to the notion of courtly love, but I rather think that even if I had been acquainted with it, had grown up believing in minstrels and troubadours, I should not have recognised my own behaviour, which had more in common with the Middle Ages, or even the Dark Ages, than with the twentieth century.

My mother, who never telephoned me at the office, managed to get hold of me one evening. Her call exasperated me, as I was just about to leave the flat, but I love my mother, and I detected a note of anxiety in her voice which was uncharacteristic. I shrugged my coat off again and settled down to listen to her, my eye on the clock, as if there were little time left to me before I was due to leave.

'Alan? Are you all right, dear? I've had some trouble getting hold of you.'

'Of course I'm all right, Mother. You can always reach me at the office, you know. I'm out rather a lot in the evenings at the moment.'

'Well, I'm glad you're having a good time, dear. But actually this might be a matter you need to deal with officially. I've had a rather disquieting letter from Sybil. She seems to think that you were instrumental in selling her house.'

'Did you remind her that I am not an estate agent?'

'She has, as you know, only the vaguest idea of what you do. She seems to be rather more confused than she was, although she was never exactly lucid.'

'I had nothing to do with the sale of the house, Mother. Sarah sold it. Doesn't Sybil speak to her own daughter?'

'It appears that she has trouble getting through to her.' In this I was prepared to sympathise. 'She said that the only time she managed to speak to her Sarah told her that you had organised the lease of the new flat.'

'So I did. Perfectly routine piece of business. That was the first I knew of her selling the house, or rather having sold the house.'

'Sybil says she shouldn't have done it.'

'But she did. None of this has anything to do with me.'

I could hear my mother's hesitation at the other end of the

line. 'Don't you think you should have asked her about this, dear? Of course it's none of my business, and of course I don't appreciate the legal niceties, but I do see that Sybil has a point . . .'

'I simply negotiated the lease on Sarah's new flat. I didn't ask her about the sale of the house because at that stage it was no longer relevant. The conveyancing was perfectly straightforward: there was no mortgage, nothing to delay the matter. I saw no reason to refuse to act . . .'

'That seems a little precipitate, if you'll forgive my saying so, darling.'

'Mother, I do this sort of thing all the time. I'm not responsible for all my clients' actions. I don't ask them to unburden themselves, search their hearts, unearth their motives. I don't ask them what sort of terms they are on with their mothers. Anyway, why didn't Sybil think to enquire before all this happened?'

'You know Sybil. She can't cope with change. She can't even anticipate it. She obviously thought that Sarah would go on living in the house, probably as a married woman. She had no idea . . .'

'What has this got to do with me?'

'I'm coming to that. If you're satisfied that there is nothing for which you feel in the slightest bit responsible there's no need to worry. Although with Sarah I should have advised caution. She was never reliable: always the quick and easy answer to everything. Or no answer at all. And she never got on with her mother. In a way it's just as well that the girls moved down to that place of theirs—I believe that in every other respect they're quite happy—because there would have been trouble with Sarah sooner or later. But it was a little callous of her, don't you think?'

'Are you sure she didn't tell Sybil she was selling the house?'

'She may have done.' My mother brightened as this thought took hold. 'In fact she probably did. But you know Sybil when she thinks she has a grudge. Remember how she reacted when Humphrey married.'

By this time I was kicking moodily at the chair leg. 'I still don't see where I come into it.'

'I'm afraid Sybil has got it into her head that you engineered the whole thing.'

'But I didn't.'

'So I told her. But she said she intended to write you a stiff letter. I know you'll know how to deal with that; I just thought I ought to warn you. She won't do anything, of course: in fact she's always been rather frightened of you. Big men frighten her—she's that sort of woman. Thankfully few of them survive. It's interesting how times have changed . . .'

'Mother, I'll deal with it, I promise you. It's just that I was on my way out . . .'

'I'm so sorry, Alan. Of course I'm being a nuisance. When will I see you?'

'I'll try and come over on Sunday. It's just that my evenings are rather taken up at the moment.'

There was a pause. 'What are you doing?' I asked finally, a question I usually avoided. I did not want to know about my mother's life, which I saw as empty, wistful. I had longed for her to remarry, so as to ease the burden of her solitariness onto shoulders other than mine. And there was a claimant, a thoroughly respectable bachelor who lived a floor above her in Cadogan Gate and who continued faithfully to escort her to the theatre even when she had turned down his proposal.

'But why don't you accept?' I protested when she told me. 'You could have been a wife instead of a widow.' For I imagined widows indulging in ceaseless sentimental tears, whereas all the widows I know now lead aerobics classes. She had smiled, and said something that terrified me. '"Was it not her position in life to be his mother?"' 'What?' I said. 'What are you saying? Of course you're my mother, but that's not a *position* . . .'

'I was quoting, dear. Lady Mason says that in *Orley Farm*. I love it, as you know.'

'What are you doing?' I asked her.

'Reading.'

'Not *Orley Farm* again? You must know it off by heart.'

'*The Claverings*. I'd forgotten how it ended. Just write Sybil a gentle but firm letter, dear. But once she gets hold of an idea . . . Come to lunch on Sunday if you can. Are you eating?'

'Of course. I have lunch with Brian or a client most days. And I have breakfast in this coffee bar down the road. I don't need much in the evenings. Are *you* eating?'

'Rather too much. Jenny sees to that.'

'I'll see you on Sunday, Mother. I've got to go now.'

'Good-night, dear. Until Sunday. And I'm sure you'll know what to say to Sybil. God bless.'

I walked to the window and looked out. It was a fine evening in late autumn, my favourite season of the year. There are a few pedestrians at my end of Wigmore Street once the office workers and the dental nurses have gone home: the music lovers at the Wigmore Hall do not make themselves felt until much later. At the back of my mind I was aware of overstepping some sort of mark, and I was unsure whether this was professional or moral. As I said, I was unversed in the idea of love, and the theories surrounding it. I think I knew that it was subversive, even at that stage, before I had been completely overtaken. But when I speak about being overtaken is this not simply to exonerate myself, as if I were a passive instrument—not even an agent—at the mercy of powerful and indifferent forces? The one lesson I learnt from the whole affair was that one is responsible not only for what one does but for what is done to one. But I think I also knew relief that at last I had the ideal pretext for contacting Sarah, instead of waiting for her notional party. There was no reason, apart from the inability to get through to her on the telephone, why I should not simply have invited her to dinner. I did not do this because I was not ready for her. I was still at that stage which I now recognise as adolescent. I wanted to move straight from my imaginings into a full-blooded affair. With an affair I knew I should be on safe ground. I did not want to have dinner with her, to get to know her. I already knew her, or what I wanted to know of her. Besides, I was afraid of a refusal.

Sybil's letter arrived the following morning. It appeared to have been dashed off with extraordinary energy on several sheets of dark blue writing paper. I scanned it hastily before leaving the flat: it contained many admonitions but no threats. 'Scandalous' was underlined several times, as was 'Thoughtless' and 'Impertinent', this last embellished with three exclamation marks. The letter seemed to issue from a correspondence already fully formed in Sybil's head, as if I had previously written to her, outlining my feeble excuses for disposing of her property. Since she had, as it were, already established my side of the argument, I saw no reason to get involved, and told myself that it would be prudent to have no hand in the matter. My conscience was almost clear, though a little tender, my duty, as I saw it, was to instruct Sarah as to her obligations towards her mother, or, if that were impossible, to write to her, and occasionally to answer the telephone. This promised a certain amount of pleasure, although it was not the romantic pretext I sought. I really would have preferred to meet Sarah on neutral ground, devoid of all contingencies, but this was again an illusion, possibly a delusion, as if the only circumstances in which it would be possible for us to come together were to be situated in the confines of a dream. From this I was able to deduce, but much later, that my feelings were admirable, exalted no doubt, but doomed to remain unrealised.

It was a fine morning, with an early mist just dissolving into early winter sunshine. I was halfway to the office before I remembered that I had had no breakfast, strode back again, drank my coffee, ate my toast, and was still early for work. At some time during the morning I dialled Sarah's number, and, as usual, got no reply. At this point it occurred to me to wonder why I was making such a fool of myself. I was nearly thirty, neither decrepit nor disadvantaged, and yet I seemed doomed to assemble these rickety structures of possibility around a woman whom I hardly knew and who probably only thought of me, if think of me she did, as some kind of dim adjunct to a family with which she no longer had any contact. For if I retained anything from Sybil's letter, apart from her general condemnation, it was a sense that as a parent she was unlikely to have had much contact with her offspring for some time.

From Sarah's point of view I could judge the unwelcome nature of Sybil's erratic vigilance: this was not a mother in whom an independently minded daughter could or would confide. I was uncertain about mothers and daughters, but I knew that even my own loved parent sometimes made me sigh with impatience. How much more so, then, would that seductive child-woman reject a mother who was not only completely solipsistic but aesthetically unpleasing. I only ever seemed to have seen Sybil in the heather mixture coat and skirt in which she visited my mother, her short bristly hair crowned with her trilby hat, yet in her youth she must have possessed something of the aura that her daughter had inherited. After all, she had once been a bride: presumably the tension that gathered her face into a permanent frown had not always been there. Even so it was hard to see how

Sarah had developed her more artful personality from the genetic elements at her disposal. That she was unique, a *lusus naturae*, fitted in with my perception of her, one which I was somehow unwilling to abandon. It harmonised with my curious state of impotence, justified my unwillingness to confront her on any kind of rational pretext. Yet Sybil's letter provided me with just such a pretext, perhaps the only one I should ever have, and it was with only the slightest tremor of impatience at what seemed to be a duty I was only half minded to discharge that I picked up Sybil's letter and left the office for Paddington Street.

The day had passed in a dream; I could hardly remember how it had passed or what it had contained. Most of what it had contained was speculation, yet in the street that speculation had turned once more to dreaming. I almost wanted to postpone this meeting so that I could continue to enjoy my fantasy undisturbed. And yet when I pressed Sarah's doorbell I had no hesitation in assuming that she would answer it, although for once I should have preferred her not to. This was to change, of course, as events and expectations themselves changed. Within seconds, as it seemed, she stood facing me, her white face startling in the half light of the hallway. She looked abstracted, though not thoughtful; her abstraction issued directly from her habitual self-absorption, yet had nothing self-indulgent about it. I was struck with the thought that I had misjudged her, that she was not as light-minded as her careless manner and habits would suggest. If I were to sum up my impressions as we stood on either side of the door it was that she was a serious person who was in flight from seriousness, who sought frivolity, insouciance as an escape from whatever occasionally dulled her eye or drained her colour. As she stood staring at me, as if she had no idea how I came to be there, or on what pretext, she seemed to be having some difficulty with herself, pushed her heavy hair away from her forehead with an old woman's gesture, and swayed from one foot to the other like an actress warming up in the wings. When she said, 'You'd better come in,' her voice was almost resigned.

I was appalled but hardly surprised by the confusion in the flat, a confusion too long established to be temporary. In fact it seemed like a bivouac, as though inhabited by squatters, yet what furniture there was—a pale leather sofa, a gilt-framed mirror propped against a wall—seemed opulent and slightly inappropriate. The floor space of the small sitting-room was covered with the writhing flexes of two telephones, one of which was ringing as I entered. It would not, I knew, be answered, nor was it. A large stock of old copies of *The Times* and the *Financial Times* obscured the seat of the rather pretty reproduction Louis XV chair to which I was vaguely directed, but I remained standing, as did Sarah. She wore a loose flowered dress and her feet were bare. Again it seemed difficult to capture her attention, although we were the only two people in the room.

'Would you like a drink?' she said suddenly, as if coming out of a dream.

'Later, perhaps. I've come because I had a letter from your mother, which I think you should know about.'

'I doubt it. She writes to me too, you know.'

'She seems to think you shouldn't have sold the house without telling her.' Put like that Sybil's case seemed unanswerable.

'Well, I did. If she'd wanted to keep it she shouldn't have pushed off and left. Not that I wasn't pleased to see her go.'

'But did you tell her what you intended to do?'

She shrugged. 'I told her when I'd done it. That seemed more to the point.'

'She seems to think I should have known about this. I

think she's got it into her head that I masterminded the whole thing.'

'I shouldn't let that worry you. Her head's always been stuffed with conspiracy theories. That's why she was so impossible to live with. One of us had to go. I'm only glad it was her. She's probably mad, anyway. Who in their right mind would volunteer to live in an old folks' home?'

'I understood they had their own flat,' I said.

'But it's one of those horrible outfits with a warden, for when you fall out of bed and break your hip.'

'Have you seen it?'

'Oh, I've seen it all right. Sinister. Beautiful country house, or must have been once, inhabited by people on Zimmer frames. They're all right, the two of them. They've got what they wanted, though why they wanted it is a mystery to me. They're still active, Marjorie still drives. You can just see the Disabled stickers on all the windscreens, can't you? If you ask me they're both crackers. Always were.'

Her face was scornful, as if the elderly could only conjure up feelings of disgust. She was also ashamed, I could see, because her mother and her aunt had deliberately chosen old age and in so doing had turned their backs on everything she stood for, youth, beauty, desire, as if these things were unmentionable. She appeared to think that they had done her a monstrous wrong, for which she would defy them with all the means at her disposal.

'If you could perhaps write to her, without dropping me in it,' I ventured.

At this her attention switched abruptly to me, her scorn undiminished. 'I never even mentioned you. Why should I? I hardly know you. I'm not sure I even want to know you.'

'All right, all right. I'm not trying to interfere . . .'

'Of course you are.'

'Well, I am. But why should I be blamed for something you should have sorted out?'

'You don't get it, do you? She writes me letters like that. I dare say she writes them to a lot of people. She's crackers, like I said. Anyway this is boring. Is this why you're here?'

'Partly,' I said. 'I've been trying to get you on the phone. I wanted to ask you out to dinner.'

'Oh, you did, did you?'

'Why should that annoy you?'

She shrugged again. 'Everyone asks me out to dinner.'

'What of it? And anyway, I'm not everyone.'

'You can say that again.'

'Are you always as rude as this?' I asked, bewildered.

At this she grinned and said, 'You'd better have that drink.'

I stayed with her that night, of course. Apparently it was as easy as that. As I seemed to have envisaged a mythic pilgrimage, a romantic conquest of imponderable obstacles, it might be said to have constituted an anticlimax. But only on the level of my more febrile imaginings. On the level of verifiable reality it was the revelation for which nothing had quite prepared me, conducted in silence, with what seemed like supernatural energy on both sides. I took this unbelievable gratification to be mutual: indeed no further proof of our inevitable conjunction was needed, or so it seemed to me. I never questioned my desire for Sarah, nor, oddly enough, hers for me. Any declaration, I thought, would have clouded the issue. Since she accepted me, for whatever reason, I sought no explanations from her. Thus I was never to know the reasons for her compliance. But then again I had the proof, and my memory would furnish me with details which she, perhaps, could not or would not have confirmed, had we ever indulged in one of those conversations which our activities served to demonstrate as being otiose, only resorted to by others less superbly matched. I was constrained through shyness, though I might have enjoyed such loving gossip, whereas she was silent through a form of impermeability, as if to give herself away might constitute an almost terminal weakness. And yet I was sure of her. She had given me all the assurances I needed. She had no further need to give an account of herself, at least, not to me.

In the morning I did not even care that I was unbathed, unshaven, that I should have to spend the day like that. This did not greatly disturb me, although normally it would have done. An alternative hygiene had replaced the obedient disciplines of the days, weeks, months, years that had gone before.

'I'll ring you,' I said. 'Please pick up the phone from time to time.'

Her face had resumed the strange clouded expression of the previous evening. Her stare did not seem to take me in, or to take in what had passed between us. I refused to let this annoy me.

'See you,' she said vaguely.

'When? Shall I come this evening? We could . . .'

'Have dinner, I know. Don't be a bore, Alan. Don't *cling*. I'll see you around. Right now I want to have my bath.'

I was aware of the strong smell of her hair, stronger after a night on the pillow. When the door closed behind me I found myself, somehow, in the street. I began calculating how and when I would see her again, though I knew that this would not be easy, that she would only see me when she wanted to. Throughout the day I could smell her hair. I telephoned several times. Each time there was no answer, yet I had an image of her, sitting in the flat, on the floor, perhaps, willing the sound to stop, the silence to be restored.

6

Mother's boy-friend, Aubrey Fairweather, was there when I called on the following Sunday. A thin patrician-looking man who was always content to take no for an answer, or so I had assumed, he visited Mother punctiliously, never outstaying his welcome. In a crisis, if he ever acknowledged such a thing, he would rather drink an exquisitely dry sherry than a double brandy; his most familiar gesture was his careful insertion of a cigarette into an amber holder, a gesture which seemed to belong to the age of drawing-room comedy, as did his Paisley cravat and his sleek silver hair. Some years older than my mother, he had taken her refusal to marry him with a contained smile, and had the grace, or the persistence, to continue to bestow his presence on her, thereby indicating his superior nature. I rather liked him. His effete appearance gave no hint of the fact that he was a great traveller: even now he was liable to disappear for a couple of months. 'China,' he would explain on his return: 'Peru.' He also had a house in France, near Cagnes. I thought he had his bachelor life well organised. I could tell he was no good for Mother. He was sensitive and civilised; so was she. What she needed, I thought, was a more robustly male presence, but so far none had presented itself.

Nevertheless I warmed to Aubrey, who looked delicate but was probably made of teak. I was also sorry for him, for his deliberate gestures and careful appearance. I thought these characteristic of men who had survived their years of active experience and were forced to roam the world in search of lesser delights. I was filled, at that stage, with the memory of Sarah, and the awesome revelation of our matching physical temper. For the first time in my life I had met a woman with that rare sort of genius, effortless, uninvented, almost unconscious. This was the gift she possessed and I had been its recipient. Like Julian Sorel in another context my virtue had been equal to my happiness. This phrase had puzzled me ever since Mother had persuaded me to read the novel, another of her favourites. She had blushed and said, 'It means that he acquitted himself well, and no further explanation was needed. I'm sure you see the beauty of that Alan.' I had, in fact, although I had thought the novel difficult. Yet along with its crankiness went a sort of excitement, which convinced me that its author had been young and ardent and romantically fulfilled, even though his hero had ended in prison.

Sitting in my mother's drawing-room with those two well-behaved people I could feel my youth threatening to overwhelm me. I wanted to get up, pace the room, throw open a window, leave at once for a long walk. I did not want to listen to Aubrey's measured sentences, or my mother's faithful and polite interjections. Yet when I was seated at the dining-table, and we were all three eating my mother's excellent roast chicken, followed by her equally excellent lemon tart, I succumbed to a feeling of family solidarity, a feeling to which I was willing to admit Aubrey on a temporary basis, largely because I was so filled with benevolence towards the elderly, whom I pitied for no longer having access to the happiness I had so recently known. I pitied them both for their very politeness, which I thought must be a regrettable substitute for impulses which had died with their youth. They seemed to have no idea that they were unfortunate or benighted, but I found myself looking for and finding signs of impending old age in their heightened colour, the satisfaction with which Aubrey plied his fork, their savouring of the sweetness of the lemon tart and the last mouthful of wine. After the coffee I knew that Aubrey would go upstairs to his own flat and pass out. I always left soon after lunch so as to let Mother have a rest. I had no wish to see her asleep, thinking it would detract from her dignity. Also my restlessness would not permit me to stay silent until she woke up. The terrible stillness of Sunday afternoons, the impression I had of sleep settling on elderly people everywhere in this corner of London, combined with the habitual dead calm of the streets, afflicted me with a melancholy which I was ill-equipped to bear, made me feel uncared for, as if those who should be caring for me had abdicated their responsibilities, leaving me alone and without resource. On the afternoon of this particular day, of course, I intended to go straight to Paddington Street, a fact which must be kept from my mother at all costs. In fact it was she who introduced Sarah's name, as she straightened the collar of my jacket and brushed my sleeve.

'You wrote to Sybil dear?' she said. 'And you managed to have a word with Sarah?'

'As a matter of fact I thought I might go round there this afternoon,' I replied, and with those words felt an onrush of the fiery joy with which Sarah's name was now associated. There was also a certain amount of sweetness in the fact that I had been open with my mother, who at that stage certainly did not suspect my involvement. I never liked to lie to my mother, though I considered certain aspects of my behaviour too likely to shock her. The fact of this partial confession— that I intended to call on this particular woman—alerted me to the possibility that in ideal circumstances Sarah and my mother might be contained in the same thought, that Sarah's name might be introduced quite naturally into any conversation I might be having with my mother, as if she were a bona fide relation, or as if she were my wife. I did not see why I should not marry her, although I could see why she would not marry me. There was the question of getting her to concentrate for a sufficient length of time on myself, my history, my attributes, all of which appeared to be of no interest to her. Her engagement with me was confined to the physical, and for the moment I found this so exciting that I preferred to think of myself as a lover pure and simple, that illusory family framework fragmenting even before I had time to reflect on the possible benefits of squaring the circle, never far from my conventional mind. I had no desire to marry, nor was there any pressure on me to do so. My mother, I knew, secretly valued the fact that I was unattached. I had wanted to make her feel included in my secret life, but there was an impropriety in this. I had probably left the condition in which it was natural for me to confide in my mother far behind, with my school-days and my first holidays away from home.

Now I must be tactful, for I had naturally entered an area of concealment. Nevertheless I felt an odd pang of regret for that spontaneous openness that had once been mine and which I was conscious of laying to rest on that particular Sunday, as I looked at the two gallantly wakeful elderly faces surveying me with carefully concealed indulgence. Mother's face, when she kissed me, was warm: she hated me to see her looking less than her best. Aubrey shook my hand, as he always did. I waited until he had turned the corner of the staircase back to his own flat. Their relief when both of their doors shut was almost palpable.

I marched briskly across the park to Marble Arch, through Old Quebec Street to Portman Square and up Baker Street to Paddington Street. There was no reply from Sarah's flat. This did not greatly discompose me; I had not really expected to find her at home. I had no idea what young women did on Sundays in London; possibly I had thought that they drove out to visit friends in the country. Then I realised that I did not know the make or number of Sarah's car, for I assumed she had one. In fact I knew nothing about her, how she spent her days, how she earned her living, how she saw her future. She presumably had enough money from the sale of the house to live on quite comfortably, yet the flat had been half furnished, and the droopy flowered dress that she had worn had looked as if she had picked it up from a market stall. Of her two expressions, the one morbid, the other indifferent, I preferred the former. Combined with her long crapy red hair it gave her a pre-Raphaelite air of brooding intensity. Yet, apart from brief intervals of animation when she was with friends, she was not intense: she was almost frustratingly superficial, confining her remarks to what could be avoided, refusing communication on any other level. What had made our nights together so exciting had been their very wordlessness: there had been enactment of an almost magical kind. It was that memory that was to sustain me through the days that followed, when I hoped, but did not expect, to hear from her, and when, in my own bedroom, I could almost hear the ringing of her unanswered telephone. Even this acted as an intriguing reminder of her silence, which seemed to me then to be superior to any gift for conversation. Indeed, her very taciturnity, the fact that at no stage would she explain herself, even when explanations were most urgently required, consigned her to a special category of passively demonic women who are usually death to a man's peace of mind, as Sarah was to be to mine.

On the following morning Brian came into my office, waving a square card of the kind used for wedding invitations. 'Had one of these?' he asked.

I took it. 'Sarah,' it said. 'At home. 5th May, 6.30–8.30.'

I hated it. I hated the pomposity of the engraving and the coyness of 'Sarah'. Above all I hated the fact that nothing like it had come in the morning's post.

'I expect mine's at home,' I told him.

'The thing is, I don't know whether to go or not.'

'You could always take Pamela,' I said nastily.

'Felicity's parents particularly want to see us at the moment. They're rather insistent. Weddings, you know. I feel rather overlooked, to tell you the truth. Oh, she's a marvellous girl, and we've known each other for ages, but I'm not sure I want to get married. I like women too much, you see.'

'I've noticed.'

'And I don't want to stop.' He produced this truth manfully, as he had at school, when owning up to a misdemeanour. Together we contemplated Brian's future as a solidly married chaser of other women.

'I don't want you to go to this party, Brian,' I told him. 'There's nothing in it for you.'

'I'm not sure about that,' he said. 'Why, you mean you . . . ?'

At that moment, to my intense relief, the telephone rang. When I eventually replaced the receiver I concentrated my energies and stared at Brian fixedly, in an attempt to forestall his next question.

'And have you . . . ?' he asked, intrigued but not hostile. 'Ah. I see. Right.' I could see him thinking furiously, planning, for all I know. I am very fond of Brian, as he is, I think, of me, but I do not share his views on women. To Brian every woman is an unrepeatable offer, waiting to be snapped up: he is a confident acquirer of new friends. And it seems to suit him; he has a sunny disposition and an even temper and an aura of confidence that tells you that he was once his mother's favourite. Nor does his behaviour lose him any friends. I have seen him prospecting, and there is a sort of grace about him even at those times, the sort of grace in which I have always been deficient. I am stolid and prudent and slightly behind the times, ill-equipped for subtlety or light-heartedness, and yet I know that I am capable of passion. This is my secret, to be revealed to only one other person. I had always thought that my behaviour would speak for me, so that I should have no need of embarrassing explanations. So far I had avoided them; now there was no point in disguising the fact that Sarah had breached my defences. I was in thrall to her, and encouraged so to be by the very fact of our physical virtuosity. This to me was love, love that had no need of words, pleas, arguments, justifications. To love wordlessly, to meet on a level of arcane comprehension, of mysterious communication not visible to others, still seems to me the highest good. That is when one is truly known, or so I tell myself still. Perhaps it was self-serving of me never to make a declaration, but I knew that if I did Sarah would merely raise a sardonic eyebrow. I told myself that she felt as I did, and in this alone I am persuaded that I was not wrong.

I checked the second post carefully: nothing. I declined Brian's invitation to lunch, saying that I wanted to do some shopping. This sounded silly even to my ears, but in fact I did go to a shop and buy a large bunch of pink lilies, which smelled as insistently as a chapel full of incense. These I took round to Paddington Street, where the door was opened instantly, as I had known it would be, by a girl whom I recognised as Sarah's docile friend Angela. Sarah, wearing a towelling bathrobe, her marvellous hair newly washed, materialised silently behind her.

'Hello,' I said, cursing the need to use my voice. Words seemed to me as problematic as they must have been to primitive man. 'I thought you might like these.'

'Oh, aren't they *lovely*?' said Angela. 'I'll just put them in water, shall I?'

With her momentary disappearance I sought to embrace Sarah, and was relieved to feel her response, when her friend returned, bearing a vase. She flushed as if she had witnessed something untoward. No doubt the poor girl was in an agony of embarrassment; the air was thick with the scent of our closeness, and it was evident that a third person's presence was not required. Sarah remained calm, even amused, not altogether displeased by her friend's discomfiture and my heavier breathing.

'We were just discussing my party,' she said, as if I knew all about it. 'Angela's doing the catering. She's frightfully good at that sort of thing.'

'I think it's important that the hostess should be free to circulate,' Angela put in. Her colour was beginning to fade, yet she looked unhappy. I wondered briefly if she were always so sacrificial, and if so what infallible instinct had guided her towards Sarah, who gave no prizes for constancy and devotion. Angela was the meek girl-friend whom every confident woman learns to use as a foil, probably when she is still at school. She would, if seen on her own, be thought pretty, with the sort of blonde hair and fair skin that tend to look colourless when their owner is not in perfect health and a little too suffused when she is. She was the third person to know of our attachment, the first two being Sarah and myself.

'And am I invited to this party?' I asked, determined to attend even if denied entrance.

She shrugged. 'Sure.' In comparison with her unhappy friend she was an icon of impassivity, as she stood there in her white bathrobe, her feet bare, on her face a familiar brooding expression, her skin matt, as if her heavy hair had drained the colour from it, her hands hanging loose at her sides. Her friend was dressed in the sort of clothes my mother would have applauded as suitable, a grey pleated skirt, a red jacket, and a white blouse with the same sort of pie-frill collar that I remembered vaguely as having seen before. The three of us stood somewhat awkwardly in the middle of the room, Angela and I being unwilling to be the first to leave, until I said, 'Well, I suppose I'd better be getting back to work,' hoping to call forth the same sort of declaration from Angela—Sarah clearly was not going anywhere—but, 'I'm lucky, I only work part time. I get time off in the week for going in on a Saturday morning.' Then I was moved to ask her what she did. It appeared that she was a secretary on an architectural magazine with offices in Bloomsbury and that she lived in a flat which she shared with two other girls, in Bedford Way. This information seemed to me so juvenile and depressing that I immediately discarded it.

'I'll look in this evening,' I told Sarah. She gave no indication that she heard me. It was Angela who saw me to the door.

The afternoon passed without incident. By six o'clock I was back in Paddington Street. As if warned by some attendant spirit, I did not expect to be admitted, nor was I. There was no answer to my ring, and when I lifted the letter box and peered in, the flat was dark. I knew that there was no one there, though I date the beginnings of my distrust from that moment. My ridiculous position, squatting down outside the door, should have told me that I was beginning to be in error.

That was how I always thought of questionable behaviour, as being in error. Faintly I could smell the lilies, the scent of which now seemed to me baleful.

I wandered home, though I knew I should go back later that evening. I thought of telephoning Mother until I realised that she and Aubrey would be settling down in front of *Coronation Street*, to which they were both addicted.

'Isn't it time he got a set of his own?' I had asked her.

'He doesn't approve. He says television is one of the blights of modern civilisation.'

'And yet he watches that rubbish.'

'Well, you see, darling, it's so frightfully good. So well acted. And the people seem so friendly in that part of the world. Aubrey has often remarked on this, and as you know he's been everywhere.'

I decided to leave them to it, and went round the corner for a quick meal, after which I felt unaccountably tired. All this was proving a strain. Knowing that I should not sleep, and preferring unfinished business to no business at all, I went back to Paddington Street and met the same black silence. I reached home just after eleven and slept exhaustively. I always sleep well when I am disheartened.

I saw her again, but all too infrequently. Those meetings were to be our last, though I did not know this at the time. I can impute no fault to Sarah, have never blamed her for her absences, which never quite took the form of refusals. Nor was she entirely indifferent. Rather, she was unknowable, enjoying our comings together as much as I did, but not appearing to remember them, perhaps judging them as acts which would pass naturally into oblivion. It was only when I had lost her, had lost the possibility of ever seeing her again, that I began to dwell obsessively on her absence I never fantasised about her, never thought that I glimpsed her in the street, never reacted when a woman with the same colour hair walked in front of me, never smelled her phantom scent. I became aware of absence in the most dolorous and unexpected ways, yet even then I never pictured her with another man. Her gift to me was her singularity, so that in my imagination she was always alone, communing intently with herself, or perhaps not even thinking at all, simply existing, out of my reach. I never knew what she thought of me, because I never asked her. Even in hindsight I do not entirely regret this. I never made a fool of myself. If my expression was ever soulful and pleading it simply vanished into the black hole that was her lack of overt response. On that other level we knew each other perfectly. Like a satellite that fails to return to earth, our adventure was unfinished but beyond human retrieval systems.

Her party, when it came, was dreadful, as I knew it would be. A deafening sound system had been installed, possibly by one of several young men, to whom I was not introduced. The room was full of people, all making a great deal of additional noise, among whom I made out her friend Berthe, to whom shouting and shrieking were a natural mode of discourse. The maidenly Angela squeezed past me from time to time, proferring plates of food, on which she had obviously spent the whole afternoon: pin-wheels of cream cheese and asparagus, tiny sausages which needed the accompaniment of a bowl of mustard, smoked salmon on brown bread, crudités, with another bowl, this time of mayonnaise, none of which was either necessary or appreciated. I felt sorry for her. Being somewhat superfluous myself, I could see how she had taken on this task in the hope of being popular. She was the sort of girl to whom her mother says, 'Accept every invitation. You never know when you might meet someone.' So far she had met no one, except myself, and I had come to the conclusion that I was out of place. I was not unhappy, merely bored. I never enjoy these gatherings, and this seemed to me worse than most. I was annoyed, too, to see that Sarah was enjoying herself, shrieking with the best of them, though this was becoming increasingly necessary in the crowded room. In this mode she struck me as ordinary, undistinguished. I preferred her silent, even when her mouth remained closed on the words I longed to hear.

'You're very quiet,' said Angela, who now seemed to me to be permanently at my elbow. 'Is there anyone you want to meet? Not that I know everyone. But doesn't Sarah do these things well? I think it's a success, don't you?'

She seemed anxious for it to be a success, as if it were her own party. Perhaps she had been invited to think, or had merely assumed, that this was a joint affair, that it was her natural role to provide for the guests, in the vain hope that they would pay her some attention. If she had thought that, she was disappointed, although her disappointment was disguised by a hectic flush and a mask of fearful animation. She seemed as out of place as I felt. It occurred to me to ask her what the connection was between Sarah and herself.

'We were at school together,' she said. 'I've known her all my life.'

In which case, I reflected, it was a friendship doomed to be one-sided. Sarah was the kind of woman who does not need female friends, only the occasional sparring partner with whom to exchange recondite information. This function was obviously filled by Berthe, who waved to me across the room. I would have approached her, thinking her intriguing, though much too noisy, had it not been for Angela, whom it would have been rude to desert.

'Don't mind me,' she said, 'if you want to circulate. I've got my hands full. Has everybody had enough to eat, do you think?'

The food lay around almost untouched. Drink, on the other hand, was being consumed on a scale with which I was unfamiliar. The atmosphere was thick with smoke.

'I shouldn't worry about the food,' I told her. 'You've done splendidly.'

'I'd better take it back to the kitchen, then. Oh, you're not leaving?'

'Well, yes. I brought some papers home with me that I ought to look at tonight.' That at least was true.

I slipped out into the beautiful night, in which even the sound of a police siren made a relatively civilised noise. I was halfway down Paddington Street when I heard footsteps behind me and turned to see Angela, her ghostly white blouse and flowered skirt enhanced by the light of a street lamp. Politely I waited for her to catch me up, reflecting that she was actually rather pretty. In the dark she seemed fragile, her waist and ankles thin, her hair almost bleached.

'Which way do you go?' she asked, a little breathlessly.

I told her that I lived in Wigmore Street, to which she said, 'Oh, then you're quite near Sarah.' I said that my flat was convenient for my office in Gloucester Place, to which she replied that she too lived near her work in Bloomsbury. After this there seemed nothing more to say, and we walked on in silence.

'I can't take you home,' I said. 'I've got this work to sort out before tomorrow. I'll find you a cab.'

'Oh, that's all right. I'm in no hurry. It's rather pleasant to walk after stewing in that room, isn't it?'

'Didn't you enjoy yourself?'

'Oh, of course I enjoyed myself. It's just that I'm a bit of a loner. I love walking in the country. I love reading. Do you read a lot?'

'Not really. What sort of books do you read?'

'Oh, anything. I've been known to pick up two or three paperbacks just for the weekend.'

This seemed to me so damning an answer that there was nothing further to say. By now we were in Wigmore Street, passing the coffee bar where I ate my breakfast. I was glad to see that it was closed.

'Is that your local?' she asked.

'I sometimes eat there,' I replied.

'Oh, how interesting.' Her voice trailed off, as if she were thinking of something else. She seemed quite ready to get into the cab I hailed, as if exhausted or preoccupied. I lifted my hand briefly as the cab passed me, and then thought of her no more.

Ringing Sarah the next day, or rather attempting to ring her, took the best part of a morning. When I eventually got through it was to be told that she was going away for a bit. 'Anywhere special?' I asked. Possibly America, I was informed. To see friends. To my enquiries as to when she was leaving the answers were vague. 'I'll want to see you before you go,' I said temperately. 'I'll come round this evening. Will you be there?'

She said she thought so, but not to count on it. That evening found me once again peering through her letter-box. Then I went home and dialled her number. There was no response. For the first time in our history the sound awakened in me not merely frustration but bafflement, estrangement, distress. It was as if I were in a permanently empty room, and as if a ringing telephone, by some unknown decree, were doomed to ring unanswered throughout eternity.

7

Shortly after that evening I had a remote perception of Sarah's absence. It affected me like a sudden fall in body temperature, or a diminution of oxygen in the atmosphere. My feelings were a mystery to me. To fall in love with someone who refuses all communication was contrary to my nature, which is nothing if not practical. I had always thought that my life would follow a pleasant if undistinguished pattern: success in the profession, harmonious family relationships, and eventually marriage and children. I was modestly successful, certainly, and I was devoted to my mother, but I did not see myself married, since Sarah was the only woman I desired, and Sarah promised only the most fugitive of contacts, no sooner offered than taken away, leaving no trace, and with every absence growing more elusive.

If I felt any satisfaction with my part in this liaison it was largely for having taken up a challenge, and for having flown in the face of all my precepts, professional and otherwise. I had the distinct impression that my modest store of principles was diminishing: I was ready to behave uncharacteristically in pursuit of this empty centre of my life, a pursuit which I rather thought might last for ever. I was ready, in short, to devote myself to her, although I knew that such devotion would not influence her in any way. There was always present the sheer difficulty of impinging on her consciousness, of that attention always withheld, and it was precisely against this sense of occlusion that her physical response seemed so miraculous. Yet in my more collected moments I was aware that I knew very little about her, as indeed did her mother. Another letter from Sybil had arrived that morning; the scope of her grievances seemed to have widened. Now she complained about her daughter, and behind the complaints I sensed a genuine impotence. Would I see to it that Sarah kept in touch? 'From a professional point of view, Alan, your words are bound to have an influence.' I had apparently been promoted to magistrate, or perhaps rural dean, with cure of souls. I wrote back, on a purposely vague but I hope affectionate note, saying that I had seen Sarah, that she was well and happy, and that I was sure that she would be in touch. If I did this it was because Sybil now derived additional importance from the fact that she was Sarah's mother.

It must have been a few weeks later that on entering the coffee bar for breakfast I saw Angela, seated expectantly at a table, an empty cup in front of her. My astonishment was hardly feigned; on the other hand it was not her fault that she wore that look of bright expectancy. Not her fault, perhaps, but just possibly an error, as was the fact that she made no apology for invading my privacy in this manner. For I regarded this half-hour as unconditionally mine. Even the proprietress, Mrs Daley, knew not to engage me in conversation. My coffee appeared without commentary, followed by my toast. I was only just aware of the hand placing the cup and plate on the table, leaving me to uninterrupted perusal of *The Times*. Bachelors enjoy these small privileges, even when they are distracted, as I had to admit I was, although I viewed my condition as morbid. For that very reason I made an effort to behave normally, or as normally as was possible in these abnormal circumstances.

'Hello,' I said. 'This is a surprise.'

'I just thought it would be nice to see you again.' She reddened then, with one of her frequent blushes. My only thought was how transparent she was. She made no attempt to hide the fact that she had to all intents and purposes followed me. Such directness was a novelty after the feints of Sarah's behaviour, and I suppose I felt relief that cards were for once on the table. In the harsh light of the café she was pleasant to look at; her colouring was fresh and her eyes bright. When she felt me looking at her she undid her headscarf and shook back her hair. She regarded this manoeuvre as defiantly seductive and blushed again, furiously, when she saw my face relax into a smile.

'So, what are you up to these days?' I asked her. It seemed only polite to take an interest in her life, although she seemed already to have produced it for my inspection. I thought I could guess the rest: that she had until recently lived at home with her parents (I was wrong here: her mother was a widow, like mine), that she was not altogether happy living in a flat with two other girls, that she was the one who stayed home and washed her hair while the other two went out, that she was frightened by her companions' promiscuity, or what she thought of as promiscuity, that she had lost her virginity late and reluctantly, and that she needed stronger personalities to protect her from the shocks of this rough world. Her attendance on Sarah was entirely characteristic, although she may not even have liked her. Probably attraction and repulsion were the same two sides of every coin for her, and fear would be uppermost in her mind at every new encounter. It had no doubt taken an enormous act of courage for her to confront me like this, for it was a confrontation, of that there was no doubt. She was laying herself open for my inspection, and I could not help but feel touched. I was also irritated. There was an element of pleading in her rather too bright expression. I thought she might burst into tears if I were not gentle with her. I recognised the obligations to be gentle as a chore, and thought of Sarah with yet another pang. With Sarah I was not obliged to be gentle. I may have been importunate but that was my choice: I could also be selfish, brutal, joyous, triumphant. She had given me tacit permission to please myself and in so doing to please her at the same time. That was her gift to me: pure unreflecting pleasure, for which I felt there would never be any substitute.

'I expect you're very busy,' said Angela, as if she knew that all men were perpetually busy.

'Well, I dare say you are too,' I replied. 'After all, women do most of the work these days, or so they tell me. The girls in my office don't let me get away with any assumptions about my importance, or rather lack of it.' I was making heavy weather of this, I realised. I simply did not know what to say.

'I meant to tell you—that's why I'm here, really. I took those lilies home with me. I hope you don't mind.'

'Didn't Sarah want them then?' I asked carelessly.

'She said the smell gave her a headache. When I went back the next day to clear up she said to throw them away. So I took them. You're not cross, are you?'

'Not at all. And, anyway, Sarah's away, I believe.'

'That's right. America. She's wonderful, isn't she, the way she just acts on impulse? I mean she hasn't got a job or anything. I know she's quite well off, but you'd think she'd invest her money or something. I know I would. But she seems determined to enjoy herself while she can. I suppose you can't blame her.'

Angela obviously did blame her, just as she blamed her prodigality in every other respect. Though she had no proof of this she must have intuited it correctly.

'Any idea how long she'll be away?' I asked. 'Or when she's coming back?'

'Not really, no. You never know with Sarah, do you? At least I don't. She makes me quite dizzy sometimes.' She laughed merrily to show that she bore no malice. I revised my earlier opinion: I could see that she disliked Sarah quite intensely.

'I rather need to know how to get in touch with her,' I said.

'My goodness, are you another one of Sarah's conquests?' Again the merry laugh. This girl, I could see, this *maiden*, had been severely shaken by her friendship, if friendship it could be called, with a woman whom she knew to be superior to herself in one crucial respect, and brooding on this superiority had made her clumsy in her approach to men. Her wholesome aspect, her evident lack of experience, which might have attracted a much older man, embarrassed me, and made me very slightly antagonistic. I did not appreciate this lack of subtlety, although paradoxically it was being paraded for my benefit. I knew that unless I injected a note of sobriety into the proceedings there might be some hectic and unwelcome attempts to tease me. I have seen men beguiled by this sort of nonsense, which I associated with children's birthday parties. I put it on a level with tickling: certainly I wanted no part of it.

'Sarah is a distant relation of mine,' I told her, picking up our two bills. 'Her mother has asked me to keep an eye on her.'

'Oh. Oh, I see. Well I can't help you there, I'm afraid. She didn't tell me when she was coming back. I expect she'll just turn up when she feels like it, don't you?'

As she walked out of the door in front of me I noticed the slimness of her legs. Otherwise her physical presence hardly registered, although I had every opportunity to appreciate it since she turned up again the following day, and the day after that. Soon Mrs Daley, sensing perhaps my irritation, would answer my silent enquiry with a barely perceptible nod towards the corner of the room where Angela was modestly but insistently installed. I was left in no doubt that she had me in her sights. This so alarmed me that for a week I went to the trouble of cooking breakfast at home, but this entailed remembering to buy bread and eggs, and carrying a plastic bag to the office, to the disapproval of Mrs Roche. Then one morning I found that I had run out of coffee, and felt vaguely ashamed of myself for so obviously avoiding this quite harmless girl. Mrs Daley was quite aware of my state of mind. By the end of three weeks she had ceased to nod conspiratorially to me and now busied herself polishing spoons. She had decided to believe that Angela was my girl-friend. Unfortunately Angela did too.

'See you tomorrow,' she always said as we left. And she had already given me her telephone number at home and at work, and had asked for mine. I was obliged to give her the office number, saying that there was no point in ringing me at home, as I was hardly ever there. 'Where are you, then?' she said. I winced, and told her that I spent a lot of time with my mother, noting with a sinking heart that this fallacious information was yet another point in my favour.

As a matter of fact Mother did ring me one evening and

asked me to come over, as she had something to discuss with me. I imagined that this had something to do with her investments, on which matter she habitually deferred to me, although she was quite capable of managing very well on her own. As I trudged through the park I felt vaguely uneasy. Looking back later, I saw that this was premonitory; at the time, however, I merely looked forward to eating one of her delicious suppers and listening to her news, to which I need pay little attention. She was a supremely tactful woman, who had no doubt spoilt me in this respect: she saw that she must not burden me with information of any significance until I had eaten, and never before she had satisfied herself that I was comfortable. Therefore I was largely unprepared to find her so nervous and so abrupt. Scarcely had I taken off my coat than she ushered me without ceremony into the drawing-room and indicated a chair. I sat down warily, thinking that I must be in for some additional duties. All I could think of was Sybil, presenting Mother with some intractable family problem which I should have to sort out.

'My darling,' said my mother hesitantly, 'I have something to tell you.'

'Are you ill?' I said, alarmed.

'No, no. It's just that Aubrey and I were married this morning.'

'What? You mean you didn't tell me? Warn me, I should say.'

'I made up my mind very quickly,' said this woman who had once claimed that her position in life was to be my mother. 'Of course it will make no difference to my feelings for you. In my heart you will always come first. And Aubrey has been so kind: that's why he stayed upstairs—he knew I'd want to see you on my own. We'll move in together when we get back.'

'Back from where?'

'From Cagnes, darling. He has this little house, and we're going there soon, perhaps next week.'

'For your honeymoon,' I said, trying to come to terms with the fact that my mother was not only going to marry this man but to sleep with him as well. I felt like Hamlet, though as far as I could see (and I had to concede this) Aubrey was not in the least like Claudius. Then I got to my feet and kissed her and was rewarded for my effort when she wiped her eyes and put away her handkerchief and gave me a shaky but happy smile.

'What decided you?' I asked. 'After all this time.'

'Such a silly thing. I was out with Jenny, on one of our afternoon excursions. Perhaps I was a little out of sorts, or perhaps I wasn't listening, as I usually do, to Jenny's chatter. Suddenly I caught sight of the two of us in a long mirror in one of the shops, and, Alan, I saw two old women, arm in arm, with obviously nothing better to do with their time than spend it in department stores, in that terrible over-heated atmosphere. I could feel Jenny's arm weighing me down. And I suddenly thought, "I don't want to get old like this. I want a sense of renewal. I want to be with a man again."'

'And is that what Aubrey offers you? A sense of renewal?'

'He offers me kindness, care, generosity, and a social position. And perhaps the last is the most important. A woman on her own is rarely respected for what she is, and not always for what she does. She has to make a strenuous bid for recognition if she wants to merit attention, even in this day and age. And she is not always treated kindly, particularly when she is no longer young. I look in the mirror these mornings and I am shocked. And to think that I was once admired for my looks! And I notice little things about myself that tell me that I'm getting older. I dread the winter, dark nights, wet leaves on the pavement. I could so easily fall, or Jenny could, pulling me down with her.'

I sensed a new regard for self, where previously there had been only selflessness. I took her in my arms and comforted her, until her renewed sobs had subsided. I longed for her as she had always been, and was to be no longer.

'So perhaps you'd give Aubrey a ring this evening, when you get home, darling, to offer your congratulations? And there'll be a few people for drinks on Sunday, just to avoid the awkwardness of writing to everyone. Not that there are too many of our old friends left.' She meant, I knew, the friends that she had had when she was married to my father.

'Jenny will miss you,' I said. I felt in that instant for everyone who would miss my mother, for I did not doubt that she would quickly become absorbed in her new life. 'I suppose you'll be travelling more,' I went on. 'Aubrey's always off somewhere, isn't he?'

'I've told him that he must go on his own, that it will be good for us to take occasional breaks from each other. Then you and I will be just as we've always been, darling.'

'Until he comes back,' I said.

'Oh, Alan. Be kind, dear. After all, one day you'll marry and leave me on my own . . .'

'I should never do that.'

'Oh, yes. And perhaps sooner than you know. And I don't want to be alone any more than you do. And it will be good for you to know that you don't have to worry about me. Aubrey will do that.'

'Are you fond of him, then?' I asked.

'I am, yes. And he is fond of me. That's always a comforting thing to remember. I think we shall be very happy once these awful announcements are behind us. You won't forget to ring him, will you, dear? And Sunday for drinks, twelve noon.'

Only the empty park, I thought, was wide enough to contain my thoughts, which were of rage and loneliness, as if I were an infant. Yet gradually I calmed down and began to see matters more objectively. There was no point in not being glad for Mother. Everything she had said made sense. I knew and liked Aubrey, to whom I must this very evening offer congratulations, as if I were a hearty senior in a club frequented by old buffers. What made me sad was a comparison of Mother's situation with my own. I had no one. At that moment the thought struck me that Sarah's absence might be permanent, that she might never come home, that if she did she would continue to be as elusive and as uncommitted as she had always been. A new notion was making its insidious way into my consciousness: that this was unworthy behaviour, that one did not wander affectless through life, ignorant of or indifferent to one's influence on others. I thought that I deserved better, or perhaps needed more than an occasional casual recognition of my enslavement. For she can have been in no doubt, despite my plucky offhandedness. And I had thought that I was sure of her response, of that light so persistently hidden under a bushel. Strange how the Biblical phrase came back to me, I who had been devoutly secular all my life. I wanted my reward on earth, now more than ever. I was aware of spiralling self-doubt, like physical nausea, threatening to overwhelm me. The force of my distress made me feel literally queasy. I could not wait to get back to the safety of my flat.

It did not occur to me to wonder at the discrepancy between my equable public persona and the private turmoil that assailed me whenever I was engulfed in my own thoughts. Never having encountered this turmoil before I chose to believe that it was customary in the circumstances, and that others had been similarly assailed before. Nothing had prepared me for it, but I had no proof that it was unprecedented. Certainly the dichotomy was worse when I was alone, as I was now; on the other hand, nothing would have induced me to ask advice. Suddenly it all became intolerable, and I was as forlorn and bewildered as I had not been since early childhood. I took a sheet of paper, and, almost without thinking, began a letter. Dear Sarah, I wrote. I seem unable to reach you, and this is now a problem, in many ways. I long for you, but for the first time without hope. You had seemed to me once to be part of my future, or rather part of an everlasting present that would become that future, yet you barely deign to acknowledge the present, let alone that future. I want you in my life, yet you remain obstinately outside it. Perhaps it is time for me to take my leave, no longer to let matters remain unfinished, but to finish them. In my heart you will always come first. (I remembered my mother saying this.) I will make no further attempts to contact you. You know where to find me if you ever need me. But you will understand if I no longer wish to spend my life running after you, or even to remain on my own. (This last remark was sheer bravado. I must have thought I could torment her by hinting at a rival, several rivals. This I knew would not severely disturb her, but I left it in. It felt mildly dangerous, provocative.) I am yours devotedly, in spite of, or rather because of, everything, Alan.

Then, feeling noble and calm, and quite resolute after my recent distress, I telephoned Aubrey and wished him well. He was very pleased.

'We shall always be glad to see you, Alan. Don't leave it too long. And of course the house in France is yours whenever you want it. You'll be with us on Sunday? I'll look forward to seeing you then.'

The following morning in the coffee bar I ordered eggs with my toast in an attempt to make myself feel better.

'Gosh, you look awful,' said Angela, her eyes widening in sympathy. 'Has something upset you?'

'My mother's getting married. No, she's got married. She was married yesterday morning. I still can't believe it.'

'How absolutely frightful for you,' was her response. Frightful for *me*, I noted. She had instinctively got it right.

'They're giving a small drinks party on Sunday,' I told her. 'I don't suppose it would amuse you . . . ?'

'I'd love to come. I'll pick you up, shall I? I'd love to see your flat. Then perhaps we could walk across the park. I'm a great walker.'

In the light of what was to come, all I can offer was the fact that I had posted my letter to Sarah, and consequently did not want to be alone, or to be seen to be alone, in case news of me should ever get back to her.

In fact I was glad to have Angela with me on that Sunday, when Mother and Aubrey were the centre of attention, and I had no function except to assure friends that I was delighted for her. I felt like a bridesmaid at the wedding of her oldest friend, aware that life would soon separate us. I was of course glad to see Mother so happy. I saw her glancing speculatively at Angela, who once again made herself useful handing round the canapés. I wondered if the poor girl faced a lifetime of doing this, at least until someone rescued her and elevated her to a position superior to that of handmaid. Strangely, Mother did not seem to appreciate her assiduity, and at one point took a tray from her and told her to sit down and drink a glass of champagne. The only other people sitting down were Humphrey and Jenny, Jenny looking doleful, Humphrey nearly asleep. I could see why Mother wanted to enjoy a form of life rather more removed from their orbit than would have been possible had Aubrey not been at hand. One makes significant decisions sometimes on the strength of insignificant pointers. One look at Jenny's swollen feet told me more about those afternoons that had been deemed so pleasurable than Mother's remarks about status and respect had been able to do. As she had said, she had once been admired for her looks and even now was an attractive woman.

'Doesn't she look lovely?' whispered Jenny. 'I'm so glad for her. Of course I'll miss her.'

'But she'll still be here,' I assured her. 'Although we can't expect her to be here as much as formerly.'

'Oh, no, Alan. It won't be the same at all.' There was a finality to her tone that spoke of past disappointments, past betrayals. 'Come, Humphrey. It's time for us to go. You'll come to see us, Alan? Humphrey is so fond of you. As I am, of course.'

'Still waiting to show you my clocks,' said Humphrey, as Jenny manoeuvred him to his feet. 'Come any time. Always pleased to see you. And Anthea, of course.'

I wondered who Anthea could be until I saw Angela faithfully posted on Humphrey's other side. She was invaluable in awkward or dreary situations, although ill at ease with people of her own age. She took Humphrey's other arm and kissed him goodbye, at which I saw Jenny give her the same lightning appraisal that had momentarily arrested my mother's happy exuberance. Jenny's expression was considered, as if she might be sorry for one so inexperienced, but at the same time devoid of indulgence for that lack of experience. I remembered that she had been a working woman, possibly a woman who had lived on her wits, and that this event, my mother's marriage, signified for her the end of something she had come to treasure: equality. With Mother she had been allowed to think of herself as a lady. Now she was on her own again.

The party broke up at about two o'clock, and soon we were out in the dead calm of the Sunday street, a calm broken only by Angela's breathy enthusiasms. She thought everything was marvellous, my mother amazing, Humphrey adorable. I suddenly found this hard to bear. She was no companion for my forlorn state. I thought only of the letter I had sent to Paddington Street, and cursed myself for having sent it. It seemed to me then that my moment of lucidity was no substitute for a lifetime of hope and expectation, fallacious though both might have been. I had a headache; I felt vaguely sick. I remembered how I had tried to avoid Mother's parties all my adult life. My ungracious mood must have communicated itself to Angela; certainly I did nothing to disguise it. I took her home in a taxi, refused her invitation to coffee, and walked back. In the flat I resisted an impulse to sleep, and settled down to study some papers. These too I eventually pushed aside and spent the rest of the afternoon watching a football match on television. I have no interest in football, but I could think of nothing better to do.

At what point does destiny reveal itself? I woke up the following morning with a temperature. I plodded into the office, feeling dreadful, and was sent home by Mrs Roche. It was only the flu, I told myself, but I had never been ill, and did not know how to take care of myself. I remembered a vague injunction to drink plenty of fluids, but I did not have the strength to make myself a cup of tea, and cold water made me feel worse. Eventually I went to bed and tried to sleep, without success. Some time in the middle of the night I realised that I was unnaturally hot, and also that I had not cancelled my appointments for the following day. Regardless of the hour I tried to ring Brian, but there was no answer from his Dorset Square flat. If I were to die I thought it important that someone should know. I could not bring myself to disturb Mother; that was my last sensible thought, and I was rather proud of it. But by the morning all reticence, every shred of self-respect had vanished. That was when I telephoned Angela.

And she was there, miraculously, and within an hour. Home-made lemon barley water appeared on my bedside table. I did not hear her leave: at some point it occurred to me that she must have pitched camp in another room. She was an excellent nurse, and I clung to her gratefully. When the fever left me I saw a small suitcase in the corner of the bedroom and realised that she had to all intents and purposes moved in. I wondered how she would take it when I intimated to her that I would be perfectly all right on my own once again. In the end I was too weak. Or perhaps I lacked the necessary resolution. Perhaps she knew what she wanted and I had temporarily forgotten what it was that I had always wanted. I said nothing. That was how she came to stay. She had sponged my burning body, she had seen me naked. My helplessness gave her a new authority. I could not but remain grateful for the care she had shown me. Helplessly I felt a weight descend on my shoulders, the weight of domestic quietude. By the time I was on my feet again we seemed to have become engaged.

8

Illness serves as a corrective: one emerges from it sober but diminished. One learns that one's continuation cannot be taken for granted, or, as the poet puts it, never glad confident morning again. My brush with mortality—and it was only a bad attack of the flu—made me grateful and tender-hearted. Above all I was grateful for Angela's care, which remained constant. I accepted the fact that she now took charge of my comfort and, incidentally, of my flat; I would arrive home in the evenings to find her scrutinising swatches of fabric and colour charts. She was overjoyed, not only to have become engaged, but to have become engaged before any of her friends had managed to do so. And I think she loved me, in her rather juvenile and utterly conventional way: I was, as men go, a good catch. And I? I loved her pretty hands and feet, the camomile smell of her hair. I loved her domesticity, the stateliness with which she presided over my household affairs.

She gave up her job immediately, although I urged her not to; I was alternately becalmed and disconcerted to think of her sitting at home all day, although she seemed to think this perfectly natural. When she was not shopping, for which she dressed herself carefully, as other women do when they meet a friend for lunch, she was lying on the sofa reading one of her reassuring novels. When I bent over to kiss her on my return from the office, the look on her face was one of purest gratitude. It disarmed me, but I could not always suppress a feeling of irritation. It seemed to me that she had abdicated her independence and thus turned her back on all the advances that women had made. It also limited our conversation. 'What sort of a day did you have?' she would ritually say, and when I described an interesting case I could see that I was talking to myself. She preferred to think of us in a genteel country setting, in a house called The Old Rectory, or The Old Post Office, in which she, in a flowered skirt, and one of her eternal blouses, would bake bread or entertain guests of the squirearchical class. I did nothing to disabuse her, although I liked my flat. Vaguely I envisaged a move some time in the future, but when I saw how much pleasure the fantasy gave her I quietly laid the plan to rest. Reality, I knew, would always let her down.

She spent my money freely, as if it were her birthright. I could hardly object to this, since she cared for me so well, but I was sorry when my terracotta walls became an inhospitable vanilla, and my Hessian curtains were replaced by a William Morris print. The flat became transformed into a clinic, one of the many clinics in this area of London, and Angela into a sort of superior nurse. Yet her happiness disarmed me. She regarded her new status as entirely rewarding; I was aware at times that she was a little girl playing at being grown up. To confuse the matter, she did not behave like a little girl but as an unconvincing adult, one who lives the part for which she has been cast. Being engaged, to Angela, meant acting like an engaged person, rather than like a woman who is going to be married. Indeed, she was in no hurry to get married, as if the prospect displeased her in some way; what she really enjoyed was this role-playing, which had its beguiling moments even for myself. I liked to think of her concern spreading to every corner of my domain. I was sent out every morning like a schoolboy, while Angela set to with Hoovers and dusters, before arraying herself for a morning's shopping. This too was a semi-official activity. In order to buy half a pound of butter at Selfridges she would traverse Wigmore Street with a wicker basket over her arm, for all the world as if she were living in that market town in which she felt herself to be an honorary inhabitant. She listened fervently to *The Archers*, and rustic accents greeted me when I returned from the office.

But I was also greeted by a smell of fine cooking, and the meal that was produced was invariably delicious. I went out less: as Angela pointed out there was no need. On my way to work I greeted Mrs Daley at the coffee bar with a guilty wave as I hastened past. I was always early, and thus was able to work more effectively than ever. I was grateful to my professional life for posing few problems. If I was aware of anything that might eventually check my enthusiasm, it was at this stage too unformed to contain much anxiety. I too was amused by the novelty of my situation; I was touched and flattered by Angela's admiration. Above all I felt safe with her. I looked back on my affair with Sarah as a derangement, an inconvenience. I retained an image of myself peering through the letter-box of her flat in Paddington Street and felt little more than impatience, embarrassment. If I thought about her at all, it was with antagonism. Yet in my dreams, with Angela lying chastely beside me, I saw her strange closed face, the face that could so disconcertingly change to a mask of hilarity when in unimportant company, yet remained impassive even in the act of love.

Of course comparisons were inevitable, although I did nothing to encourage them, suppressing my thoughts as best I could. Anyone could have told me that suppressing thoughts is the best way to ensure their irruption at a later date. Angela was frightened of men; her trust in me, who she knew would never willingly harm her, was undermined by a certain primitive fear of the male animal. She was docile in my arms, but she was also ineradicably embarassed by the reactions of my body. I tried to explain that these were involuntary but she would turn her head away and a few moments later brightly talk of something else. Her pleading expression, which had been turned on me at our first meeting, had an unwelcome effect on me: I found it stimulation, so that our love-making was perhaps more violent than it should have been, until I came to realise that this was precisely what frightened her, as it might have frightened any inexperienced woman.

Her lack of experience puzzled me: it was in direct contrast to her wifely or womanly activities. In the daytime, safe from the terrors of the night, she was all confidence and competence, and I found her more and more beguiling. Yet I was forced to acknowledge the fact that my value to her was primarily as the essential component in a fantasy of married life that had been lovingly cherished ever since she was a little girl. As a lover I was as good as any other, since all were unwelcome, something to be endured, the price to be paid for a position for which she had secretly planned since our two lives had collided. Both of us were preoccupied by secrets. For Angela a tense kind of emotional bargaining took place: if she consented to do such and such a thing then she might claim a reward, the reward of freedom and respectability. My own thought processes were not essentially different: if I surrendered all my anarchic longings I could successfully engineer my emergence as a prime example of conformist man, housed, fed, cared for, my continued existence successfully guaranteed.

I accepted this. I have always been fairly conventional, and perhaps that was why I found Sarah's frustrating behaviour, her unaccountability, so intriguing. Initially I was pleased to think of myself as restored to order. In this respect I was perhaps more self-deluding than I knew. My mother, in her new realistic mood, did not really find Angela to her taste, although her manner towards her was welcoming. As a new wife herself she appeared to have a surer grasp of a couple's secret life than Angela and I did. Angela's fussiness, her awkward compliments, grated on my mother, who appeared to wonder why the prospect of marriage did not confer more dignity, more comprehension. She found my complacency equally puzzling, as if I had become middle-aged overnight. Aubrey was in favour of the match, not only because he wished me to be taken in charge by someone other than my mother. Angela flirted with him, as she did with Humphrey, elderly men being devoid of any kind of threat on her primitive scale of imaginings. She was wary of my mother, of her sophistication and her indulgence of the male, which she sensed, as she had always sensed another woman's potential response; she placed herself under Aubrey's protection when we went to Cadogan Gate, and his exquisite courtesy and basic self-satisfaction were equal to the task of putting Angela at her ease. For when she felt threatened or misunderstood, the tears would gather in her eyes and her face would lose its colour. I found this phenomenon so alarming that I perfected a whole armoury of disclaimers, so that in any situation and at all times I was able to reassure her that all was well.

The person with whom she felt most at ease was Jenny, whose initial doubts had been laid to rest by Angela's fervid overtures. Perhaps they were true soul-mates, or perhaps Jenny was a severe case of thwarted maternity. I remembered how she had coveted Sarah, and how Sarah had shrugged off her unwanted care, so that Sarah's visits to Humphrey had been planned to coincide with Jenny's afternoons out with my mother. She was thus doubly duped, and some realisation of this might have made her wary of new friendships. But she was lonely for young people, and if Sarah were so long absent then Angela would be more than acceptable as a replacement. Perhaps life with Humphrey was not quite all she had been promised, although when speaking of him she was touchingly loyal; perhaps she had simply not acceded to age as successfully as her elderly husband had done. My mother had always marvelled at her girlishness, her hopefulness. Whatever the reason, she adopted Angela as her new companion. Both professed a liking for Selfridges, and before long that was where Angela was wont to spend her afternoons, in the company of Jenny, whom she seemed to regard as a surrogate mother, although she had a perfectly good mother of her own, living on the outskirts of Maidstone. I noticed that although she professed great love for this parent, she would rarely make time to visit her, too protective of her new authority to wish to see it undermined. In the end it was I who insisted that we visit Mrs Milsom, although after an excruciating weekend in her red-brick box of a house I was not keen to repeat the experience.

Her mother was a tremulous but obstinate woman who deferred to me flatteringly on every conceivable subject and who did not appear to notice the extreme discomfort in which she lived. All the rooms in her house were small, so that the dining-room was filled by the dining-table, while three chairs and a television occupied the sitting-room. This last, however, was rarely used, as the kitchen was the largest room in the house, and I guessed that meals had been taken there prior to my arrival on the scene. A steep staircase led to three tiny bedrooms and a single bathroom. The garden was large and sloped down to a small stream, and it was there that Mrs Milsom spent the best part of her days, battling with weeds in all weathers. Her dust-coloured hair and her anxious unadorned face might have prefigured what Angela would have become had she not taken refuge in another life. Oddly enough there was no love lost between them. They were perpetually on the brink of some trivial argument, and the exasperated sweetness with which Angela addressed her mother might have alerted me to the strength of certain ani-mosities in a character which still seemed to me open, trust-ing, even childlike in its transparency.

Brian did not like her. This worried me, for Brian's approval was always necessary to me. Of course he was too well mannered to say that he did not like her, nor may he have formulated his dislike in any conscious way. His dislike was entirely characteristic: he simply did not find Angela attractive. He would not have wanted to make love to Angela had they been under house arrest at the Ritz for forty-eight hours. For Brian to abstain from his usual speculations on being introduced to a woman was a bad sign; a worse one was that although he had met her before he did not remember her, or indeed had never noticed her. Yet she was pleasant to look at, fresh, artless. It may have been the artlessness that put him off. Once, when she called in at the office with her market basket over her arm, he made an excuse and left. In Brian's simple view a woman should know how to play the great game and give every sign of that knowledge, rather than pose as Little Red Riding Hood. I think he felt genuine distaste for one so unformed, rather as my mother did. Both were more concerned for me than for Angela, which made my desire to protect her even more ardent. At the time I could not see that there was anything wrong with this, or that there was anything the matter with Angela. I told myself that Brian was used to a different sort of woman, and that both of us must abstain from criticising each other's tastes. This caused a very slight distance between us, for the first time in our long friendship.

He did his best to enlighten me, without being so cross as to ask direct questions. Instead he said cunningly, 'You ought to take Angela to Paris for a week-end. You're getting set in your ways.' To Brian, Paris was the touchstone of any love affair: if a woman did not respond to Paris, and to her lover in Paris, then she was beyond redemption. He may have thought that I shared this belief, an irony in the light of what was to come, though not one I have ever appreciated. Looking back I can see that he was maddened by my domesticity, worried by my new caution. Every morning I would treat him to an account of the previous evening's meal, as if I had just been promoted to a normal diet. He too reflected on the length of our friendship, and dreaded to see it banished by a woman whom he rightly suspected of jealousy. I may have been aware of this; I no longer know. Perhaps I already felt that any jealousy on Angela's part was justified. Certainly I knew and trusted Brian enough to know that he would never shame me into saying something untoward. In that way we were able to remain friends, despite an habitual reserve. To break this would have signified an infringement of all the codes by which we had been educated. I had a singular, and perhaps sinister conviction of doing the right thing at this time. I felt invulnerable because I was behaving myself. My conscience was clear, which no doubt made me complacent, insensitive to the feelings of others. Had I been in my normal state, which verges on the sceptical, I should have paid more attention.

When the invitation to Brian and Felicity's wedding arrived, Angela decided that we must give a dinner party, so that our own status as a couple should not go unregarded.

'Is this really necessary?' I asked. 'They know we're engaged. Anything more formal tends to be embarrassing.'

'It's customary,' she replied. 'And it's customary to offer a gift.'

I thought this was ridiculous. I had not 'offered' a gift to Brian; I had merely kissed Felicity warmly and gone back to work. The very faintest suspicion of melancholy stole over me as I watched Angela hauling down long-unused dinner plates and champagne glasses ('We must have champagne') from the top shelves of cupboards. I was perhaps beginning to regret my quiet evenings, particularly those evenings when I could slip out to Paddington Street and find Sarah, sometimes willing, more often not at home. My regret was almost abstract. I wondered if I really wanted a woman in my life on a permanent basis, let alone a woman who would turn my life upside-down. I no longer knew my own kitchen, since Angela had provided us with a servant, by dint of persuading Adelina, who did the washing-up at the coffee bar, to work for us. Secretly I was appalled by the amount of money being spent, although I could afford it. I just thought that life had been simpler when I was unattached, with the proviso that being unattached was synonymous with being available. Like most men, I contemplated affairs with equanimity, or had done before I met Sarah. The great argument in their favour was that one's home generally remained uninvaded, so that one could return to peace and quiet and one's own standard of living. I had been unprepared for the sheer busyness of life with Angela, particularly as she seemed to have imported so many of her clothes, and, until I threw it out, her teddy bear.

Yet I remained impressed—still—by the energy she

expended on my behalf, although unwilling to acknowledge the fact that I was required to expend a great deal of energy in return. If I did not pay enough attention to the matter in hand, if, for example, I wanted to read the evening paper, there was a very slight tendency to sulk. The tears, which were quite frequent, I could cope with: they made me feel protective, but I disliked being taken over. If I thought of another woman at this time it was not Sarah but Simone, my hard-headed sunny-tempered companion in Paris, with whom it was so easy to enjoy life, who never bore a grudge, and who was even able to tolerate partings with a certain style. On the other hand, Angela would do me credit in her way, was in fact quite ambitious socially, and would see to it that this dinner party, to judge by her preparations, would impress our guests, or rather Angela's guests, since I was merely there to acquiesce to arrangements which had been maturing in Angela's mind for some time, and for whom Brian's wedding invitation acted as a stimulus, or perhaps an irritant: I feared the latter, since Angela and Felicity were not guaranteed to hit it off. Felicity was a clever, sharp-featured girl, with all the right connections. Brian was her weakness: her brittle upper-class authority literally melted when he looked at her in a certain way. I had seen him look at other women like that, but I said nothing, having long ago decided that Felicity could fight her own corner. But Angela, who could only oppose softness to Felicity's hardness, was not comfortable with her, as I had reason to observe. Nevertheless Felicity's presence was ineluctable; indeed I rather thought the dinner was in her honour, a view which Felicity herself shared. Brian had already learned the trick of mental absence, perfected through many a tedious discussion. Only his ineffable smile would signal to me that his thoughts were elsewhere.

The other guests were Aubrey and my mother, and Jenny

and Humphrey. I thought it kind of Angela to invite this couple until I remembered that Jenny was her new friend. My mother, it occurred to me, might have been a little offended at being passed over in this way, but I doubt if she knew that Angela and Jenny spent so much time together. And if she had known would she have minded? My feeling was that she would have deplored the amount of time that Angela spent in Jenny's company, thinking back with something like horror on those afternoons once deemed so amusing and so suitable for an unoccupied woman like herself. I could not help noticing the fact that her marriage had given her a new dignity, a new assurance. She greeted Brian and Felicity warmly, and introduced Aubrey with pride; she kissed Jenny and Humphrey as if they were mere acquaintances, as if Jenny were no longer the honorary sister or sister-in-law she had once been, and her greeting to Angela was affectionate, but no more than that. It was Jenny who enthused, exclaiming rapturously over the salmon and wild rice, the tropical fruit salad, and the apple cake that was served with the coffee. It was indeed a splendid meal, worthily accompanied by the Montrachet and the Beaume de Venise which were my contribution. Only the coffee was not strong enough: it never was. I remembered Brian once saying that if a woman could not make a decent cup of coffee she was likely to be no good in bed, and avoided his eye. Fortunately he was beguiled by Aubrey, as was Felicity. They were going to Thailand for their honeymoon, and Aubrey was telling them exactly what to see.

It was a success, but the sort of success that makes one feel inordinately tired. Indeed, I tended to feel tired quite a lot about this time, not at work, but as soon as I got home. When I was tired Angela was the ideal companion, anxiously supervising my intake of nourishment, the quality of my sleep. It was precisely when I was less tired that I found her something of a problem. I became aware that my advances displeased her, though I had learned to curb my enthusiasm. She claimed that I hurt her, so that I became careful and circumspect. It was at times like these that the spectre of Sarah revived and took on flesh and blood, so that it became impossible to sleep. Sometimes I found this intolerable, though I said nothing. Finally I renewed an old prescription the doctor had once given me for a mild sleeping pill. That way we both got some rest.

I remember very little of our wedding, which took place in the village church which Angela had not frequented since early childhood. The reception was held in a marquee in her mother's garden. The early spring sun shone fitfully through heavy cloud, but 'At least it's not raining,' as the guests cheerfully assured each other. Angela, in voluminous white, had been given away by her uncle, Frank Clark, Mrs Milsom's brother, who, to judge from his ramshackle appearance, was not a frequent visitor to the Milsom household. Her mother, I thought, had done things well, and, having seen to everything single-handed, was almost wild-eyed with the strain. She struck up a friendship with Mother, who at one point, when the celebrations were successfully under way, led her into the kitchen and made her a cup of tea. I was very touched to notice that Sybil and Marjorie had travelled up from Dorset. For a moment I wondered what they were doing at Angela's wedding, until I remembered that it was my wedding as well. It was Jenny who took Angela up to her bedroom to change. When I was sent up to find them I discovered them both sitting on Angela's bed in tears. The discarded wedding dress, an irreducible mountain of white taffeta, was hanging on the outside of the wardrobe, as if it might be put on again at any minute.

'Why on earth are you both crying?' I asked.

'So sad,' said Jenny, dabbing her face, a face now looking much older. 'I had hoped that Sarah might be here.'

'I sent her an invitation,' said Angela. 'I sent it to Paddington Street. Don't cry, Jenny. She'll be home soon. After all, I'm the one who's going away.' Aubrey was lending us his house in Cagnes for the honeymoon. The thought of this provoked a fresh burst of tears.

'You're both tired,' I said. Actually I was the one who was tired. I was exhausted. If Brian, as my best man, had not looked after me so well I think I should have stolen away to find an empty bedroom and gone to sleep. We were going back to Wigmore Street that evening and flying to France the following day.

My last sight, as we bumped off in the car, was of Sybil and Marjorie, rather more elaborately hatted than usual, peering at us through the side window and flinging a handful of confetti. Marjorie, leaning painfully on her stick, raised a hand to wave. 'Who on earth is that?' asked Angela, arranging her pleated skirt at its most becoming. I did not have the energy to explain the ramifications of the Miller family, which was after all Sarah's family; too much fervour had worn me out. I longed for nothing but a cup of good strong tea, preferably drunk in complete silence. Angela, I knew, would sit up half the night dispatching pieces of wedding cake, the very cake that was giving me such unaccustomed indigestion. I wondered if there were any precedent for a bridegroom wanting to spend his wedding night on his own.

In England the weather had been uncertain, overcast days declining into soaking rain. In France it was hot, gloriously hot. The spring light was so brilliant that Angela complained that it gave her a headache. I, on the contrary, felt as if I had shed a skin, not only of winter heaviness but of conformity. I was up at six every morning, humming happily in Aubrey's kitchen, making coffee as strong as I had always thought it should be made. I took my cup out onto the little terrace and inhaled an air filled with the sharp scents that I loved, the scents of France. I envisaged days spent wandering about the little town, until I remembered that I was on my honeymoon, and went indoors to make the tea that Angela preferred. She looked charming as she awoke from sleep, the morning light enhancing her fair colouring. Aubrey and Mother had left the house ready for us; there were enough supplies to last a fortnight. There was literally nothing for us to do, and I was impatient to go out; this however did not appeal to Angela, who had inspected the house and declared it not to her liking. She would have preferred an hotel, she said; apparently an hotel was more 'customary'. Also she felt Mother looking over her shoulder, though Mother had scrupulously tidied all her things away. She got up slowly, although she had always bustled about in the early mornings in Wigmore Street. I offered to go out for bread for our breakfast, but she asked me to wait so that we could go out together. By this time I was hungry and impatient to begin the day, but she claimed that she had no appetite when we sat down at a café table and toyed with her coffee while I guiltily wolfed croissants.

When I suggested driving somewhere for lunch she said, 'You go. I'm a bit tired. I'll just go back and read my book.' Again with a feeling of guilt, I hared off, like a child let off school. When I returned in the afternoon, after a solitary lunch, I would find her lying on the sofa in the *salle de séjour*, her book discarded by her side.

'You should get more air,' I told her. 'Don't waste it, just lying there.'

But she protested that her stomach was slightly upset, that France always did this to her, and that she would be all right if left on her own. She seemed oddly withdrawn, as if the paradisal place were somehow not up to her imaginings. I felt obliged to keep her company, although I craved the heat and light of the majestic day. When she consented to come out with me for an aperitif she was dismissive of the passing show which so enchanted me. 'This place doesn't suit me,' she said. 'I shall be glad when we get home.'

Aubrey had said that we could stay as long as we liked—I had thought three weeks. But at the end of the first week Angela could barely tolerate the place and was talking about our looking for a house in Sussex or Hampshire where she thought it would be appropriate for us to live.

'But why move?' I asked her. 'There's no hurry. And anyway you don't know anyone in Sussex or Hampshire. And I should have to commute. Unless of course I spent the weeks in Wigmore Street.'

'Oh, you couldn't leave me on my own. After all, I shouldn't know anyone to begin with.'

'That's what I've just said. Don't try to do everything at once. You like the flat, don't you? And you've got Jenny to go out with.' Although I could see that Jenny's company might pall after a time. Poor Jenny! Eternal makeshift, eternally on the margins. I thought of her in tears, in Angela's bedroom, as I had last seen her. Her tears had seemed so heartfelt, as if she had finally realised that she had no daughter of her own, and as if she knew that Sarah would never be that daughter. And the ungrateful girl had given no sign, not to Jenny, not to me.

By the time we got ready to come home, after a mere nine days, Angela told me that she was pretty sure that she was pregnant.

9

The hardest lesson to learn is that everything is subject to change. My reversal of fortune was brought home to me not by any dramatic circumstance but by the distinctly un-friendly attitude of Mrs Daley at the coffee bar, where I was once again obliged to eat breakfast. Blaming me no doubt for the defection of Adelina, she would plant my coffee on the table in such a way as always to spill a little in the saucer. Thus, a refugee from my own home, it appeared that I was not to be allowed to enjoy hospitality elsewhere. Another of Mother's novels came to mind, one over which we had both puzzled, although I suspect that men find it more palatable than women. This was Goethe's *Elective Affinities*, in the Penguin edition, a seemingly passionless story in which cou-ples change partners with those of their best friends in a calm and unadventurous fashion, as if they were obeying a scientific law, or a law of nature. No damage is done, no jealousy is caused, and civilised behaviour is maintained at all times. My mother had remained anxious after reading it, and had passed it on to me for my opinion. My opinion was that if these matters could be accomplished without undue emotional expenditure then so much the better. But I had felt uneasy after reading it, as if it contained subversive material. And I already knew that without love one was condemned to that same aridity that prevailed in the novel. What I did not yet know, not in fact until I had been married to Angela for three or four months, was how to deal with loss of love, how to negotiate a passage to that same civilised behaviour that was held to be desirable in Goethe's novel. I did not know how to behave when my spontaneity was so rigorously checked, when I had become a guilty stranger in my own home. I blamed myself, although I had not changed. I still cherished my wife, felt protective of her. Yet at about this time, in the space of those three or four months, I knew that I had never loved her, and now never would.

Nor, I think, did she love me. Certainly she treated me with hostility, as one who had inflicted on her a monstrous wrong. Her fear of men had if anything increased now that her body was no longer her own but was inhabited by an embryo which she seemed, from the very beginning of her pregnancy, to regard as an incubus. I had been delighted by the prospect of a baby, although aware that our way of life would be threatened, and the anxious care which I now felt obliged to dedicate to Angela in all her waking moments would soon have to be diverted to someone even more helpless. In fact I should have been almost happy, bemused yet excited, had Angela not come to this strange decision that I was entirely responsible for her condition.

'But you were on the Pill, weren't you?' I asked her.

'No, I wasn't.'

'But if you didn't want a child . . .'

'I still don't. I'm not strong enough. I've got my hands full looking after the flat.'

'I remember when you used to look after me,' I said, only half jokingly.

'Yes, well, now it's your turn.'

After a pause I said, 'You're a perfectly healthy woman, you know. The doctor confirmed that everything was normal. Only he thought you weren't getting enough exercise. Perhaps if you were to get up you wouldn't feel so tired.'

'I know how I feel, thank you.'

For she would stay in bed for most of the morning, and I think would have spent the day there, had not Jenny arrived every afternoon to take her out for a walk. When I came home from work it was to a smell of cooking which indicated that Jenny, not Angela, had been busy in the kitchen. The smell was of onions, vinegar, a coarser, less appetising smell than I was used to. Sometimes I traced it to a portion of stuffed cabbage that had been left on a plate for my dinner, which I ate hastily, in the kitchen, while Angela watched television.

'Have you eaten?' I would ask, sounding like my mother.

'I had something earlier, with Jenny.'

'Listen, darling, I wish you wouldn't spend so much time with Jenny. She's a perfect dear, I know, and she's very fond of you, but if you would just vary your days a bit more you'd feel more normal. I know it's all very strange—for me too—but don't you think you might be a bit more positive about it? And anyway, why Jenny? Why not my mother? Or your mother, come to that? Do you want her to stay here? You're not frightened, are you? There's nothing to be frightened of.'

But I could feel her fear, and her resistance, when I tried to hold her. Her resistance even spread to my mother, who telephoned every day and suggested a visit. Angela, however, thought she detected condescension in my mother's tone and repudiated her suggestions. This hurt me, and no doubt my mother as well. My mother was always referred to as 'your mother', never 'Alice', let alone 'Mother'.

'Your mother telephoned' was her usual response when I asked her if she had seen or heard anyone other than Jenny. 'She said to give her a ring sometime. Only not now: I want to listen to this.' Soon Mother and I were telephoning each other in office hours, which was unsatisfactory for us both, since I was sometimes in the middle of a meeting, and had to tell her that I would talk to her later. Sometimes we thus missed each other for a day or two, which added to my feeling of strangeness. To be out of touch, to eat breakfast in a café, to swallow my dinner in the kitchen—none of this would have mattered if Angela had appeared to love me. I say 'appeared' because I was too aware of her dissatisfactions to ignore the evidence that the emotional climate had changed. I loved her new fuller body, but was not allowed to touch it. This worried me disproportionately. I even rang Angela's doctor to ask for reassurance on this matter, which I thought that he, as a man, might be able to dispense. Unfortunately I was put through to the practice nurse, who regarded all women, herself included, as victims, and whose contribution to my enquiry was a suggestion that I purchase a tape of whale music 'to take the tension out of the atmosphere.' I was so cowed that I actually did this, with the result that mournful but not necessarily musical hoots accompanied my plate of stuffed cabbage, and proved as adhesive as the very faint smell of onion that clung to the kitchen curtains.

'Are we all mad?' I asked my mother, when I eventually got through to her. 'Are all pregnant women like this? Why does Jenny have to cook my dinner? Is there any way of dissuading her? She doesn't seem to want me to look after my own wife, which I can surely do perfectly well. Angela seems to have entered some kind of female Order, with Jenny as Mother Superior . . .'

'If I am speaking rather softly, darling, it's because I don't want Aubrey to hear. It looks so rude if I leave him and go into another room when you telephone. I have had to learn new rules, as you have had to do. No, I'm not happy about the situation, but there seems very little for me to do. Angela doesn't care for me, unfortunately.'

'Oh, come, Mother, she's not herself at the moment . . .'

'I may have told her that she was taking her condition too seriously. I seem to have upset her. Oh, it'll all blow over once the baby's born—I'm really sorry I mentioned it.'

'I'm a bit worried about Jenny's part in all this.'

I could hear my mother sigh at the other end of the line. 'I don't see as much of her as formerly. My time belongs to Aubrey now. And Jenny feels hurt. What you don't understand, Alan, is that Jenny is in search of love, not for herself, but for others. Does that sound strange? You have to remember that she has no family, that she has always been an orphan. For that very reason she may have invested too heavily in her friends, and been eternally disappointed that they did not feel for her what she feels for them. To me she was touching, and yet when she attached herself to me I knew that I should let her down. She used to say, "I do so long to see Sarah," and when I tried gently to explain that Sarah was young and rather thoughtless, and that there was no real reason for Sarah to respond to Jenny's eagerness, she would look at me with an expression of genuine bewilderment. She thinks that needs are reciprocal, you see. And yet underneath it all she is bitterly disappointed.'

'When I got home last night she was in the kitchen, wearing an apron. Then I had to take her halfway down Wigmore Street and put her into a taxi. What has Humphrey to say to all this?'

'I'm sure she's not neglecting Humphrey. She simply sees Angela as a higher priority. Because Angela absorbs all her love she thinks that Angela loves her. It's a false equation, I know. I think your best bet is to tolerate it as calmly as possible. After all, Jenny's providing the sort of practical help that Angela thinks she needs.'

'But you've bought all the baby clothes, and stuff like that . . .'

'The least I could do, the most that I was allowed to do. What I can't do is fuss. That's Jenny's function. I don't like it either. I don't like it from Angela's point of view or from Jenny's. You will see how dependent on each other they've become.'

'My part in all this is apparently reprehensible. Women hate me. That nurse at the practice . . .'

'Yes, you told me about her, dear. You're not getting superstitious, I hope? Women don't hate you, don't be ridiculous. It might do you good to get to know women a little better. Anyway, you've got Brian.'

'Felicity is also pregnant, I have to tell you. She seems rather pleased. As for Brian, I hardly know him. Euphoric, I think is the word.'

'I'm so pleased for them. Cheer up, darling. After all, there's every reason to feel proud of yourself . . .'

'Oh, really, Mother.'

'And don't worry about Jenny. I'm sure you'll find some tactful way of discouraging her. Although she'll be bitterly hurt, of course.'

'Why does she love Sarah? It's quite clear that Sarah can't stand her.'

My mother sighed again. 'Women like Jenny love because they need to love. Indiscriminately. Sarah is an honorary niece, part of her honorary family. In Jenny's fantasy families love each other. She thinks it appropriate that she love Sarah.

And the irony is that although she knows that her love is one-sided she never gives up hope that one day Sarah will recognise the true worth of this person who loves her. It's almost mystical, isn't it? Like a nun, or a saint.'

'It's aberrant.' There was a silence. 'Any news of Sarah?' I asked finally.

'Sybil had a postcard from New York. But that was some time ago. I should think she's due back fairly soon.' There was another silence. 'Such an odd summer, isn't it? No sun to speak of. And quite chilly in the evenings. Of course we are nearly in September. You won't be going away, I suppose?'

'I doubt it. Though I'm owed three weeks.'

'You remember that Aubrey and I will be spending September and October in Cagnes? It's so lovely at that time of year. Of course we'll be back before the baby is due.'

'Oh, that's a long way off. Late November, early December.'

'Alan, I've just had a thought. Why not take Angela away for a bit? That would be a tactful way of easing Jenny out of the flat. Why not get the car out of the garage and drive around? You could stay in decent hotels. It would do you both good. I worry about you, darling.'

'I could, I suppose. But I doubt if I could persuade her . . .'

'I thought you said she wanted to live in the country. That's the ideal pretext. You could say you wanted to look for a house. Or indeed really look for a house, somewhere to spend the weekends. Though that would mean we'd see even less of you.'

'That's actually quite a good idea. The first priority is to rescue Angela from Jenny.'

'Why not do it as soon as possible? This evening, if she's still there. There need be no awkwardness. Just tell her that you'll be in touch when you get back. That way she won't be hurt.'

'Mother, you're brilliant. I'll let you know if and when we go. Though I suppose we'll have to, in case Jenny finds out.'

'Poor Jenny,' said my mother. 'I'll give her a ring. Goodbye, darling. I'm so glad we've had this talk.'

That evening I got home early. I found Angela on the sofa, reading. Sounds from the kitchen informed me that Jenny was in possession. Without removing my jacket, although it was a cloudy, humid evening, I went in and removed from her hands a casserole containing something strongly aromatic and unsuitable for such a warm evening. The blue eyes looked at me trustingly while I told her that Angela needed a change of scene and that I should be taking her away for a couple of weeks. I placed the casserole on the table, intending to throw away the contents and take my wife out to dinner.

'You've been wonderful, Jenny,' I said, but these valedictory words were a mistake; my meaning was clear. Her expression of trust altered, became distant, hardened. I could see that my rejection had done some obscure damage, or that I had left her without a function other than that of being companion to an elderly and never very interesting man who would now have full command of her time and attention. 'Humphrey will be happy to see more of you,' I said heartily. The look she gave me was tinged with contempt.

Wresting her away from Angela was easier than I had anticipated. Once she had received my coded warning she was on her dignity. To Angela her departure was little more than another contrariety in an already tedious day, but by this time *The Archers* had started, and it was over the voice of Jill Archer, perfect wife, mother and châtelaine, that Jenny took her leave.

'I'll get you a taxi,' I said, feeling guilty.

'Goodbye, Alan,' was her reply.

I marched back into the living-room and told Angela to

change her dress as I was taking her out to dinner. She looked surprised but made no objection, and we left the flat in a precarious state of neutrality. My plan, unfolded during dinner, of 'just driving along the coast, stopping somewhere for the night, staying if we want to,' seemed sufficiently vague and permissive to win a mollified assent. 'And then,' I added cunningly, 'you always said you wanted to live in the country. We could look around for a house.' At this she brightened. 'We start on Friday,' I said.

So began our late and last summer, a typical English summer, cloudy, tentative, overcast, neither warm nor cool, maddeningly indecisive, but touching, even moving. I thought at the time that I should remember it with nostalgia, although little trace of it remains. Our holiday began inauspiciously, with a pretentious hotel in the New Forest. This was run by a couple down on their luck, who thought their lineage could justify the forty-minute wait for a cup of coffee or the musty smell in the chintz-hung bedroom, imperfectly disguised by bowls of pot-pourri. After that I decided that we would rely only on professionals, and we spent a couple of mildly agreeable days in Bournemouth, at a five-star hotel thronged with cheerful Jewish couples. Angela loved it. As I watched her features lose their worried frown I understood her at last. She would have liked to live here, and change for dinner every evening, and discuss her health over the teacups with cordial Jewish matrons. Yet she was sufficiently in agreement with me when I suggested moving on, and for several days we drove through placid countryside, spending our nights in the nearest equivalent of our recent hostelry, not speaking much, but harmoniously silent. At night we slept deeply, side by side, as if we had been married for a hundred years. Angela forgot about her condition, which no longer seemed to bother her. We appraised each other silently, not daring to endanger our precarious friendship.

When the weather turned dull, and cooler, we headed for home. It was then that I found the house, suddenly alerted to the fact that we needed this excuse to justify occasional holidays, or for the children that we would have. I should not have seen it had I not got out of the car to buy a paper. Opposite a row of small traditional shops stood a seemingly delicate but doughty-looking house which announced itself for sale. This was confirmed by the newsagent. The owner, he said, had gone to live abroad and was willing to include the contents in the price.

'What is this place called?' I asked him, and was told that it was Shoreham-by-Sea. And the house was called Postman's Cottage, which should satisfy Angela's taste for authenticity. We inspected it together, and everything seemed acceptable, from the four square armchairs to the flowered cups and saucers in the kitchen cupboard. I bought it with unprofessional speed, cutting corners in a way I should never allow my clients to do, but it was worth it to see the thrill of ownership on Angela's face. This new pleasure was not given exaggerated expression. 'I'll need new curtains,' was all she said, as if she had earmarked the house for her own. In the end it was I who derived the most benefit from it, but I was prepared for this. It seemed a lucky chance, and consequently a lucky house. We returned to London contented, and with at last something to talk about.

Nevertheless, the world settled once again on my shoulders when we were back in London. I dreaded a return to that valetudinarian regime that had obtained until our recent departure. I wondered how the breach with Jenny would be repaired, for breach there had been; I wondered how Angela would occupy her time now that she was getting heavier and less keen to be seen in public, at least without me. She moped a bit, was withdrawn, remote from me in a way that I found puzzling. I could not reconcile her present lack of interest with the fervour she had shown when we first met. I feared that her dissatisfaction would be brought to bear on our baby, who was to be a girl, provisionally called Helen Alice Margaret. I felt acutely sorry for this baby, who would not have an understanding mother, or at least a mother attuned to the good things in life. Angela seemed not to have taken in the full implications of her condition; she ate extravagantly or not at all, took no exercise, and spent most of her time indoors. Often she waited for me to come home before going out to do the shopping. I got used to carrying her basket. Her brooding air made her relatively mute, and trying to engage her in conversation over a dinner-table—for I insisted that we eat out fairly regularly—was hard work. She was not ill, she was not noticeably suffering, yet the only emotion I could feel for her was anxiety. This alone would have inhibited me, had my ardour not died at source.

One morning I entered the office and smelled an unfamiliar scent, something heavy, probably by Guerlain. I stood stock still, feeling my heartbeat and my pulse rate increase. I pushed open my door: Sarah was sitting on a corner of my desk reading the paper, her short black skirt riding up her thighs, her mane of crinkled red hair falling over one shoulder. No more fitting image of Luxuria could possibly be found. 'Hi,' she said, and folded the paper. I moved nearer to her, so that I could smell her hair. The waxy odour was less strong than I remembered it; today it smelled of something aromatic, a dressing of some kind. I drew it back over her shoulders and filled my hands with it. For a moment we gazed at each other, not speaking. Yet when she spoke her voice was cold.

'I got your letter,' she said. 'And your wedding invitation.'

'My letter?'

'The one in which you so nobly said you couldn't live alone.'

'I think I said I was tired of waiting for you.'

'Same thing, isn't it?'

'But you were never there. Night after night I tried to contact you, and even when I did you didn't always feel you were ready to see me. And that bloody telephone, ringing and ringing. I was going mad, I think . . .'

'So you got married.' Her voice was level, but I could tell her anger was mounting.

'If you had been there . . .'

'Tell me, Alan, why should I have been there? What exactly did you offer?'

'You could have had me.' I was appalled at my ineptitude. I was not prepared for this conversation; it was precisely the conversation I never wanted to have. And it was my own stupidity that had led to this.

'I could have had dozens like you,' she said. I ignored this. I was sorry to have brought her down to my level.

'And how's dear Angela?' she asked, picking up the paper again and scanning it.

'Angela is pregnant.' I had to say it, though I thought I should faint, as the paper was laid aside, and the icy eyes scanned my confusion.

'Actually,' she said, 'I'm thinking of following your example. Getting married, I mean.'

'I see. Have you known him long?'

'Yes. He's a friend of Berthe's father. An industrial chemist. Very wealthy. He's asked me several times.'

'What's his name?'

'De Leuze. Pierre de Leuze.' She picked up her bag and strolled towards the door. 'Goodbye, Alan.'

'I must see you,' I heard myself say. It was as if someone else had issued these words, in a wondering but considered tone. The words themselves came as something of a surprise to me, but not the feeling behind them. All my sorry desire, now tinged indelibly with guilt and duplicity, was made plain to me, but was not to be ignored.

She halted by the door. 'What were you suggesting?'

'I'll come to you this evening.'

'I shan't be here. I'm going to Paris to stay with Berthe. Maybe I'll get engaged. I need a *man*, Alan, a *man*, someone to take care of me.'

'Not me.'

She was silent.

'I must see you,' I repeated. 'I'll come to Paris. Meet me there. I'll come next Monday and stay for a few days. Meet me there next Monday. At least give me that.'

She turned slowly, her hand on the doorknob. 'Where will you be?'

'At the George V,' I said, again to my surprise. I had never stayed there in my life. I was opposed to it on principle, a luxury pad for the seriously rich. A moment's consideration would have told me that my behaviour was unreal, and worse, ill-informed. And yet I had to have her. She had brought me nothing but sadness, was accountable for all my mistakes, would be accountable for the worst mistake of all, the one I was about to make, and yet there was no going back. I never even managed to tell her that I loved her, since that would have been an anticlimax, given the storm of dread and desperation that possessed me.

'I'm not promising anything,' she said.

'Please don't say any more. Please be at the George V next Monday. Please go now. I can't endure seeing you like this . . .'

My sentence was destined to remain unfinished for tears, the kind of onrush of tears to which an infant is subject threatened to overwhelm me for a woman I now saw to be nothing out of the ordinary, a lazy, careless, rather difficult woman, neither clever nor generous, a woman whose very presence was unsatisfactory, but whose absence was worse. I felt as if the whole conduct of my life was in disarray, as if I had turned my back on those sensible and pleasant advantages with which I had grown up, and turned to criminal activities. And yet I think that I was never meant to be a criminal. I loved the law, I loved my country and its now perhaps blurred traditions, I loved my mother and the memory of my father. Even my wife, whom I did not love, aroused pity and indulgence in my heart. I was prepared to forswear all this, to put myself beyond the pale of acceptable behaviour, perhaps never to be allowed back, simply because there was no mistaking the strength of my wholly irrational longing. Perhaps it was so strong because it was irrational, so very far removed from my own home life, with its timid surges of feeling. For some reason—odd, but then everything was odd—I saw Jenny's face, the face that had changed from confidence to arid disappointment. A good woman, a woman who lived to serve others, and doomed to be unfulfilled. I did not want to be like that.

I heard Sarah's steps clicking on the black and white tiles of the entrance, heard Brian's delighted, 'Well, *hello!*' heard her uninflected 'Hi,' and buried my face in my hands. Seconds later he put his head round my door. Seeing me he looked alarmed. 'I'm all right,' I said. 'By the way I shall be in Paris next week. At the George V.' He understood at once, but our long friendship kept him silent. 'When will you be back?' he asked. 'Very soon,' I told him. 'If I can get back.' This too he understood.

Angela was not so understanding when I told her that I had to meet a client in Paris. This was almost true: Sarah had once been a client. On the other hand, one more falsehood was neither here nor there.

'You can't leave me alone,' she protested.

'You're only five months pregnant.'

'Six, actually. Well, six and a half.'

'You mean . . . ?'

'I didn't know at first.'

'And you said nothing?'

'I thought it best.'

'You could ring Jenny,' I said weakly. 'Ask her to keep you company.'

'She said something about going to Dorset. Humphrey wants to see those two old women.'

'Come on, darling. You'll be fine. I'll only be gone a night.' I was willing to halve my pleasure in the interests of morality. 'I'll be back before you notice I've gone.'

This might even have been true. But if she had begged me to stay I should have stayed. This did not happen. She shrugged her annoyance and went to bed. Throughout that sleepless night I silently begged her to prevail on me. Then I too gave up, as I also wanted to, and got out of bed to drink glass after glass of water, as if I were consumed by thirst.

10

As I rehearsed this epochal scene my thinking became magical, taking no account of actual circumstances. In my projection of it everything would serve my purpose, which was undefined but not on that account to be ignored. I would arrive in Paris a free man, having left in abeyance a wife to whom I would return by the simple expedient of reinhabiting the body of which I had taken temporary leave. My wife, or rather my erstwhile wife, would, like the dolls in *Coppélia*, be brought out of her temporary suspension, which would obtain during the period of my absence, by the very fact of my renewed presence. I would arrive in Paris at about six o'clock, having caught a plane at about five. I did not take into account the time difference, since time was also there to serve my purpose. Some faint uneasiness clouded this part of the proceedings but I dismissed it as nugatory; if obliged to I would adjust. I would take a taxi to the hotel, inspect my room, find it more than satisfactory, shower, change my shirt, and order a drink. Sarah, I imagined, would not be with me before nine; as she was staying with the Rigauds I imagined that she would be obliged to eat dinner with them. Whether or not this were true, I had the hour of nine fixed in my mind. This would give me time to take a nostalgic stroll and no doubt eat something myself, very little, since at nine o'clock I would order chicken sandwiches and champagne from room service. Thus everything would be civilised, in sharp contrast to the image I still had of myself peering through the letter-box in Paddington Street. The rest of the evening and the night remained a blank in my mind, but they would be memorable. When I returned to London it would be with a feeling of completion, of triumph, and thus renewed I should be able to shoulder my burdens once again.

My first brush with reality occurred on the plane. I was seated next to a man whose terrible agitation disturbed even the whisky in my glass. I stole a glance at him, unwilling to involve myself in his dilemma, but there was no ignoring the fact that he was either ill or in the grip of a nightmare. He was a man of about my own age, dressed in a cheap raincoat and childish-looking brown shoes: those two items, however, were the only signs of normality about him. His eyes were tightly closed and his fair-skinned face was a dusky red and beaded with sweat. From time to time a low moan escaped him and he clutched his briefcase convulsively, leaving damp handprints on the leather.

'Are you all right?' I asked reluctantly.

He opened his eyes and turned his head minimally in my direction, as if fearful of movement.

'Phobia,' he gasped.

'Claustrophobia?' I enquired sympathetically.

'Travel. Motion.'

'You mean you're frightened of travelling?'

'Petrified.'

'But there's no need. We'll be landing in ten minutes, and then you'll be all right.'

'No. I have to get on the bus.'

'The bus is as bad as the plane?'

'Worse. No, not worse. As bad.'

'Where do you have to get to?'

By way of reply he handed me a card bearing the name of a hotel in the rue d'Assas.

'What happens there?'

'They come and collect me.'

Who 'they' were I did not seek to ascertain; it was their job to look after him. We were both silent for a short interval, but when the plane gave a preliminary judder he clutched my arm. Unthinkingly, naturally, I gave his hand a pat.

'You could take a taxi,' I suggested.

'I'll never manage,' he said, and indeed he looked to be in extremis.

'Would it help if I took you to the rue d'Assas in a taxi?'

'Please. Thank you.'

He quietened down slightly after this, introduced himself as Derek Masterton, representative for a soft drinks firm, and moaned again as the plane landed. I had to guide him from his seat, as he seemed barely capable of negotiating the gangway on his own. Standing behind him on the endless escalators I could see his legs trembling, though once in the open air he seemed to recover slightly.

'Have you always been like this?' I asked, as we stood in the queue for taxis. I glanced hastily at my watch; it was seven-fifteen.

He told me that he had had a breakdown after the death of his wife the previous year and that it had left him with this monstrous fear which descended on him whenever he had to travel by public transport. He said that when he was back in London—and here a fresh burst of sweat indicated his terror of the return journey—he was going to resign from the soft drinks firm and apply for a grant to study for a degree at the Open University. His dependence on me was growing, along with a shakily renewed confidence. I pushed him rather roughly into a taxi and told the driver to be as quick as he could. The car filled with the smell of Derek Masterton's sweat as we glided through the dusk. A steady rain was falling, making our progress slower than normal, although it would not have been very fast in any case; the rush-hour looked to be in full swing. My head was filling with urgent calculations: hotel, bath, telephone call to the rue de Rennes. Derek Masterton's heartfelt thanks reached me in an abstract murmur as I deposited him rather summarily in the rue d'Assas and told the driver to go to the George V. It only then occurred to me that I should have booked a room. This had somehow not seemed necessary in the trance of my imaginings. Only now did I begin to wonder whether the whole adventure would have been better had I not decided to act it out. But I had never before been given to fantasising; life, real life, had been easy for me, and I was known to have a good practical intelligence. I resolved firmly to insist, if necessary, on my right to a room, although there should be no need, surely, to insist. I summoned up my normal state of resolution and was thus almost confident again as I stepped out onto the forecourt of the hotel.

The rain, which had been falling as a steady drizzle, put on a sudden spurt as I dashed for the hotel entrance. I was surprised to see, instead of uniformed flunkeys, a number of stocky men in ill-fitting suits both outside and inside the hotel. They considered me for a moment or two, and then, at an invisible sign from someone deep in the foyer, let me pass. I went up to the desk and demanded a room with bath for two nights, two in case the so far unimaginable happened and I was to be allowed to spend the following day wandering through Paris with Sarah, showing her where I had been so happy in my youth, telling her—at last!—something of my own story, actually having a conversation with her, as I had never managed to do. Somehow it had been necessary to get her out of London in order to do this. This part of the fantasy was again rather hazy and required a good deal of concentration, so that I hardly registered the fact that the receptionist was telling me that no rooms were available. I protested. Two of the stocky men began to approach. '*Je regrette, Monsieur, l'hôtel est complet.*' Repetition did not dull the impact of these words. I was escorted to the door by two of these men, whom I dimly identified as bodyguards. I stood outside, in the rain, still accompanied, until some kind of signal was given. A long black limousine, with a blue and white flag flying on the bonnet, seethed out into the night. Very slowly I picked up my bag and began to walk. On my watch the time stood at eight o'clock.

In my head a childish voice of encouragement took over. Perhaps the George V had been a mistake. All I had to do was find another hotel, something a little more modest, convey the address to Sarah, and wait for her there. I was less familiar with this part of town, so I walked absent-mindedly, without my usual sense of direction. It was now raining heavily, and I had left my umbrella at home. Besides, umbrellas played no part in this odyssey; the weather was to have been warm, enticing, in this second week of September. It was to have been my favourite season, in my favourite city, to which, of course, I had been bound to return. I should have been young, or younger than I actually was, as young as I remained in my memory. My steps led me into a dark street, in which I could see the blue lamp of a police station. At the very end of what seemed more like a cul-de-sac I saw a trembling neon sign: Hôtel du Balcon. No balcony was visible. The street was momentarily identified by the lights of a passing car as the rue Clément Marot. The neon sign outside the hotel was fitful because it seemed about to expire. This did not strike me at the time as particularly significant. I went in, asked for a room, and was given one with alacrity. It was eight-fifteen.

I threw my bag onto the bed of a medium-sized room, badly lit by numerous bulbs of singularly low wattage. I searched in my pocket for Berthe Rigaud's address and telephone number, which I immediately dialled. There was no answer. The childish voice in my head told me that the entire family had gone out to dinner; my task now was to take a taxi to the rue de Rennes and to slip a note under Berthe Rigaud's door. This would in any case be more discreet than telephoning. I was not sure how much Sarah had confided in her friend; there was the matter of Berthe Rigaud's father's friend, this man de Leuze, who wanted Sarah to marry him. If he were there Sarah would not want him to know of my presence. I went down and asked the man at the desk for a sheet of paper and an envelope. Wheezing, he bent down, searched for a few precious seconds, and came up again with a crimson face. He appeared to be in the last stages of emphysema. Clearly everyone with whom I was doomed to come into contact was morbidly afflicted. I snatched the paper from his hand, scribbled my message, and ran out to look for a taxi.

After five or six minutes it became clear that there were to be no taxis. I began to walk, or rather to run. I ran down the Avenue Montaigne to the Place de l'Alma, where luckily a couple got out of a taxi to go to dinner at Chez Francis. I flung myself in the back and gave the driver the address. He told me he was on his way home. I refused to move. We sat there, deadlocked, for what seemed a very long time, until I handed over a hundred franc note, at which he silently drove away. Lights glimmered through blurred windows; dimly the shouts of the pleasure-bound reached me. I revised my plans: we should dine Chez Francis, like that couple to whom I was indebted for the taxi. We should have our walk, that very night, romantically, in the rain. For a while this fantasy was even more attractive than the earlier one. The rain on Sarah's hair would bring out that marvellous feral smell that I craved, had never ceased to crave. In the rue de Rennes I gave the driver another hundred franc note and watched him drive off. The rain had momentarily stopped; the sky was clear enough for me to make out scudding clouds. To my left shone the lights of St-Germain-des-Prés; I had a sudden desire to drink a cup of coffee at the Flore. I took my letter out of my pocket and scribbled on the envelope, 'I shall expect you at ten.' Then I pressed the button for the concierge. I had recovered my resolution. 'Rigaud,' I said firmly. *'Deuxième gauche,'* was the reply. As I bounded up the stairs I heard some words floating up behind me. It was not until I was outside the door, on which a brass plate announced 'Jean-Jacques Rigaud. Notaire,' that I decoded them as, *'Mais il n'y a personne.'*

There was no answer to my ring, but then I had expected none. I pushed my letter under the door, and then, filled with renewed energy, bounded down again. Outside the heavy street door the air was sweet. I toyed with the idea of a drink at the Rhumerie, for old times' sake, then, almost regretfully, settled for a coffee at the Flore. I told myself that if so far everything had not gone exactly to plan then at least I had made some quick decisions. My clothes were drying on me, although the shoulders of my raincoat were still damp. I reminded myself that I had still to take a bath and apply unguents. I was lucky with a taxi, and was back in the Hôtel du Balcon at nine-thirty.

Then I settled down to wait. I had managed to buy a paper, though my eyes skimmed over the words without taking them in; I saw something about a visit to Paris from the President of Israel. After taking off my clothes the effort of putting them on again seemed almost too much for me. I had not brought pyjamas; they had no place in my scenario. I sat down on the bed to wait, perfuming the slightly musty air of the room. I fought an impulse to lie down on the bed and sleep—I had not slept the previous night—and although I remained resolutely upright I must have dozed. When I came to it was exceedingly quiet and I was exceedingly hungry. I wondered how Derek Masterton was getting on, perhaps dimly regretted that I was confined in this manner, when I could be out in the beautiful streets, innocently eating and drinking, as if this were an entirely normal interlude, as if I could return to London with a clear conscience. I had bought cigarettes for Sarah, and although I did not smoke I smoked three. When I looked at my watch I saw that it was just after eleven. Then I must have dozed off again, for when I woke up I was lying on the bed, still fully clothed. I got up and brushed my hair. I read the paper again, including the television programmes, although there was no television, and even if there had been I should not have had the patience to watch it. The door to the room next to mine opened and closed, and muffled conversation could be heard, together with the clink of the key dropping onto a hard surface. I cleared my throat ostentatiously, as if to warn this couple to make no further noise. Obediently the conversation stopped. Minutes later there was a groan, as if of exhaustion, and then the sound of bedsprings. I glanced at my watch. It was nearly one o'clock.

I took my key and went downstairs. There was another
man behind the desk, no healthier than the first. This one
had his collar undone and was reading *L'Equipe*. I summoned
up an insouciant smile.

'*Il n'y a pas eu d'appel pour moi?*'

'*Mais non, pensez-vous, à cette heure-ci.*'

'*C'est une urgence.*'

'*Vous êtes médecin?*'

'*Non.*'

'*Alors.*' He shrugged and went back to his paper.

I spent the night in that sepulchral hotel sitting on the
bed. It seemed like a vigil, and for a time it held reality at
bay. The reality, when it came, seemed no more or less hallu-
cinatory than the rest of the episode. There had been a mis-
understanding, or perhaps no understanding at all. I had
either been taken for a fool, or, more likely had made a fool
of myself. The same mischance that had attended all my
meetings with Sarah attended me still. After a while it was
almost with relief that I knew that Sarah was not coming,
that she would never come. My conscience, through no will
or intention of my own, was made clear. All I had to do was
to expunge the memory of this visit and return to my real
life. I could pass it off: there were one or two people in Paris
whom I could see, to give myself an alibi. One rather important client, for whom I had successfully completed some
business the previous year, had told me to contact him if I
were ever in Paris. He lived in Neuilly, kept a flat in London;
all I had to do was telephone him, make enquiries as to the
outcome of his transaction. Solicitors do not normally chase
their clients, but I hoped that he would take my attentions in
the right spirit. It was tenuous, but it would have to do. I
would not go back to the rue de Rennes; indeed I would
never set foot there again. I did not want to see Berthe
Rigaud, or Sarah. I told myself that I should never see her

again, and that this suited me very well. I did not know how I could face her. She had reduced me once again to confusion. I could only hope that others would not see my confusion stamped permanently on my face.

There was no need now to hurry. I could stay in Paris for at least another day. I could have my nostalgic walk, though I recognised that the time for nostalgia was past. I would telephone Neuilly, perhaps suggest lunch, and spend a few necessary hours recovering. I was a solicitor, the least romantic species on earth. After a decent and no doubt painful interval I would return to my original status, that of respected citizen and married man. My path in life had been traced for me before I had ever known Sarah, and no doubt it suited me well enough. If I had felt the need to turn aside from it, events had proved to me that I was unsuited for adventure. My recent behaviour filled me with a kind of amazement, as if it had been the fugue of a madman. I felt cold, old. I wondered at what time I could reasonably take another bath, so as not to wake the couple next door.

Still dominated by time, I calculated that if I left the hotel at six I could walk for an hour before looking for a café in which to eat breakfast. In my damp raincoat I wandered aimlessly, before returning to the Place de l'Alma and waiting for the day properly to begin. The murmur of traffic grew louder as I sat down and ordered coffee, the panorama of the city coming to life in the wide open space before me. Beyond the bridge lay the Paris I had known and loved, and perhaps should never see again with that life of the heart that had once attended me every morning of my life. I was conscious of a feeling of shame that I had behaved in so uncharacteristic a fashion. I tried to expunge the previous night from my memory, consigning it to that detritus that exists at the back of every mind, so that eventually the process of living in the present will be sufficient to obliterate it, confining it to dreams from which one awakes with relief. I did not think of Sarah at all; she had if anything only confirmed her absence from my life. My task now was to justify my presence in Paris, to legitimise my absence from London. I telephoned Neuilly, but only got an answering machine. I left a message that I would ring later, then, slightly crestfallen, got to my feet and began my day of absence.

With nothing to do, no office to go to, no one to talk to, I was profoundly disoriented. At the same time I recognised that I was not fit to go home, and would not be until I had recovered my normal composure. It had become a beautiful day, mild and sunny, with that poignant autumn sunshine that is so affecting at the decline of the year. The rain of the previous evening had brought out a strong smell of earth and grass, even of damp stone, and I followed it down the Champs-Elysées, beyond the Rond-Point, and as far as the Tuileries, where I sat down. I felt, humbly, that I should stay out of sight, but at the same time I longed for company. I did not desire the company of anyone I knew, but rather the company of small children, who, after school, would spend the afternoon in these stony gardens. Slowly I worked out a programme for the day. I remembered my father's habitual, 'What is your programme?' which made no sense to me as a small boy. Now I saw that it was part of my inheritance, together with work, duty, order. And yet I did not want to go home. The day brightened about me as I sat on my iron chair. At last, with a sigh, I got up and went in search of more coffee.

A further telephone call to Neuilly was equally fruitless. I wandered back up the Champs-Elysées, feeling guilty now that I had no alibi. Both Angela and Sarah were far from my thoughts. I found this entirely natural, yet at the same time I was uneasy with this moral obliquity. So far my life had been regular, although decisions—the decision to marry, to have a

love affair—seemed to have been made without my full volition. Now it would be necessary to ask forgiveness, or rather
not to appear to ask forgiveness, for a fault which had not
quite taken place. I must act out my assurance until such
time as it might be returned to me. I thought of our baby, but
I was not yet ready for sentiment. My feelings were too
ambiguous to permit of much room for anyone else. What I
really wanted was to be at Postman's Cottage, on my own,
for a chance to order my thoughts. That this was an impossibility, and presumably would always be an impossibility,
added to my paradoxical solitude in this city in which I had
always been accompanied.

I had an early lunch, bought some scent for Angela, and
returned to the hotel. I realised that my sleepless night had
exhausted me, and I had to resist an impulse to lie down and
let the rest of the day take care of itself. I was also slightly
light-headed with the fear that I should never again be normal, so anomalous did my present situation seem to me. I
roused myself and telephoned Brian, thinking of the office
with love, as if I were an exile, unable to enter it again.

'Where are you?' rasped his voice, breaking in on my
reverie.

'In Paris, of course. Any news?'

'I've been telephoning the George V all morning.'

'I couldn't get in. I'm at . . .'

'Never mind that. You must get back here as soon as possible.'

'What's the matter?'

'It's Angela. She's in hospital. I'm afraid something went
wrong.' His voice softened.

'The baby? Is the baby all right?'

'The baby didn't live. Premature, though that wouldn't
necessarily have mattered. The cord was round its neck.' He
sighed. 'A little girl.'

'Is this true?' I asked, my mouth dry.

'Of course it's true. Angela asked me to take her to the hospital. Apparently she felt unwell and didn't know what to do. Your mother was away, and that other friend—Jenny, is it?—must have been away as well. She didn't know where you were.' There was a significant pause, as if Brian were waiting for my explanation. 'She rang me at the flat. It was just by chance that I happened to be there and not at the house.' Dimly I brought Brian's domestic arrangements into focus. His parents-in-law had provided a small house in St John's Wood as a wedding present. Brian had retained his bachelor flat, which he intended to let, and no doubt occupy from time to time. Now, however, he spoke with the voice of one observant of the moral law. 'I'd left a file there,' his voice went on. 'I picked it up and was about to leave when the phone rang. Thank God Felicity wasn't with me. I don't want her brought into this, Alan.' His voice was stern again.

'Angela. Is Angela all right?'

'She will be, of course. She was pretty frightened, poor girl. Although I don't know if she took it all in. When I went this morning she was asleep. With a bit of luck you'll be there when she wakes up. If you leave at once, that is, as I assume you will.'

'I must ring my mother,' I said, my mouth dry.

'Don't waste time. Get back here. And don't do this sort of thing again, will you?' Then, in an altered voice, 'I'm sorry, Alan.'

When I replaced the receiver there was a terrible silence. I contemplated the scale of my punishment: that it should be visited on Angela was almost too cruel for me to take in. I think perhaps that I did not grasp very much as I sat once more on the bed in that fusty room. Yet in the very few minutes left to me before I should be forced into action I realised that I had it in me to be a father, that to be a father was a natural, and inevitable, part of my real, my normal life. I think I felt more for my baby in that hotel room than I had ever felt it possible to feel. When I thought of the cord round its throat I had to tear at my collar as if I were being strangled. I wept then, but there was no time for weeping. I picked up my bag, went downstairs, paid the bill, and wandered outside in search of a cab. I have no memory of arriving at the airport, of changing my ticket, of sitting in the departure lounge. I had the impression, once again, that my mind was no longer under my control. My thoughts were of my dead daughter, whom I saw quite vividly, as though I had been there when she died. Except that she had not lived in the first place. I understood why people used euphemisms for death. 'He passed away', they said. 'He went peacefully.' There was no euphemism, however, that would apply to this particular death, a death in limbo. It was only with a last effort of will that I was able to get up and board the aircraft.

Derek Masterton was on the plane, eyes closed, once more in agony. I went and sat next to him. As we gained height and his ordeal began I put out my hand and touched his arm. It was my one good deed, perhaps the one good deed of my entire life.

11

To remember Sarah was to remember something—scarcely someone—inert and dangerous. I had been impelled by that very inertia to inaugurate an unaccustomed and untypical course of action which had led to my downfall. Poetic similes would not be out of place, though I was not in a poetic frame of mind. I was abashed by the swiftness of my punishment, for never for a moment did I not take all the blame. My wife, her face closed against me, her lips tightly shut in a grimace of rancour, held me entirely responsible for the baby's death, as did everyone else, or so I thought. My mother, white-faced and faltering, did her best not to blame me, but Aubrey was not so restrained.

'This is a bad business, Alan. What on earth were you playing at, leaving the poor girl alone like that?'

I had no answer. 'Playing', or something very like it, was

exactly what I had been doing. The words 'antic' and 'ludic' seemed appropriate when applied to my recent behaviour. I thought that Aubrey was mistaken if he intended to cast me as a villain. I was not wicked, or rather I was not simply wicked; I was aberrant in the way of someone who is not quite right in the head, led astray by a force he cannot comprehend. I did not comprehend it myself, nor did I intend to scrutinise my state of mind, or to 'work through' my feelings, as the current wisdom would have one do. My expression must have been appropriately idiotic; at any rate Aubrey regarded me without indulgence. I remembered that I had spoilt his holiday, another crime which would call for further expiation on my part.

This exchange took place outside Angela's hospital room, in lowered voices. In Aubrey's tone I could detect a note of sheer dislike, which saddened me, and no doubt compounded my mother's sadness. Although she had never cared for Angela, although she was now Aubrey's wife rather than my mother, her feelings for me were intact, though loyalty to her husband kept her silent. Aubrey insisted that they go back to Cagnes, to which I could raise no objection. My part now was to accept others' opinion of me; the time had not yet come for me to stand up for myself. Besides, I had no defence to offer. I stood silent, as waves of disapproval reached me in that antiseptic atmosphere. 'My poor boy,' murmured my mother, as Aubrey led her away. After that I was entirely alone.

Besides, it was Angela who now had precedence. I felt an unwelcome reluctance to re-enter her room, remembering her look of spite, and her breath, foul from the anaesthetic, which she unleashed in my face, with the words, 'It's your fault!' How much she knew, how much she suspected, were matters I should have to put straight if ever the right moment arrived. The fact that she had only ever seen the baby as an inconvenience did not lessen the exaggerated regard in which she was held by everyone, doctors, nurses, visitors—Felicity arriving with an armful of flowers but evidently warned not to stay too long—or the distaste with which these same people viewed me. The doctor who had delivered her took a more robust and no doubt more masculine view.

'Pity you couldn't have been here,' he said. 'Still, these things happen. There was nothing you could have done. She would have lost the baby in any case. You can have others, of course, but I should treat her very carefully for a while. She's quite fragile, you know.'

'But she'll be all right, won't she?'

He looked evasive. 'There's bound to be a reaction. Some degree of depression is inevitable. She doesn't seem to realise that the birth was compromised in any case. I'd like to keep her in for a bit. Of course she'll need your support.'

I thought this ridiculous. Angela was a healthy woman. It is the duty of the normally constituted to live, and to live abundantly. This is not within the power of everyone. It was Angela's duty, as I saw it, to regain her strength, to come home, and, after a period of quietness, to take up the burden of her life again, of our life, though I doubted if that would ever be the same. For the time being she seemed thoroughly at home in the hospital, allowing the nurses to wash her as if she were a child, refusing to get out of bed, even when she was fit enough to do so. I would arrive at the hospital in the evenings to find a nurse brushing her hair or arranging her bed jacket, for all the world as if she were a proud young mother. This seemed to me exceedingly dangerous, and I tried to rouse her, to alert her to the true facts of our situation. No doubt this was premature; in any event my suggestions were met with a storm of tears which brought the nurses running. Her tears were now so habitual that I gradually accepted them as part of her normal behavior. When they ceased they were replaced by an expression of sly contentment. 'You weren't here, were you?' she would say. 'You don't love me. You never loved me anyway.' Though I could not refute these words they left me heavy-hearted. I would turn to leave, with a bag of dirty washing under my arm. 'You'll come back, won't you?' she would say, the tears threatening again. But there was no need to ask. She knew that I would come back, that I was tied to her as never before. I knew it too.

'I'm putting her on anti-depressants,' the doctor said. 'For a month or two. And she's mildly sedated. You'll keep an eye on all this, won't you?'

'She doesn't seem to want to come home.'

'That's to be expected. She feels safe here. Post-natal depression's a funny thing. It can lead to a form of regression. Certain physical signs . . .'

'Such as?'

'Panic, loss of appetite, sleeplessness, agoraphobia. She'll recover, of course, but it may take time. Your support is what she needs.'

'She doesn't appear to want it.'

'It'll pass,' he said, but without conviction. 'It was a pity you had to be away. She seems to blame you for the entire business. And me, of course. Tell me, had she always been quite well? Mentally, I mean.'

'Yes, of course. Although . . .'

'Yes?'

'She seemed to change once we were married. She was perfectly happy when we were engaged. Then she had to grow up.'

I felt mean as I said it, but it seemed to me to be true. That dependence on Jenny, about which I had never felt comfortable, now appeared to me in a slightly more sinister light. At the same time she had entirely rejected her own mother, who seemed to have lost interest in her directly after the wedding, as if she were now entitled to honorary retirement. She had paid one visit to the hospital, had told her daughter to count her blessings, a singularly infelicitous remark in the circumstances, and had gone home again. I realised, in the interstices of the doctor's somewhat ambiguous remarks, that he was not quite happy with the prognosis.

'How long can you keep her here?' I asked.

'Well, obviously, we can't keep her indefinitely. She's in danger of becoming institutionalised. We try to guard against that.'

'But when will she be well?'

He looked at me carefully and then looked away. 'She's perfectly well now,' he said, echoing my own conviction. 'But she's got it into her head that she needs help. Well, she does, of course, to a limited extent. But there's still a lot of work she has to do on her own. Is there anyone at home? Besides yourself, I mean.'

'I'm the one person she doesn't seem to want.'

'You must accept that, though I know it's hard. Better to keep your distance for a bit, get someone in to keep her company. Don't leave her alone too long.'

'What are you telling me?'

'Just that. Time is on her side. As I say, she's a healthy young woman. And there's no reason why she should be kept here. If you could take her home at the end of the week?'

He turned on his squeaking rubber heel, as if his responsibilities were now at an end. I watched him disappear down the corridor. I went in to Angela, who was listening to *The Archers*. On her face was the beatific look it wore when entering the world of her favourite characters. I waited politely until the programme ended, but when I tried to take her hand she snatched it away.

'Dr Morrison says you can come home at the weekend.'

'Of course I can't come home. I'm not well.'

'You're perfectly well,' I said gently.

'How do you know? You weren't here, were you?'

'I'm here now. Try to live in the present, darling. This place is no good for you. You don't belong in a hospital. You look fine, quite recovered.'

And indeed she did look perfectly well, her cheeks pink, her hair slightly longer than usual. She looked almost as she had looked when we first met in the coffee bar, all that long time ago. Only now there was a new passivity about her. I always found her in bed, although she should have been up and about. I could see no sign of the depression the doctor had warned me about; that, I thought, might come later. Rather she seemed oddly defiant, sometimes humming under her breath, as though to ignore me, or to downgrade my presence.

'We could go down to the cottage,' I said. 'You could finish the curtains.'

'Don't tell me what I could do. I'm not well.'

'Angela,' I said gently. 'Please come home. Come back to me.' There was no answer. 'What went wrong?'

'I fell, didn't I? I fell in the kitchen.'

'Why did you fall? What happened?'

'I don't remember. I'm tired now. Please go.'

And indeed she suddenly looked tired, as if her memory had snagged on something uncomfortable, unmanageable. The sense of her words did not come back to me for a very long while, and even when they did I tried my best to ignore them.

Now that I have so much time I ask myself what blind biological urge prompted her to avail herself of a partner, and then, when the obligations of marriage were forced on her, to renounce the entire condition, as being too much for a still childish temperament. I had always known that she was immature, but had not understood that her immaturity was limitless. I understand now that there are women whose fear of men will always hinder their understanding of them, and will, of course, occlude their sympathy for them. Such women need men as a support, a protection, but they can offer only minimal support in return. Angela would quite probably have felt more comfortable with an older man, even an old man, one who would cherish her, but not threaten her with penetration. I have seen such couples, the husband, no doubt impotent, babying his wife and delighting masochistically in her tantrums and caprices. Such play-acting, which is appalling to witness, is a necessary part of their transaction. If Angela had entered such a union her tendency to regress would have been legitimised. But precisely because she was a healthy young woman she had harboured certain ineradicable desires, certain archaic wishes, and with the unthinking force of nature had set her sights on a partner of similar age and physical appearance. Unfortunately such impulses died once the conquest had been achieved. The white wedding dress, the marquee on the lawn of her mother's house, had marked the conclusion of the exercise.

I did not accept this explanation for a long time, although it would have flattered me to do so. What it did throw light on was my fascination with a woman whose characteristics and whose *modus operandi* were precisely the opposite of those which delineated Angela. Sarah was not a particularly likeable woman; she was, in addition, inarticulate and unreliable. But she was not afraid of men. She was not necessarily dishonest in her dealings with them. She was their equal, as shifty and as elemental as are most men in their dealings with women. When she had wanted me it was without subterfuge; she had no personal plans which involved taking me over, subjugating me in order to pacify or neutralise some unresolved conflict in herself. She thus represented a vista of freedom, no doubt entirely illusory, although the illusion may have been that of her partner, in this case myself. Yet she had not waited for me. It was precisely because she had not waited for me that I had been tempted to pursue her. Whereas Angela's pursuit of me, which I had thought touching, had yielded little more than passing satisfaction for either of us, Sarah exerted no effort whatever. What Angela saw now was a husband to whom she was not only indifferent but nearly hostile. With the social satisfactions of her marriage inevitably declining, with a body which had been physically altered, her fantasy was eclipsed. Perhaps the involvement had always been with herself, rather than with a companion. Her friendships had been fleeting, founded on suspicion. I had early on in our life together come to see that she trusted no one who treated her as an equal. She accepted protection, mine included, and if she had entered my life in the first place it was because I was weak and ill and could do her no harm. Once I was returned to life and health she knew that I would threaten her dangerously precarious equilibrium. It was a self-fulfilling prophecy.

My life, as I left the hospital each evening, was illuminated only by the faintest glimmers of insight. Anything more explicit would have constituted yet another disloyalty. In any event I had more practical matters to consider. When I had returned to the flat I had found it in a state of disarray which I had not previously noticed, although it must have been deteriorating for some time. Perhaps the over-bright discipline of the hospital had left me unprepared for the layer of dust in the bedroom, and the shiny marks on the kitchen floor, as if something had been spilled and carelessly wiped away. Perhaps this was why Angela had fallen, although she normally spent little time in the kitchen, leaving it to Adelina, and latterly to Jenny. There was a smell of stale cooking, though no cooking had been undertaken when I was away: on the table was a half-eaten bowl of corn-flakes, soggy with bluish milk. In the bedroom the bed was unmade.

I was alarmed by this neglect since it suggested that in my absence Angela was disinclined to care for the flat she had once cherished. I cleaned up as best I could, changed the bed, and parcelled up the dirty sheets for the laundry. I opened the windows wide, though it was a damp and misty evening, and made myself a cup of milkless tea. It occurred to me that I was not going to be able to manage on my own. My grief, which was profound, had drained me of energy, even of the desire to bring matters to a successful resolution. Indeed, I did not see how this could be done. We had more or less admitted that our marriage was over, yet now more than ever was I obliged to remain married and to care for my wife. I saw us declining into one of those awful conspiracies in which one partner becomes the *souffre-douleur* of the other, the situation only, accepted—and tolerated—because of that inexpungible guilt for which there is neither forgive-ness nor indeed excuse.

I would cherish and protect Angela, largely because I had betrayed her, and she would make use of me precisely for that reason. This state of affairs would have obtained even without the tragedy of the baby's death. With the instinct possessed by the insecure and the suspicious she knew that, given the choice and the opportunity, I would prefer another woman. It hardly mattered that she had no proof that the other woman was Sarah; it hardly mattered that I had only left her for one night. What mattered to her now was to engineer her return to victim status and to punish me. I accepted my punishment because I felt that I deserved her resentment. I could only hope that with the passage of time that resentment would change into indifference. One thing caused me intense pain: I should never have a child. Angela would not consider it, and I could not blame her. My light-mindedness had unfitted me for the role of father. This she knew and even welcomed.

In the meantime there was the problem of how we were to live. Clearly we could not do so without an intermediary. Angela would take some time to recover, and should not be condemned to recover on her own. She had lost touch with most of her friends, and her mother was a broken reed. It was then, with none of my former reluctance, that I thought of Jenny, although I doubted whether she would look favourably on my request for her renewed attendance. She was away, I knew; I did not know when she was expected back. I decided to wait until the weekend. I would delay Angela's return until the Sunday night, and make my call then. I was sure that Jenny would respond to Angela's need, not so sure that she would respond to mine. I only knew that some sort of temporary solution must be found and I could think of no other.

We were obliged to spend one night alone together before Jenny could come to the rescue, which would be on the following day. That one night was enough to emphasize our estrangement. Angela insisted on my moving my things into the spare room, and it was clear that she intended to spend her time in bed, both day and night. When my exhortations fell on deaf ears I gave up. I thought it ignoble that a woman in these enlightened times should retreat into a form of voluntary invalidism, and I began to view my wife dispassionately, as if she were a character in a play, rather than as someone who was my partner for life. Of her post-natal depression I could see no sign: what I did see was a form of passive derangement. I think it was clear to me even at that stage that she did not intend to get much better. Intent on one of her novels, occasionally humming under her breath, she paid me no attention whatever, except to say, 'I'm tired,' or, 'Leave me alone. You don't know how I feel.'

'You must get up, darling,' I would urge.

'When I'm better.'

'But you are better. You're perfectly all right.'

'I'm still weak.'

'You'll get even weaker, lying in bed.'

'Leave me alone. You don't know how I feel.'

It was therefore with relief that I welcomed the presence of a third person, with something like gratitude that I accepted my portion of stuffed cabbage, or some cabbage derivative—living at the Hôtel du Départ had not done much for Jenny's cooking—leaving the two conspirators in Angela's bedroom with the door firmly shut against me. For they were conspirators, the motherless child and the childless mother, engaged in a monstrous pantomime of filial and maternal affection. While I saw Jenny's presence as inevitable, I also came to see it as malign, at least in its effect on Angela. I would leave her in the morning still in bed; this I acquiesced to as being within the limits of normality. I would return home in the evening to find her in bed again—or still—her hair newly brushed, a suspicion of make-up on her face, but all this for her own benefit rather than for mine. Jenny, apparently in the best of spirits, would greet me warmly, our previous misunderstandings forgiven and forgotten. She would assure me that Angela had had a good day, but that she must not get overtired.

'Perhaps if you could encourage her to get up and go out, Jenny? You both used to enjoy going out . . .'

'She's not ready for that, Alan. I don't think you understand what she's been through.'

'But that's all over. It was very sad, for me too . . .'

'It's always worse for a woman. If you want to sit with her don't stay too long. I want to give her her pill before I go.'

For Jenny was both mother and nurse, though I had to keep reminding myself that Angela was a young woman with no known disease but an apparently inexhaustible desire for guardianship. Both were united in a distaste for men which in Angela's case, and perhaps in Jenny's too, had hardened into alienation. I did not intend to add Jenny's case history to my repertoire: I merely noted that she had probably viewed her marriage as Angela had done, as a release from obscurity, a legitimation. Now, apparently, she had found a new métier as surrogate mother, a role in which she blossomed, to judge from her bright eyes and assumption of control, or empowerment, as the rather useful word describes it. She would arrive every day at about two o'clock, bearing in her shopping bag certain delicacies for Angela and something that she had cooked the previous evening and which I would eat for dinner. We were thus assured of nourishment, even if it were not wholly to our taste, or rather to mine. Another of Angela's worrying symptoms was her refusal to eat what I thought of as grown-up food, that is to say lunch or dinner. She existed wholly on ephemera, nursery foods presented to her on a tray by myself in the morning, before I left for work, and Jenny in the evening before she left. This diet was probably sufficient for one who spent her days in bed, but it added to an increasing process of infantilisation. Also I suspected Jenny of indulging these tastes, and even adding to them, with cakes brought from the *pâtisserie* she patronised, and which she appeared to enjoy by proxy, having denied herself the pleasures of the table in the interests of her figure.

I viewed this partnership with the purest horror. I dreaded my return home in the evenings, when I would busy myself with the washing-machine and the Hoover, for Jenny, naturally enough, would undertake no household duties, and in addition, or perhaps as a further sign of lack of interest, would leave the kitchen untidied. Her curatorship was markedly partisan, though to be fair I think she acted innocently. Certainly she was free from malice. She was simply obeying some blind impulse not only to serve, but to protect, and in this particular scenario I was the unacknowledged threat. Their two views of the situation exactly coincided. Of my own feelings, my own sadness, there was no acknowledgement. This hurt me greatly, since I had too much pride, or too much guilt, to proffer my situation for their perusal.

'Everything all right at home?' Brian would say. 'Getting on all right, is she?'

'Fine, fine,' I would answer. I knew that he was not deceived, but I was not about to make a bid for his sympathy.

'Perhaps you'd both come to dinner,' he said. 'I'll get Felicity to give Angela a ring.'

'I should leave it for a bit,' I told him, and told him more than once. 'She still gets very tired.'

'You should take her away,' people urged. 'A change of scene would work wonders. For you both,' they said, these kind people, neighbours, colleagues, for although no complaint had ever passed my lips I had lost weight, no longer appeared as presentable as I had formerly done, and was frequently sleepless. At night, in the spare room, I wept, stifling the sounds in my pillow. To my horror we both appeared to be going downhill and I seemed to have lost the will or the capacity to put matters right.

It was a momentary insight into my own condition that emboldened me to speak firmly to Jenny on one particularly harassing evening. I knew that what I was doing was reckless, but I was tired and hungry for normality. I took her by the arm and led her into the sitting-room, where Angela could not overhear us. Under the stark centre light we were accuser and accused.

'This can't go on, Jenny,' I said. 'You're making her into an invalid.'

'She is an invalid, Alan. You don't understand . . .'

'She's a perfectly healthy woman who refuses to get out of bed, and you're encouraging her.'

'I see.'

'You're indulging her, Jenny. This is *folie à deux*.'

'I see,' she repeated, with some hauteur. 'Thank you very much, Alan.'

'Of course I can never thank you enough for your kindness.'

'So you're telling me to leave.'

'Jenny, do understand. I want my wife back.'

'Do you?' She looked slyly. 'You were after Sarah, weren't you?' For an instant a younger, more speculative woman considered me, a hint of irony in the faded blue eyes. 'Did you see Sarah? Did you see her in Paris?'

'No, no, I didn't.'

I could feel the flush of shame creeping all over my body. I bundled Jenny roughly into the hall, fetched her coat and her shopping bag, and opened the front door. She stared at me, while various half-formed suspicions grew in her mind. My further guilt was thus firmly established, and, what was worse, was acknowledged by two people. I no longer knew how guilty I was. All I knew was that I should never again feel innocent. I now see that age would bring about this change in any case. Then I was merely aware of a feeling of entrapment. That, of course, is what guilt really resembles, the blind alley of one's own consciousness, with no alleviation either from another person or from oneself.

'You don't want me to come tomorrow, then?'

'Not really, no.'

I forced myself to kiss her on both cheeks, hoping that this would urge her on her way. Her final humility maddened me. She should have been angry, she should have accused me—I longed for such accusations to be out in the open—

but she chose to smile and look at me with an uncertain expression on her face. Then, 'She takes her pill in about an hour's time.'

'I'll remember. Thank you, Jenny.'

I marched in to Angela, and said, 'You can stay there for now, but tomorrow you are getting up. And you'd better be prepared to pull your weight again. Jenny won't be coming any more.'

She stared at me. 'But I can't do without her.'

'You can and you will. Believe me, this is all for the best.'

But she took no notice, turned her face to the pillow, and began to cry like a child.

'Don't forget to take your pill,' I said, and left her.

This continued for three weeks. Angela wept and I exhorted. She remained in bed, and soon her hair and her nightdress began to look untended. I bought prepared dishes from Marks and Spencer which she ate greedily and carelessly, like an old lady or a very young child, the corners of her mouth gleaming with sauce. Then she would apply a thick layer of lipstick, she who had used so little. Streaks of old make-up appeared on the pillow; the room began to smell. She refused to let me near her, even to change the sheets. I called the doctor, who was non-committal and said he would look in again. One freezing night I staggered into the spare room, dropped my clothes on the floor, and fell into a deep sleep. That was the night that Angela took the rest of her pills. She was dead when I went in to her the next morning. There was no note. That my poor girl had decided that she wanted nothing further to do with me was my final punishment.

12

It was Aubrey who suggested, or rather who strongly recommended, that I go away. 'This has broken your mother's heart,' he said consolingly. Mine too, I reminded him. He considered me, as if weighing the sincerity of my words, then, having perhaps decided that I was, for a very brief moment, to be trusted, his expression softened.

'We must all recover as best we can,' he said. 'I'll look after Alice, of course. Don't worry about her. Worry about yourself, but worry constructively. Get some exercise, some decent food. I know the place for you—I used to go there myself when I was out of sorts. It's a place called Vif, on the border between France and Switzerland. There's very little to do there but walk and sleep, and that's just the sort of thing you need. They know me quite well there. If you like I'll give Monsieur Pach at the hotel a ring. In fact you can leave the whole thing to me, tickets, hotel, currency. I'll drop them into the office; that'll save you a bit of time.'

For he was anxious to get rid of me, not because he disliked me, but because I was associated with disaster. He was, for a man of his relative sophistication, surprisingly superstitious. I saw that look on other faces: the hastily lowered gaze turned resolutely into one of cordial sincerity, the caution of the approach—could it possibly be avoided?—and the neutral, numb-seeming words of condolence. I had become an embarrassment, even an irritation, and my presence was not welcome.

I therefore took the hint and avoided most of my friends, all of whom professed themselves anxious to see me; perhaps they were, but I could anticipate the conversation, the avoidance of one particular subject, and I felt protective of their naïve kindness, far more protective of them, in fact, than of myself. Only Brian and Felicity were precious to me, Felicity even more than Brian, whose unfailing presence in the office next to mine constituted a consolation in itself. Felicity spoke of Angela's death quite simply as an event destined to pass into history, and thus to an extent without affect. I dined with them quite often, either in St John's Wood, or, at my invitation, at a restaurant near their house. I trusted them so deeply that when their baby son cried in the nursery I did not even mind. It was as if their adult presence, so matter of fact, so devoid of exaggerated sympathy, served as a bulwark against my hurt.

In any event I was scarcely aware of hurt, only of shock. This had a curious effect on me: I became polite and humble, searching people's faces for the reassurance I could no longer find in myself. When I looked in the mirror I saw that my expression was one of pleading. If I lived at all in those first months I lived automatically, eating without hunger in order to combat fatigue, walking carefully to work in order to afford myself some vestige of healthy activity. There was one change: I slept a lot. I became a sleeper of heroic duration and consistence. In the early evening I thought of my bed in the spare room with longing, but waited until a suitable hour before I would permit myself to pull the coverlet off the bed and undress with a sigh of relief. I camped out in the flat, using only this temporary room and the bathroom. I ate out, when I did eat; sometimes I went for a walk in the dark, to use up the time before I could decently go to bed. Sleep was what I most wanted. It seemed to be the only need I would ever have again.

One evening I returned home to find that Mother had been in, had removed Angela's clothes from the wardrobes and stored them in the cupboards in the spare room, and had stripped the beds and changed the sheets, removing every sign that Angela had ever occupied our bedroom, along with vestiges of her infinitely tragic life, her novels, her pills, even the flowered towels she had bought for our bathroom. I almost resented this. By inviting me to occupy my flat again, as I had occupied it before my marriage, it seemed as though my mother was being insensitive. But this very slight clumsiness did not offend me. It embarrassed me. I felt apologetic about taking my ease in the big bed, thought the spare room more appropriate. It was not that I was afraid of Angela's ghost, for whom I felt pity and protection. I was simply aware of her absence as something irreparable. I did not blame her for what she had done, because I recognized that what had happened was an act to which she had put her name, that she had acted in character. That her life had excluded me for an appreciable time I accepted, however regretfully. I told myself that our parting was inevitable. I went through this reasoning every night. Then I entered sleep as others enter religion.

When Aubrey dropped an envelope containing my air

ticket and a quantity of French and Swiss currency onto my
desk I looked at him blankly; I had forgotten where I was
going, and why. My lack of assurance unsettled him, pro-
pelling him into reluctant sympathy.

'You need the break, Alan. You're still a young man, too
young to spend your life brooding. Some fresh air will do
you the world of good. Your room is booked. You'll telephone as soon as you arrive? Try to sound positive when you
speak to Alice, won't you?'

I detected an anxiety for my mother behind this desire to
get me out of sight. It occurred to me that he loved her, and
that this late love had rattled his normal composure. He was
uneasy with me, too scrupulous to blame me for causing
trouble, but unable to care for me in what he viewed an
enormous indiscretion. Indeed I felt the same way that he
did; my guilt had disappeared, to be replaced by a high
degree of social embarrassment. It was for this reason that I
acquiesced in his plan for me. The name of the small town to
which he had consigned me—Vif—seemed appropriate,
since my nerves were *à vif*, that is to say, flayed. Since I was
no longer at home anywhere, except in my dreams, which
were, curiously enough, peopled with characters I had
known in childhood, I became resigned to going away. It
seemed only polite to do so. And somewhere, at some level,
there may have been a hope that Aubrey's reasoning was sufficient, that all I needed was some fresh air and exercise, and
that if I absented myself I would expiate my fault (since it
remained mine) and would go some way to being forgiven.

'It's only two weeks,' said Brian, to whom I confessed the
terrifying blankness of my mind. 'Though why you couldn't
just go to the cottage I don't know. I suppose by pleasing
Aubrey you're pleasing your mother . . .'

'That's it,' I said thankfully. 'That's why I'm going. To
make them feel comfortable.'

'It might be all right. I recommend running, preferably before breakfast. Take something to read. I'll ring, of course, or Felicity will.'

'She's been marvellous.'

His face softened. 'She's a good girl,' he said. 'I know you'll be all right, Alan.'

What he meant to say was that he hoped I'd have better luck next time. This did not offend me; in fact it encouraged me. If Brian thought it permissible to turn the page then I would think so too. My view of love at this time was wistful, as if happiness in marriage would be forever denied to me. Briefly, fugitively, I glimpsed a time when I might deplore my choices, might give a sad but impatient shrug when I considered how badly my emotional investments had turned out. Indeed, for a somehow heartening moment I consigned both Sarah and Angela to the past. Of the two of them it was Sarah who inspired the greater distaste. I was once again on the side of the virtuous; wholeheartedly I saw the point of virtue. Since obedience was a virtue I would go away, but I would endeavour to go away without my memories. I had always been a fairly robust character; if I were condemned to live alone then I would try to make a good job of it. Nevertheless, when I left the office and knew that I should not see it for two weeks, I felt something akin to panic. A solitary life is not for the faint-hearted, and I wondered whether, as Brian thought, my luck would ever change. Bracing myself, I made what farewells were in order, my features set in a rictus of determination and assurance. Then I was out in the street, bound for sympathy.

I dozed on the flight to Geneva; evidently sleep was to be my new occupation. Following instructions I went down the escalator in the airport and found the train that was to take me to Vif. By this time it was evening and I could see little from the windows, but I was aware that the train was climbing. It was the nadir of the year, a misty early February, when the days are still short and the promise of spring seems remote. I stumbled out into the dark and a profound silence. Then, beyond the station, I found a café, and sat down, my bag beside me. I was shocked into consciousness by the completeness of my exile, and for a moment I felt renewed panic, not knowing what to do with myself. Then I picked up my bag, found a taxi, and told the driver to go to Aubrey's hotel, which seemed to me to be some way out of town. I noticed very little of my surroundings that first night, although I have come to know them well ever since. The proprietor, Monsieur Pach, a small immaculate man with white hair and hands folded like a monk, asked after Aubrey, whom he appeared to know well, and told me that the weather was warm for the time of year. He melted away silently, then just as silently returned with a map of the region and a small brochure detailing some of its delights: the Château Fort, the Promenade du Soleil, the Belvedere, with its *vue panoramique*, the Hôtel de France with its Sporting Club, and the English Tea Rooms.

'*Et là-bas,*' he said reverently, '*vous avez la France.*'

The brochure also told me that the region had been popular with English visitors since Queen Victoria had spent a few days at the Hôtel de France in the company of her eldest daughter. This seemed appropriate. Although I had only been there a couple of hours I detected a certain womanishness in the ecclesiastical calm of Monsieur Pach, the brooding care with which my soup was served by an elderly waiter. I felt amused and exasperated: was this what Aubrey thought I was good for? I went up to bed feeling larger than usual, feeling my muscles tense once more. I would walk, I would run, I would return to remind them that I was not yet to be written off. Naturally I slept well that night; sleep was not the problem. But I slightly dreaded the morning and the day before me, when I would feel the full weight of my leisure, or of my penance, which ever it was to be.

There were very few people about. That there were any people at all was attested by the thwack of balls from the tennis courts of the Hôtel de France, further down the valley. The sound, which carried easily in the still air, woke me at eight most mornings. Later, when I took a walk to the neighbouring village of Chelles, I saw a small crowd of old men gathered round a gigantic chess set on the pavement outside a café. Such people who played these games seemed mild, harmless, self-absorbed, not of a kind to pay much attention to a casual visitor. There were few distractions; that is to say there were none. I saw few people until the evening, when I went down to dinner in the hotel restaurant. Even there the most distinctive sounds were of soup spoons on plates or the mild gurgle of Apollinaris being poured from a bottle. My fellow guests were two elderly German women, a very stout man seated, as I was, at a table for one, and a husband and wife whose very gestures proclaimed them to be English. They nodded and smiled as they passed me, but otherwise ignored me, for which I was grateful. After dinner, my eyelids already heavy, I was obliged to go up to my room, which was comfortable but austere. I might return to the bar for a nightcap, but the bar, although staffed by a young man in a correct white jacket, was deserted, and I began to feel self-conscious there.

The days were easier. There was the walk to Chelles, slightly uphill, or the walk downhill into Vif. There was lunch at one of the two or three restaurants, the return to the hotel for a coffee on the glassed-in terrace, then the walk back to Vif for the English papers which arrived on the afternoon train from Geneva. These would take care of that awkward interval before dinner, or at least until it was time to take my bath. I bathed twice a day; it seemed foolish not to, with so much time at my disposal. Then there was dinner, prefaced by nods and smiles, and at the end of these long days there was blessed sleep. I was sometimes already dozing when Brian rang, and could hardly summon up the energy for an intelligent conversation. This worried him, so that he would ring again on the following evening. Hazily I would assure him that I was fine, much better. I said this entirely for his sake. What insight I had told me that I was very sad, more sad than a man of my age had a right to be. But at the same time I felt a renewed strength in my body, my legs stronger from the walking, the skin of my face taut from the keen air. I was forced to the conclusion that Aubrey's idea had been an enlightened one. My rest would do us all good, even Brian, who was trying so hard not to mention his son, on whom he doted, although Felicity did so without compunction when she came on the line. I was grateful to them both, to Brian for his delicacy, to Felicity for her lack of subterfuge.

I became an out-of-season inhabitant. 'Out of season' exactly describes my state of mind which was blessedly vacant. I could spend half an hour leaning on a wicket gate overlooking a meadow, without anyone noticing that I was there. Or I would stroll down to the Hôtel de France and simply contemplate the chandeliers twinkling through the huge plate-glass windows. I spoke to no one, and in this way may have appeared quite rude to the English couple, the Hobsons, also staying at the hotel. They at last approached me, and I was mildly grateful to them, but as I learned that they had met in this place some forty years ago, and that they came back every year on their wedding anniversary, I smiled pleasantly and offered no information in return. Finally, disconcerted by my reticence, the worried-looking Mrs Hobson, who did not appear to be greatly enjoying this annual pilgrimage, asked me if I were married. 'My wife died,' I said briefly, offering no explanation. In that moment it appeared to me that all I had to do was to proffer this simple statement of fact, both to those who enquired and to myself. Angela retreated, became Angela no longer but a girl I used to know and whom I was beginning to lay to rest. After my brief confession the Hobsons left me alone, as if affronted by my introducing a note of mortality into their holiday, which they were obliged to celebrate sentimentally, as if they had just met. This meant that they had to stay together, although Mr Hobson was allowed to read his day-old copy of the *Daily Telegraph* on the terrace, during which time his wife would scan the driveway and wait for him to finish amusing himself. They would go for a walk occasionally: I might run into them in the town. When I did so I wished them good-morning with a jovial smile, which to them might have appeared misplaced. But I had done with playing the widower; I was still young enough to feel the energy in my healthy body and to appreciate, as a thing which would vanish overnight, my tiredness at the end of the day.

But I slept voraciously, although more dreams intruded into my sleep than heretofore. They seemed to replicate each other, so that night after night I walked down an endless street, looking for an address, which I knew I must find, since my life depended on it. This walk, attended by great anxiety, led me through various London boroughs which I knew were not contiguous, and encompassed Clapham, Putney and Highgate. On the way I invaded several buildings where orchestras were in rehearsal. I asked directions of the young musicians, explained that I did not know the number of the house for which I was searching. They indicated a street that ran past factories and youth hostels, until at last I stumbled across a small cul-de-sac of pretty houses, on the door of one of which was emblazoned, in full letters, the number: Seventeen. I woke with a feeling of immense relief, not knowing what the dream meant, but with some sort of vague assurance that an answer to my predicament could be found, in the same mysterious and quasi-magical fashion.

On Sunday the hotel filled up. Families ate lunch in the dining-room, as some sort of treat or ritual. They were polite, spoke in lowered tones, the children silent and well behaved. I found that I could view these children with indulgence. I silently gave thanks, either to fate or to the deity in whom I did not believe, that I could still appreciate children, that I was not about to become squeamish or misogynistic. I began to plan treats for Brian's son, Adam, promised myself that I would look for toys for him, buy him the finest bear that the Swiss shops had to offer. I was dimly aware that solitude was making me sentimental. I thought, but cautiously, of friends and family at home, and of the moment when I should have to return to them. The families in the dining-room got up to leave, the wives slightly flushed, the husbands graceless but benign, the process of digestion comfortably under way. I imagined them going home to their spotless houses, to watch television, or to sleep. They would have been to church in the morning, have walked up to the hotel for an aperitif. I imagined this ritual being played out Sunday after Sunday. I half rose from my seat and nodded goodbye as they passed my table. They smiled back. Home, I thought; they are going home. I was already impatient for the ending of the day.

The second week passed more slowly than the first, though that had passed slowly enough. I still appreciated the gift of anonymity, though at times I began to long for company. I did not wish for the sort of company I had always enjoyed; in fact I shied away from it. Since I was in no way a fantasist it did not occur to me to envisage an ideal companion. Rather, I was aware of my unaccompanied state as anomalous, although I had endured it well enough, had even found it amusing, in a role-playing sort of way. I saw myself from the outside, a very English figure, suitably dressed in a raincoat and walking shoes, a meaningless and all-purpose smile on my face. The natives, mild-mannered and reflective people, seemed to find this acceptable, since they recognised me as a tourist of the docile variety, one who was not likely to disturb the profound peace in which they lived. I found a bookshop and bought some paperbacks, but I did not yet have the patience for reading, and sitting in the hotel, either in my room or on the terrace, made me nervous and too conscious of the weight of the quiet day. I preferred to keep on my feet, until I knew much of the surrounding countryside by heart. There was always that lowering of the spirits when the light faded, when I thought of the busier streets of London, even of my empty flat, with something like longing. But I was determined to sit out the two weeks, if only to make my re-entry into normal life acceptable to others. Those others—Mother, Aubrey, Brian, Felicity, even Jenny—had begun to retreat from me. They represented an enormous debt which I should eventually have to repay. I would sigh at this point, as I registered the paucity of my resources, and get up to walk yet again into town for the English papers.

At last it was Sunday, and my bag was packed soon after breakfast. The monk-like Monsieur Pach, for whose discretion I was extremely grateful, ordered my cab and wished me a pleasant journey. I said goodbye to the Hobsons, shook the hand of the stout man, whose name I had never learned, and waited in the foyer with the German ladies who were also leaving. Through the windows of the car the landscape, so familiar, already seemed strange, distant. The train travelled silently through stations whose names I could barely remember, and the airport, when I arrived, seemed like a glittering outpost of civilisation, transplanted to a region of strange customs and manners, remote, closed, impenetrable from the outside, inhabited by pacifists. The noise, which was muted, struck me as exorbitant. I reflected that I was now allowed to eat and drink anywhere I liked, sat down and had a *pain au chocolat* for my lunch, as if I were on leave from school, and eventually boarded the plane with something like alacrity. Everyone on the flight seemed in good health; no one claimed my attention. Without noticing, I relaxed into my former role, no longer a solitary walker, a man in every sense out of season, but a London solicitor, with attachments, with a history, but a history which no longer threatened to do me harm.

Aubrey was there to meet me at Heathrow. I thought that was decent of him, though I knew that Mother was behind it. He told me that they were expecting me for supper. In the car we were silent.

'How was it?' he said finally.

'Not bad,' I replied. 'Pleasant place. Rather a good idea of yours.' Depression was finally making its expected inroads as we drove into London. There was a further silence.

'And how are you?'

I thought about this, obstinately unwilling to give him a reassuring answer.

'Loveless,' I said.

' "*Personne ne m'aime, et je ne m'en plains pas. Je suis trop juste pour cela.*" '

'What?' I asked him, startled.

'One of those marvellous eighteenth-century women, I forget which one. Madame du Deffand, no doubt. She blamed no one for not loving her, said she was too—what is it?—Just? Fair? for that.'

I was deeply shocked. My guilt was to be re-established, it seemed. Yet I too was too just to deny it.

'Of course people love you,' he added, a little too late. 'Alice loves you. I love you.'

But I knew that he had been thinking up his quotation, and waiting for the moment when he could get me alone in order to deliver it. I said nothing, hoping that my silence would rebuke him. Maybe it did. There was no further exchange until we reached Cadogan Gate.

As we sat in the dining-room, eating ham and salad, Wensleydale and apple tart, it seemed as if the past few years had never taken place, or it would have done had it not been for Aubrey's reservations. This person was now my mother's husband, towards whom I was bound to be deferential, if only for my mother's sake. She looked tired, older. Aubrey, no doubt communing in spirit with various marvellous eighteenth-century women, made civilised conversation, mostly about his travels, and his memories of Vif. Had it not been for this the atmosphere might have been rather strained. He had his uses, I reflected, and Mother, even if tired, was cared for. They had discussed me in my absence, I realised, may even have disagreed, perhaps painfully. This would have grieved my mother, but she was too loyal to show it. Her loyalties were now divided, and she clearly found this difficult. I therefore played my part, and in the end I think she was even surprised by my levity, although she would guess the reasons that prompted it.

After dinner conversation became desultory, until, pleading tiredness, I asked them to excuse me. I did this as much for their sake as for mine. In the hall Mother disappeared, then reappeared with a shopping bag containing a loaf, a grapefruit, a pint of milk, a packet of butter, and a tin of coffee. 'Aubrey went out specially this morning,' she said, but without her usual loving smile. So he was kind, I reflected, even if his kindness was eternally subjected to his critical judgement. I thanked him profusely and left, promising to telephone. In the street, as silent as ever, I felt as if I had left home for good. But perhaps leaving home was what it was all about, this new feeling of vulnerability, as if the former protection had been removed. Perhaps all I had ever done, all anyone does, is to leave home, to experiment with life on one's own, without markers. My past experiences now appeared to me as one vast divagation, a series of inevitable mistakes. Too little is known at the outset, when others do one's thinking for one. I had simply failed, as others no doubt fail, when the fledgling judgement proves inadequate to the trials one encounters. Maybe death, when it comes, is simply another longing for home. As, despite my bag, I walked across the park, Cadogan Gate receded, not only in distance, but in memory, like the home I should perhaps never have left, in order to protect others as well as myself.

The flat seemed silent, indifferent, and no more welcoming than the hotel had done. It was, I reflected, my new home, as if I had never been there before. I moved cautiously through the rooms, careful to switch off the lights. In our bedroom, which, in a reflex, I thought of once again as ours, the air was undisturbed. I unpacked, drew a bath, wondering if I were as tired as I had said I was. In bed I waited cautiously, politely, for sleep. But that night sleep did not descend as easily as I had come to expect.

13

I became bluff, genial, to hide my loneliness. At night I read poetry, *Un Voyage à Cythère*, *The Haystack in the Floods*. I dined out most evenings, inviting my friends to restaurants when I was not at their houses, but always relishing that solitary walk home through silent streets. There were one or two flirtations, but very little came of them, apart from a transitory impression of closeness which did not survive for more than a night or two. These affairs did not take place in my flat, which was kept more or less inviolable, as if my wife still lived there. The week-ends I spent at the cottage, which turned out to be damp. I had a decent heating system installed and made various improvements, spending lavishly in order to persuade myself that it was really mine.

The chief advantage of all this was that the house was ready to receive visitors. Brian and Felicity borrowed it frequently, and in fact used it as their own when for any reason I stayed in London. I was glad of this, both for their sake and for mine. Also it made the house seem less forlorn, and I looked forward to the time when there would be two children to play in the garden, for Felicity had become pregnant again very quickly and was expecting a girl. This news did not affect me unduly; my own daughter was a case apart. In time I came to regard the whole tragedy objectively and was successful in dismissing it from my mind for a good part of every day. What remained of it was incorporated in my loneliness, the one contingent upon the other. Because of the part I had played I was condemned to go through the world uncomforted, and because I accepted this the burden remained oddly manageable, so manageable that I think few people were aware of its existence, whereas to me it was a physical accompaniment, a *doppelgänger*, and the price it exacted, or one that I volunteered, was a form of celibacy, interrupted only briefly from time to time, which I also accepted, thinking it suitable, and perhaps only temporary. I walked a great deal; walking, along with sleep, remained my chief resource.

Having, with some sorrow, realised that the long and close connection between my mother and myself was now tenuous, I was, despite my many friends, to all intents and purposes, unsupported, or rather deprived of that primitive support that one craves at such times. This did not greatly bother me, for my self-communing was so intense that it was an effort to spend many hours in company. Strangely, few people noticed this, perhaps because of the exaggerated *bonhomie* I cultivated at this time, so that I was forever patting men on the back and kissing their wives, actions which I should have viewed with some reserve in earlier days. It seemed important to manifest my gratitude to them in ways that they would understand, even if the effort left me tired.

But I also knew that these friends would reassure themselves and others that I had recovered, that I had got over the two unfortunate deaths that had made them so wary of me. In some entirely unconscious fashion I seemed to want them all in position, ready to welcome me when I decided to re-enter the world. I was in the world, of course, but my thoughts were elsewhere. It seemed important to evolve naturally from this indeterminate state. In the meantime I did my best to assure myself of continued affection, until the day arrived when I should be able to return it in good measure.

I spent my fortieth birthday in Cagnes with Mother and Aubrey and grew increasingly bored and depressed by the tedious expatriate life they had come increasingly to prefer. When I said as much to my mother she replied, 'But we're old, Alan. We're not ambitious for anything more. We like our place in the sun. You may even be the same one day. And try to understand, darling. Life changes us, moves us on, and that is the hard truth of the matter. Even so,' and here she lowered her voice, 'you know that you will always come first. That's why I try to make it up to Aubrey. Can you not show him a little more affection? He's awfully fond of you, you know.'

I considered this. 'Has he made you happy?'

'He delivered me from a solitary old age. You have no idea how that frightened me. I could see myself tottering around with Jenny until one of us got ill and had to nurse the other. Instead of which I've got the sun on the terrace every morning, and the company of a man I respect. I sound hard, I know. I cut my links very abruptly, particularly with Jenny. That reminds me, have you been in touch with her?'

'I've telephoned. She didn't sound all that pleased to hear from me. I gather Humphrey's not too well.'

'Yes, I had a letter from Sybil. Of course, he's getting on; he must be nearly eighty. And living in that very retiring fashion is not exactly healthy. She's been so good, Jenny, I mean. If I gave you one or two things to take back for her could you bear to pay her a visit? Lavender bags, honey, that sort of thing.'

I did not think that Jenny would appreciate these tourist souvenirs, and would indeed know that they had originated in a guilty conscience, but as I had my own conscience to deal with, my own amends to make, I said nothing. It was entirely possible that through our own actions both my mother and I had sacrificed someone who had been eager for our affection, perhaps too eager, in a way that had managed to be subtly irritating. Neither of us had been willing to make up for the emotional deficiencies of Jenny's life. My own debt to her was considerable, although I remembered her attendance through Angela's last illness with something like horror still. The fact that she had found it fulfilling had always exasperated me, as if there were merit in such simple sacrifice, even if the case were so questionable. At the same time I remembered her speculative, almost sly look, when she asked me whether I had seen Sarah in Paris. In the light of subsequent events that look, that question, were particularly unfortunate. In that moment her affection had seemed almost an affectation; a keener intelligence had been visible in her glance, keen enough to make me extremely uncomfortable.

It had taken courage to telephone her after the funeral. When I did so Humphrey had answered and appeared not to understand what I was talking about. I left a message, which would probably not be passed on. Nor was it; when I rang again, prompted by an unwilling gratitude for her past generosity, she answered at once, as if anxious to reach the telephone before her husband picked it up in his study. To my surprise her reaction to my call was one of indifference, as if I were someone she barely remembered, rather than the man who had once so brutally dismissed her from his home. I tried to thank her; I even wrote her a letter, to which she made no reply. She was not hostile; she was even amiable, but she gave me the impression that many pages had been turned since her days of mothering Angela. I sensed that since her most lavish sympathies had brought her nothing in return, she had decided to withdraw them, even cancel them altogether. This had made me even more uncomfortable, as it exactly paralleled my own condition. And now I was bound to present her with various trinkets from the south of France, for which she would express appreciation, knowing precisely how much the gesture was worth. I felt ashamed in advance, even ashamed of my mother, as I followed her round the market, accumulating olives and cheeses.

'Leave all that,' I said. 'Buy her something better. What about that dish over there?'

It was a terracotta dish with a green glaze round the rim, shaped like a shallow amphora, with two short handles. I paid for it myself, relieved to have found a gift that was both appropriate and dignified. I had not relished the thought of handing over anything which smacked of haste, of precisely the sort of reflex that Jenny always seemed to invite.

'You'll give her my love,' said my mother. 'Tell her I think of her.' But I could see that if she did it was of a fate she had almost not avoided. 'And let me know how she is. And how you are, my love. I'm afraid we haven't given you a very lively holiday.'

But I said that I had had a good rest, which reassured her. At her age, no doubt— but what age was she? Barely seventy, I reckoned—she may have thought that a good rest was what anyone might want. The thought saddened me, as did the sight of her waving to me as I drove off, her white hair setting off her tanned face, her hand, more wrinkled than the rest of her, holding down the skirt of her cotton dress. From the balcony outside their bedroom Aubrey, looking even older than my mother, raised his hand in a brief farewell salute.

When I telephoned Jenny after my return I got the impression that the call was answered in the same prompt, almost precipitate fashion, as if to forestall Humphrey's interference.

'Oh, Alan.' There was a pause. There was no reason why she should be friendly, I told myself. But this was disconcerting.

'Alice sends you all kinds of messages,' I said heartily. 'And something I can only deliver in person. Perhaps you could put up with me one evening? Unless you and Humphrey would be my guests . . .'

'Humphrey rarely leaves the flat these days. He's not at all well. You'd better come to dinner. Any evening next week. We're always in.'

We settled on the Thursday, and although the prospect filled me with boredom it was no more disheartening than spending an evening on my own. I added a bunch of yellow roses to the dish, which I kept on my desk, and which I would miss. She had warned me that because of Humphrey's declining health we should have to eat early. At six o'clock, with a sigh, I put the dish in my bag, and left for the Edgware Road.

It was a dull wet evening, leaves slippery on the pavement. I felt heavy in my eternal raincoat, and reflected how anomalous I must have looked in that Paris night, nearly a year ago. The gloomy pile of Humphrey's block of flats reared up out of the uncertain light, seeming to threaten the cars passing in a cloud of spray and dampening my trouser legs. It was years since I had visited Humphrey, long before his marriage; I must have been taken there by my mother when I was still a boy. I remembered the flat as dark, ugly, macerated in a stale and never renewed warmth. I must have been given something to eat on that occasion for I had an image of myself seated at an oval table under a centre light-fitting consisting of a wooden wheel supporting several rather dim tulip-shaped bulbs. I also had an impression of thick curtains drawn against the daylight, although it must have been barely late afternoon, and the ticking of innumerable clocks.

Jenny opened the door, with an expression of welcome, which though appropriate was not effusive. 'Well, Alan,' she said. 'It's been a long time.' Before I had a moment in which to offer my lame excuses she drew me nearer, and said in a lowered voice, 'You'll see a great change in Humphrey. He's very forgetful these days. Very obstinate too.' She tapped her head significantly. 'Don't worry if he doesn't remember you. He drifts in and out. It can be very difficult. After all, I'm not so young myself.' She sighed, and then said brightly, 'Humphrey! Look who's come to see us! You remember Alan, don't you? Alice's boy.'

Humphrey, rising slowly from his chair, clearly did not remember me, though he scrutinised me thoughtfully. I did not see that he was much changed from the pachydermatous creature so cherished by Sybil and Marjorie in what I now thought of as the old days. Possibly Sybil and Marjorie might have brought a smile of recognition to his face; his wife he tended to accept as a species of retainer. 'Is dinner ready?' he asked her, turning his head cautiously in her direction. Some reflex must have told him it was hardly worth the bother of sitting down again. Holding on to my arm as a handy means of support he made his way towards the door, ignoring Jenny who was attempting to smooth the creases out of his jacket. 'We don't stand on ceremony here,' he said, in a brief access of lucidity.

'No, of course not,' I replied.

'You don't mind if we eat straight away,' Jenny stated

rather than enquired. I caught a look of weariness which was immediately effaced. 'Humphrey likes to watch television before he goes to bed. Humphrey! Your favourite programme is on in half an hour.'

'Ah, yes,' he said. 'Dinner first.'

The centre light was as I remembered it, with one bulb already burnt out. Apparently it had never been replaced. We ate a mushroom quiche in all but silence. I might have been unknown to them, so little attention did they pay me.

'Mother sends her love,' I said.

'Ah, yes,' said Jenny. 'And how is Alice? Of course I never see her now. Strange, when I used to see her so often.' The wordless accusation of disloyalty hung heavy in the dusky atmosphere.

'I hardly ever see her myself,' I said. 'I've had to accept the fact that they spend most of their time in France these days.'

'*La vie de château, quoi?*' said Jenny. There was a further silence.

'Sarah came,' said Humphrey abruptly, mashing his spoon into his plate of port wine jelly. 'Always comes on her birthday. Time she was getting married, I told her.'

'Oh, she will marry, have no fear of that,' said Jenny composedly.

'Thought you were going to marry her,' said Humphrey, restored to something like life by the thought of Sarah. 'Did you marry someone else? Some other girl? Annabel?'

'Angela,' both Jenny and I said simultaneously. That was the only time Angela's name was mentioned, without it being conspicuously avoided.

'Asked her what she wanted for her birthday,' Humphrey went on. 'Said she wanted one of the clocks. Gave her that little silver carriage clock of mine.'

A significant nod from Jenny indicated a gap on the mantelpiece, between two worthless brass candlesticks.

Humphrey chuckled. 'She knew to take the most valuable. Jenny was angry.' He chuckled again.

'You should not have let her have it, Humphrey,' said Jenny, her colour rising.

'Why not? All this will come to her anyway.'

'Humphrey . . .'

'I promised my brother I'd take care of her. She'll get everything. Well, it's mine, isn't it?'

'Your programme must be starting, Humphrey.'

'Didn't someone say you were a solicitor?'

'I am a solicitor, yes.'

'I'll give you my will. You can look after it.' He looked crafty. 'Can't trust her, you know.'

'I hardly think . . .'

'Why? Haven't been struck off, have you?'

'No, no.'

'Well, come and see me before you go. Don't forget.'

I stood up and steered him out of the room. When I had lowered him into his chair, I went back to Jenny, my napkin still in my hand. Her colour was high, her expression hard.

'You see how I'm placed, Alan. Entirely alone.'

'I'm sorry.'

'I had a long talk with Sarah, well, not long, while Humphrey was out of the way. Make sure some man takes care of you, I said. Make that man marry you, I told her.'

'What man?'

'The man she's living with, of course. In Paris. De Leuze, his name is.'

'I'm out of touch, I'm afraid.'

'A very respectable sort of man, I'm told. Older than she is, which is all right now, although later on . . . But she could be a young widow, if things turn out . . .' She left the sentence unfinished. 'It's the money that's important.'

'Why won't she marry him?'

'She says she doesn't love him.' She laughed, with what seemed like genuine amusement. 'As if love had anything to do with it.'

'Does she love someone else, then?' I asked, my mouth dry.

'You'd have to ask her that yourself, wouldn't you?' she said harshly. 'I talked some sense into her, I hope.'

'I thought you were fond of her.'

'Well, of course I am.'

'Well, then, why give her such bad advice? At least, it seems bad to me.'

She put down the dish she was holding. 'Listen to me, Alan. Sarah is like me, neither daughter nor mother. There's only one way for her to earn respect. If necessary she must make the best of a bad job.' As I have, were the unspoken words. 'Respect is what a woman needs in this world.' Oddly enough I remembered my mother saying something like the same thing.

'But surely, these days . . .'

'Oh, no, make no mistake. Women get older. For men it's different. I'm sure you still have your diversions.' She regarded me without amenity. 'Men can bury their past. An unmarried woman *is* her past. Whereas a wife has a social position. A spinster has none.'

'But this is ridiculous. She's still young. There's nothing to stop her doing what she wants to. She could even have a child . . .'

She flashed me a look of triumph. 'She can't have children. She's a barren fig tree, like me. The same reason in both our cases. An early abortion . . .'

'I don't want to hear this.'

'The wrong women have the children, Alan. And even then some of them don't know how.'

It seemed as though all the bitterness of her life had suddenly risen to the surface. That bitterness was sufficient to obliterate all her affections, together with the efforts she had made to secure them. From the other room came a burst of laughter from the television, together with Humphrey's hoarse chuckle.

'And that's what I've come to,' she said, as though we had been talking about her all along.

'And Sarah?'

'I've given her my advice. I could do no more.'

'You used to be so loving,' I said. 'So warm-hearted. I hardly recognise you.'

She sat down again, smoothing the tablecloth with the flat of both hands. 'I've had a hard life,' she said quietly. 'You didn't know me when I was a girl, in Paris. Or earlier than that, with my uncle and aunt. There was no love lost in my childhood, unlike yours. I used to look at families, wondering what it was like, to belong to them. I was young, I had my love affairs, I thought they would last. They lasted as long as I was with someone who could pay the bills. Then that stopped. I always worked. And I got tired, more and more tired. Then I met Humphrey. I was overjoyed, but overjoyed because he needed me. Do you understand that? What I thought was love was gratitude. We were grateful to each other. And even that was good enough for a while. But you've seen him; he has no use for a woman. Probably never had. And I had to do without. And now he doesn't even like me. And I'm still on my own, after everything.'

'You seemed so happy.'

'I was happy as long as I was respected. As long as I had a social position. Alice made me feel, well, appreciated, normal, like every other woman with a family. I thought I could be a mother to Sarah. But neither really wanted me. No one did. Not even . . .'

'Don't,' I said quickly. 'Don't even mention her name.'

'Even she . . .'

'Please.'

We were silent. 'Sarah lives abroad now,' she said. 'She has no need of this place. Humphrey can't see that. Rather than leave it to me he'd rather leave it to those two old women of his. But no, it's got to go to Sarah. As if this were any place for her.'

'Is she in need of money?'

Jenny laughed. 'She doesn't even work. She never has. Not like me. She's dependent on that man she's living with. That's why I told her to see that he marries her.'

'Do you have an address for her?'

She looked vague. 'Humphrey's got it somewhere, but I don't know where. He hides everything from me. Her face when she took the clock! "Uncle would want me to have it," she said. I could have told her not to rely on him. I did, and look where it got me.'

At this point, and as if to refute her, or any hopes she still may have cherished, Humphrey shuffled in with an envelope. 'My will,' he said. 'You look after it for me. It's all in order.' He looked at Jenny. 'What did you say his name was?'

With a pop another of the bulbs in the chandelier expired. It seemed a fitting end to our conversation. But I was not yet to be released. At the door, with Humphrey in abeyance, she plucked my sleeve, anxious to retain me. Her breath was sour in my face, as she once again launched into her accusations and justifications.

'You see how it is, Alan. I can't leave him. I hardly ever get out these days, and I do so long to look round the shops. You can see how shabby I am.'

Indeed I had noticed that her blue dress was slightly faded, her obstinately high-heeled shoes eased out of shape by her painful feet.

'Sometimes I think I should have been better off had I

stayed in Paris. At least there I could lead a cultured life, even on very little money. But here he keeps me short. I should have known that he'd just sit back and ignore me. I should have looked at those two sisters of his.'

'Sisters-in-law.'

'And have they been in touch with me? Not a word. Oh, he telephones them. What he tells them I don't know.'

'Perhaps it might be wise to let Sybil know that he is, well, under the weather.'

'Not I! I was willing to be friendly, but one look told me that we had nothing in common.' She sighed. 'I'll tell you the truth of it, Alan. I had no family, and when you have no family you rely too much on your friends. And they let you down.'

Rather, I reflected, they could not take the weight of the deprived soul's dependence, could not bear the reproaches when a telephone call was not returned, could not fail to notice the desperation and the barely disguised aggression when a difference of opinion made itself known, could not bear to be seen through the distorting mirror of the other's needs, and would finally exchange that other for the comforting normality of a casual acquaintance.

'What do you want me to do about this will?' I asked. 'I'm bound to execute it.'

'Then that's the end of me, I suppose. I might as well go back to Paris. Of course, I'll fight it. I won't leave without a struggle.'

'Sarah might be persuaded . . .'

'I'm the last person she'll bother about.'

As this was probably true I was silent.

'You might tell Alice how I'm placed,' she said.

I picked up my bag, felt the weight of it, and drew out the dish I had bought for her in the market at Cagnes.

'She sent you this,' I said.

She looked at it with contempt. 'These things are two a penny in the south of France.'

It had in fact been rather expensive. 'Don't you want it?'

'You keep it,' she said. 'Thank you for the flowers.'

'I'll need Sarah's address,' I told her.

'I told you, I haven't got it. He's got it, only he won't let me see it. Care of de Leuze, I suppose. Although I gathered that they were moving to Geneva. He's an industrial chemist, very well placed. Not that she says much. She wrote something down for Humphrey, and now I can't get it out of him. No, Sarah doesn't have much use for me. A hard girl. No sympathy, no sentiment. And I was so willing to be friendly with her. I loved her, Alan.'

She waited for me to say that I had loved her too, but I remained obstinately silent.

'I wanted a daughter,' she said; again I remained silent.

She sighed. 'Well, I mustn't keep you. It was good of you to come, a young man like you. And still good-looking. I always liked a handsome man.'

'I'll be in touch,' I said, although I was not sure how true this was. I kissed her, at which her face brightened. She was still a woman who responded to a man's attentions, I noted, and she was cursed with a senile husband whose initial need of her had been based solely on the panic of someone adrift in a foreign city and unable to speak the language. No wonder she despised him.

I hastened down the fawn-carpeted corridors, under the dim light of various low-watt bulbs. Ancient cooking smells drifted from behind closed doors. The melancholy of London flats at nightfall! It was only Thursday, but it felt like Sunday. I did not have the courage to walk, and my taxi was enlivened by a powerful floral deodorant. I wanted a bath: I wanted to walk naked through my flat. I wanted to remind myself that I was still intact, that I had not yet succumbed to rancour and recrimination. If I wanted more than that I repressed the knowledge. That would come later. My chief feeling, the feeling uppermost in my tired mind, was one that a certain chapter of my life, the one I prized the most, had ended. I was aware that certain steps could not be retraced, however heady the impulse. I placed the dish on my desk and went to bed. That night I was wakeful, yet I did not mind. Unwillingly I glimpsed possibilities, stratagems. One speaks these days of a window of opportunity. I resolved to wait and see if even now one would open for me.

14

Towards the end of the following month I received two telephone calls, one from Mother, one from Jenny. Both told me the same thing, that Humphrey had died. Jenny had found him on the bathroom floor early one morning, and was all the more shocked in that she had heard nothing. Apparently he had taken to wandering about before she was up; he slept little, although the legend was that he slept all the time. Towards the end of his life he began to resent Jenny's presence in the flat, and liked to reassert his ownership by means of a stealthy inspection of his former domain in the early hours. This tired him so much that by the time that Jenny was making the coffee he was back in bed, and had to be coaxed into sitting up, and even later into getting up. On this particular morning he must have had a malaise and col-

lapsed, blocking the bathroom door. It was only after considerable efforts that Jenny gained access. I imagined the graceless scene: the old man, unwashed, bundled into his
camel-hair dressing-gown, and his bewildered wife, herself
dishevelled, trying to drag the body out of that confined
space. She had tidied her hair and run to a neighbour, who
rang for an ambulance and then made Jenny a cup of tea.
Jenny was apparently so overwhelmed by this act of kindness
that she burst into tears. The neighbour took this to be an
entirely commendable sign of grief and promised any further
help should it be needed. Thus Jenny began her first day as a
widow somewhat restored to the dignity she had long ceased
to enjoy as a wife.

The story of the neighbour was told to me by Jenny herself: the rest was my interpretation. On the telephone she
sounded if anything almost excited by this turn of events, a
fact commented upon by my mother, to whom I recounted
the gist of her confession to me on the last and disastrous
evening I had spent with them both.

'Well, of course, it was hardly a love match, though they
seemed happy enough, at least to begin with. Let her enjoy
this little bit of attention while she can; she certainly won't
enjoy being on her own. That's what drove her into the marriage in the first place. Poor dear. She has no gift for solitude. She'll stay on in the flat, I suppose?'

I told my mother about the will, which I had had time to
examine. It was quite in order: the property was to go to
Sarah, while Jenny had a right to the contents of the flat.
Apart from three or four clocks, whose value I had no means
of estimating, these were negligible, consisting as they did of
worn turkey carpets, antiquated sofas and armchairs covered
in faded green velvet, a heavy oval dining-table which would
be difficult to move, eight massive leather dining-chairs dec-
orated with brass studs, and a chest of drawers in the hall

which effectively blocked one's passage in and out. The contents of the bedrooms, which it would also be my duty to
examine, could hardly be more refined, and it would take
some temerity on my part to go through Humphrey's posses-
sions. I imagined a cobweb-strewn camphor-smelling hide-
out in which daylight never entered and all the mirrors were
tarnished; I imagined malodorous carpet slippers, unravelled
pullovers, antique overcoats in creaking wardrobes, and all
the dusty remains of a man whose final decrepitude seemed
to me far more shocking than his actual demise. My task, on
the occasion on which I should have to conduct my inven-
tory, seemed to loom far more depressingly than the funeral;
I thought it unfair that Humphrey should linger on in his
effects while Jenny faced the prospect of being dispossessed.

Mother was shocked but not surprised by the will. 'He was
always very family-minded, of course. He kept in touch with
Sybil, and he was on good terms with Marjorie. Indeed we
always thought that Marjorie had her eye on him. He could
have done worse; she knew his ways. It was only the accident
of his losing his way in Paris that led him to Jenny. Poor darling, she never really fitted in.'

'That, Mother, is entirely to her credit.'

'I agree, but where does that leave her now? And it seems
so unfair when she tried so hard. And she was happy at first,
so delighted to be married. She was a very good companion
in those early days, and she was so eager to make friends, to
have a family. I think she would even have taken on Sybil and
Marjorie, had they shown the slightest sign of welcoming
her, but you know how odd they are . . .'

'Quite.'

'And it was her attitude to Sarah that was so sad. She had
this fantasy—and it was a fantasy—that the two of them
would become close.'

'That attitude may have changed by now.'

'It had to, of course; it would have done so in any case, but now that Sarah's got the flat . . .'

'She may not want it.'

My mother sighed. 'My poor Alan, you don't know Sarah very well.'

I could not bring myself to discuss Sarah with my mother, so I asked her if she were coming over for the funeral.

'Of course, dear. Aubrey is not too pleased about it, but I've been quite firm. Golders Green, I suppose?'

'Yes. And I've put a notice in *The Times*. This means quite a bit of extra work for me.'

'It will be a comfort to Jenny to know that you're taking care of things. I'll see you on the twenty-fourth then, dear. Look after yourself. Aubrey sends love.'

I doubted this, though I did not doubt Aubrey's unwillingness to attend the funeral. He had scant sympathy with other people's illnesses, and as death was the logical outcome of certain illnesses he preferred not to hear about it. But he would be there, in one of his beautiful suits, to escort Mother, and I was grateful for his promised attendance, since it seemed that without him I should be the only man at the funeral and something in the nature of an unwilling host at whatever baked meats Jenny had had time to prepare. In fact I did not see who would want to be present, since Humphrey had lived out of the world so long. That was why I had put a notice in *The Times*, in an effort to drum up support. For some odd reason, though it had nothing, or very little, to do with me, I wanted no suggestion that this was a death of no consequence.

In fact, for a recluse, he had quite a turn-out. There were about eighteen people in the chapel, most of them elderly, none of whom I had ever seen before. I presumed that they were neighbours, for whom a funeral of someone they hardly knew was something of a social occasion, an opportunity to get out and meet their friends, a welcome break in the daily routine. The three frail-looking men of some distinction I took to be colleagues of Humphrey's in the jewellery trade, and I had to remind myself that at one point in his life he had been well regarded, a man among equals, rather than the faded and suspicious character I had known. Sybil and Marjorie made a late entrance, Marjorie being pushed down the aisle in a wheelchair; otherwise they seemed not to have aged by a single day. I offered Jenny my arm, since it seemed to have fallen to my lot to be her protector. She looked dignified in her black coat and spotted veil, but she was trembling, as if the full impact of the occasion had only just been revealed to her. This ugly ceremony, among strangers, reinforced her knowledge of herself as an exile, unable to summon up the brave smile, the worldly composure that the English manage to manifest even in these circumstances. She was very pale, but I thought that any grief she must be feeling was for herself and her new situation, a situation in which an outward show of tears would be misplaced. I led her to the front pew, on the other side of the aisle from Sybil and Marjorie. Then, when the service was about to begin, there was a clatter of heels, a whiff of Guerlain, and the empty space next to Sybil was taken by Sarah.

I sensed her rather than saw her; when I was able to turn my head I had an impression of modish drooping black garments, and something else, something different. Keeping my eyes rigidly to the front, I tried to decipher what I had glimpsed. There was a hat, certainly, one of those dire felt hats favoured by her mother; indeed she may have, probably had, borrowed one of her mother's hats. In the rustle that signified the end of the short service I was able to take a second look, and then I saw what had initially struck me as discordant. She had cut off her marvellous hair, which now stuck out from under the unbecoming hat in a bulky bob.

Her face, pale and sulky, was as intriguing as ever. But although she had lost her initial bloom, had in fact put on weight, so that she looked older, rather more like her mother, the effect on me was unfortunate. I longed to take her in my arms, to comfort her for her lost beauty, to let her know that she was now more accessible to me, that my previous anxieties were in abeyance, that we could perhaps at last meet on equal terms. Had it been up to me I would have crossed the aisle and greeted her, but Jenny was now trembling violently, dreading the moment when she would have to go forward and touch the coffin, fearful of what lay inside it. It was a primitive fear, or rather it was the fear of a primitive person. Around her faces which had been composed were beginning to relax, while through the open doors could be seen the suburban-looking lawns, perfect setting for a largely unlamented death.

I commandeered a car for Jenny and myself, having said a few words on her behalf to those who had attended. Her lips were too pale and too numb to utter the words inviting them back to the flat, so I did that too. On the pretext of rounding up the other mourners I spoke briefly to Sarah, asking her how she was, whether she had had a good journey, the sort of words that would pass unnoticed in a crowd. She stared at me, vaguely affronted: 'I've only come from Paddington Street, haven't I?' There was now no time for a conversation, and this was hardly the place, but I managed to say that I would look in on her later that evening, 'look in' having the right note of casual improvisation. In truth I said this for old times' sake. Although I wanted to see her, I had grown tired of my former role of ardent lover, even more my role of deranged pursuer. If I wanted to see her it was for a final reckoning, a settling of our account. I too was older, and I had lived my life without her for what seemed a very long time. I, who had grown used to solitude, had less patience for sheer absence, and where I had once built romantic fantasies around the compelling character of this particular absence I was now less sure of its potency, more inclined to treat it as a rather tiresome waywardness. I was absurdly shocked by the hat, the unbecoming hair, above all by her resemblance to her mother. I knew that when we met I would make fewer concessions than in the past. I felt tenderness, a willingness to enfold her, but also a lessening of tolerance towards her. I felt oddly in a stronger position, as if her changed appearance had turned me into a more fatherly character, and I knew in that brief moment that if we were to come together I would, I hope smilingly, forestall her caprices and insist on my own centrality in this affair, which perhaps was no longer an affair but more of a meeting between adults, in which I would have my say, so long delayed, and perhaps even now too long postponed.

Back at the flat Jenny had provided sweet sherry and fingers of iced Madeira cake, as if determined to live down to the expectations of Sybil and Marjorie. Mother and Aubrey, their brown faces giving an impression of almost indecent health and well-being in that pallid gathering, moved among the ten or eleven people now apparently willing to while away their afternoon. I found a dusty bottle of whisky and poured generous measures for Aubrey and myself, and for two of the three elderly men who had presumably been Humphrey's friends. One of them, whose mild shrewd eyes had taken in the contents of the room, introduced himself as Lionel Taylor and gave me his card.

'You're looking after things, I gather,' he said. 'If you need any advice don't hesitate to get in touch.'

I thanked him and pocketed the card: all this could be sorted out later. Jenny, her colour a little restored, sat in Humphrey's chair, apparently grateful to all these new friends for keeping her company. She seemed to me to be rather less than her usual self, certainly less than the Jenny who had so recently exposed her grievances. My mother, who noticed that she was still trembling slightly, fetched a shawl from the bedroom and placed it round her shoulders. She sat there, quite docile, until Sybil announced that they must make a move if they wanted to get home before dark. They both rose and exchanged a brief kiss—a concession on both their parts—and as if that were the sign for which everyone had been waiting, or to which they were reconciled, there was a general movement of departure. I did duty at the door, thanked everyone for coming, and assured them that Jenny would be in touch. This, I knew, was pure form: I doubted whether Jenny even knew who they were.

'You go, darling,' said my mother. 'I'll stay here for a bit. I've sent Aubrey off; I'm afraid he found it a bit of a strain.' We both knew that he had in fact found it an imposition, but this was not to be mentioned. 'I'll keep Jenny company for a little while. She shouldn't be alone. Perhaps if you could look in this evening? Just to make sure she's all right.'

I was glad to escape from that flat, in which all the lights had been on, into the somehow more acceptable confusion of the Edgware Road. I decided not to go straight back to the office but to go home, make some coffee, and sit in absolute silence for an hour. I wanted solitude, though this is frowned on in a healthy adult. The propaganda goes the other way; one is urged to get out of oneself, as if preferring one's own company were a dangerous indulgence. I wanted, above all else, to be free of attachments, of those personal agendas which are wished on one in any conversation of any depth, and which are as disruptive to the process of contemplation as a telephone ringing in the middle of the night. I was not sick, I was not melancholy: I simply demanded that I might enjoy the peace of the situation I had inherited.

I flattered myself that I behaved like a responsible and

rational being. Indeed this was a role which I had always found natural. I should do my duty in the matter of Jenny and the will, though this involved a stratagem whose implications I was not yet willing to face. Uppermost in my mind was the fact that I should very soon be face to face with Sarah, that is if she took me rather more seriously than she had taken my attempt to see her in Paris. I knew that the sheer triumph of capturing her attention would impel me to folly. I should probably ask her to marry me, and I should be equally aghast whether my offer were accepted or declined. I realised now that what I wanted from her, had indeed always wanted from her, was some kind of reciprocity, if only in the form of an explanation. It had become overwhelmingly important to me to dispel the miasma of bad faith that surrounded our relationship, and for which I was just as much to blame. At least I thought I was: the memory of that Paris escapade still shamed me. I wanted to exchange with her the sort of words adults use, not to engage myself in one more hopeless pursuit, complete with unanswered questions and missed appointments. Perhaps I simply wanted her to talk to me.

To a certain extent, I reasoned, she was innocent of conflict, certainly of the conflicts that assailed me whenever I thought of her. She existed in a state unknown to me and which I should never completely understand. Her life was an improvisation, without roots, without commitments, without guarantees: that was the difference between us. My own progress, unsteady though it was, had brought me to a sort of plateau from which I could contemplate my own follies as serious aberrations, but I needed my own company in order to do this work of self-examination. I needed silence, without the interruption of someone else's disaffections. Since I had never been able to calculate Sarah's appearances and disappearances I reckoned that life with her would soon destroy any logical structure I tried to impose. And yet she had filled my thoughts ever since I had first met her. Perhaps what I was registering was nothing more than the passage of time, to which one should pay great attention, lest one remain fixed in past expectations, without noticing how foolish one had become.

I let myself into the flat, decided to do without the coffee, and sank down into my chair. This interval which I had promised myself was turning out to be illusory, as had all my other plans. Nevertheless I enjoyed the quiet. I was hopelessly addicted to order, I realised, even to the extent of trying to introduce order into other lives. I was no prospect for a wilful girl—but she was no longer a girl. She was a rather heavy-featured woman with a shadowy lover in the background. Although I knew that I was not yet finished with her I dreaded further involvement. Hope deferred maketh the heart sick: no doubt she felt the same. I should look into her closed face and try to will her to look at me. And if the tactic worked as effectively as it had always done I should have burnt my boats and uttered an unwise and untimely declaration and thus connived at my own unreason, I who was so eminently reasonable a man.

I made a pot of tea and tried to shrug off these suppositions. I splashed my face with cold water, and after a second's hesitation changed my shirt. I drank my tea standing up, anxious now to go back to the office, where it was assumed that I knew my own mind. The brief afternoon was already merging into dusk as I walked down Wigmore Street. I should have time to sign my letters and retrieve my briefcase, without which I felt naked. Ahead of me stretched the disagreeable task of going through Humphrey's assets, or rather what assets could be subsumed under the rubric of contents and to which Jenny was entitled. This might take some time, might indeed be a difficult subject to introduce on the day of the funeral, but as a solicitor I was used to poking about in dead men's affairs. Many widows and widowers were thankful to me for discharging this task; Jenny, I knew, would be incapable of undertaking it.

I found her alone, seated at the oval dining-table, with the shawl still round her shoulders. Mother kissed her and made her promise to keep in touch, to which she made no response. From time to time she passed her hand over the table, not as a gesture of possession but as if to reassure herself of the solidity of objects. The smile she gave me was timid. I thought she had aged since the morning, and for the first time feared for her health, though to my knowledge she had never given any sign of physical weakness. I sat down beside her and placed my hand over the restless hand. With a shuddering sigh she turned to me, and I prepared myself for my inquisitorial or curatorial task. But Jenny, it seemed, was not yet ready.

'It's strange,' she said. 'I never thought I'd be frightened to be alone. Even when he was in the other room and not speaking to me it was a presence. Do you understand, Alan?'

'Of course I do. But there's no need to be frightened. You'll sleep soundly tonight and in the morning you'll feel more confident.'

'Alice was here,' she went on. 'That was nice of her, wasn't it? Giving up her afternoon like that. We had a cup of tea together. Just like old times.'

'Jenny,' I said. 'If you're ready I think I'd better take a look round Humphrey's room. You know you're entitled . . .'

She turned to me, her expression desperate. 'What's to become of me, Alan, if I can't stay here? And even if I could, what should I live on? I've got no money of my own; I've only got what he allowed me for the week in my purse, and when that runs out I shan't even be able to buy a pint of milk. Alice invited me to stay with them in France, but I can't leave the flat, can I? Sarah could come in and change the locks.'

This thought had occurred to me; I rather wondered whether to advise her to change the locks herself. But I was anxious not to step outside the law, and confined myself to asking her whether she knew what Humphrey kept in his room, whether he had a safety deposit box: questions she was unable to answer.

'I went in,' she said dully. 'But I couldn't see anything. And I didn't like to go through his things. You know he kept his door locked? I doubt if you'll find much. I've left everything as it was.' And here, to her astonishment, a sob threatened to defeat her composure. She swallowed abruptly, a handkerchief pressed to her mouth, her eyes wide with panic, as if suddenly threatened by illness.

'You stay here,' I said. 'I'll try to be quick.'

Humphrey's bedroom, or rather his bed-sitting room, was as rebarbative as I had imagined it. A coverlet had been hastily pulled over the unmade bed, which imparted its own particular aroma to the murky atmosphere. Humphrey's grey suit, out of shape at the elbows and knees, hung spectrally on the outside of the wardrobe door: on the chest of drawers lay his watch, his cufflinks, and a crusty handkerchief. Cautiously I slid open drawers, and found nothing but fuzzy grey socks and outsize underpants. Bracing myself, I slid my hand into the wardrobe, palpated several pockets, and disengaged from scarves and cardigans two pocket books with old elastic fastenings, one of which contained a considerable quantity of white five-pound notes. Sliding my hand in again I found a leather purse, heavy with the sort of coins I dimly remembered as pennies. These, however, were dated 1933. He must have kept them from his boyhood. I reckoned they were worth something, perhaps even a considerable amount.

'Why don't we have some coffee?' I remarked, back under

that centre light. 'And some of that cake if there's any left. I don't seem to have had lunch today, and I doubt if you've eaten anything.'

'Alice tried to get me to eat, but I don't want to. Will you stay, Alan? I don't want to be alone.'

I sat down and took her hands. 'It won't be so bad,' I said. 'You get used to it. And you lived alone before, didn't you? In the hotel?'

Her face softened into a smile of reminiscence. 'My little room,' she said. 'Right under the roof, the cheapest room in the hotel. But it was decent, and I had hot water, and a little primus stove, although it wasn't allowed. I could make myself a coffee in the morning. And on Sundays I went out and bought myself croissants. Nobody knew I was poor. Not like now.' The smile vanished.

'You're not poor,' I said, putting the money on the table. 'This is worth quite a bit.'

'Foreign currency?' she said. 'I don't even know what country it comes from.'

'It's English,' I told her. 'Old money. And when I've had time to find out about such things you might learn that it's worth a great deal. What about his wallet?'

'I couldn't find it. I tried his suit . . .'

'Did you try his dressing-gown?'

'No, no, I didn't, although he did hide things from me. I told you . . .'

I went back to the bedroom and searched the pockets of his dressing-gown, which someone, Jenny or the neighbour, had hung on the back of the door. In one of them I found his wallet, which contained about two hundred pounds in twenty-pound notes.

'This will tide you over,' I said. 'Put the money in your bag. Nobody's going to turn you out. Remember, they have to go through me first.'

I fished in my pocket and found the card that one of the men at the funeral had given me. I glanced at it: Lionel Taylor.

'Get in touch with this man and tell him you want to sell the clocks. Invite him round, tell him to see if there's anything else he wants. There's that Art Nouveau vase, for example. And I seem to remember being shown a box of watches when I was a boy. Pocket watches, gold ones.'

'They're in the sideboard.'

'There you are, then. That's enough for one day, I think. Time you went to bed.'

'Must you go, Alan?'

'I've still got some business to see to. But I'll be back in a day or two. Good-night, Jenny. You've got my number, if you want me. Remember, I'm quite near.'

I left, without my coffee. I felt hungry, but was too impatient to eat. I walked briskly through Upper Berkeley Street and Portman Square to Wigmore Street. I would drop my briefcase at the flat, I calculated; while there I would see if this irritating anticipation would subside. I might read a poem to steady my nerves. Tennyson was my current favourite: 'Birds in the high hall garden . . .' Perhaps the influence of Tennyson would calm me down. Yet, by the light of a street lamp, I looked at my watch, and saw that I should have to hurry. My next appointment beckoned, and I could not be late.

15

When I was very young the worst thing I could do to myself was to anticipate an ordeal. As a child this took the form of a visit to my grandmother: when I was at school it was swimming, and later examinations (which I usually passed with ease). My feeling on these occasions was not simple dread but a form of heart-break, as if I were being denied the pleasures of this world because of a rule arbitrarily imposed on me by a higher power. I would treasure my last glimpses of the street, the sun, the traffic, as if they were forbidden to me, only to be enjoyed by those for whom such rules did not exist. Prisoners must feel something like this when the gates close behind them. And the worst of it was that when I had endured the ordeal, whatever it was, the world was somehow diminished, as if my anguish had robbed it of some of its splendour. To my credit I never demanded to stay at home, with some well-worn excuse or other; my dread was an ill-ness in itself, although I knew myself to be physically intact. I would vow to myself so to construct my life as a man to avoid such ordeals, yet here I was, on this mild autumn night, walking up Baker Street either to face the last of my ordeals or the first of a long sequence of them, almost but not quite submitting to that paralysis of the will that emptied my mind of everything but the task before me. On these occasions I no longer acted; I merely submitted to events. Even as a man I underwent the emotions that had assailed me as a boy, and which I now recognised as habitual, part of my intimate economy, and no more to be shrugged off than the shape of my feet or the colour of my hair.

When under the spell of this anxiety, I would feel myself to be a sleep-walker, whose eventual waking would not pre-vent the experience from being repeated. The sleep-walker is said to wake up in time to stop him doing himself damage, but damage was precisely what characterised the whole expe-rience. The world had been altered for me through its agency, and although it might look the same I was aware of a subtle difference. The friendliness of everyday phenomena could no longer be taken for granted, since ahead of me was an event that cast a shadow over everything that I had known. My father had reassured me that everyone felt faint-hearted from time to time, but I did not believe him. It seemed to me that I was being singled out for this visitation, and the fact that I remained physically unmarked by it was if anything further proof of its mysterious power. I would set out from home in a state of grief, and no assurance of a treat at the end of the day would mitigate it. If anything I despised such assurances, for I knew that my feelings had nothing to do with my status as a child. I had been inducted into the world of loss, and having eaten of this particular apple would never be truly whole again.

Fortunately my parents paid little attention to my strange fore-knowledge which, I repeat, was not visible. Nor did it in any way subvert my performance in the noisy swimming pool or the silent examination room. In time, and no doubt as I grew older, I came to dread the feeling even more than the event it foreshadowed, as if my essential being were under attack, and I were in no position to overcome the attack, since my will, and everything that had hitherto made me what I had become, were compromised. I was no longer in control of my destiny: God was no longer benign. I grew out of it, yet I could not ignore the experience, largely because I could not decide whether it was cause or effect. By the time I went up to Oxford it had receded, become overlaid with more rational concerns. On the whole I found life easy, and continued to do so for the next ten or fifteen years, until stopped in my tracks by the intimations of that illness which had turned out to be real and which was the herald of my unfortunate marriage. That was why I had reacted so badly to it, I now reasoned, as I came level with George Street: the inner and the outer worlds had come together, and the effect of this was to make me so terrified, so undone, that I had to take refuge in another person, assuming that other person, Angela in this case, to be strong enough to bear my weight, whereas in reality she had looked to me to do the same for her.

The tragedy was that we could not console each other. Our woes were never acknowledged and so remained unknown. To me she had always appeared transparent; I foolishly had not seen that there was more for me to discover. And what she had wanted, I now saw, was some kind of confessor, to whom she could reveal secrets over which she had kept silent for far too long, since childhood, perhaps, when the boy I was then might have understood her much better than the man I had become.

The irony of my turning such matters over in my mind just as I was about to face a dilemma in my life was not lost on me, nor was the fact that I was thinking of Angela when Angela was no longer there to benefit from my new understanding. Or, rather, from my recovered memory of dread, of fate, of the road I was obliged to take, though no one could accuse me if I refused to take it. It seemed to me (and I was nearly at Paddington Street) that for once in my life I would do better to go home and commune with my dead wife, in some way to let her know that I was thinking of her even at this juncture, when I was leaving what had been our home to pursue an early fantasy to its conclusion, to destruction, one might say. I saw, quite clearly, Angela's face, her newly washed hair, and felt again that species of alienation I had known as a boy before the swimming lesson or the examination, as if the world had turned its back on me, as if I were newly excluded from God's love, as if the ordeal must be undergone with as much self-mastery as was appropriate in the circumstances. I could have abandoned the whole enterprise, of course, but I had a mission to accomplish, one that was quite specific and fairly urgent: I had to persuade Sarah to let Jenny stay in the flat, and if possible—but I did not yet see how this might be possible—to persuade her to make the flat over to Jenny, in effect to give it to her. Knowing Sarah, and her inability to answer a simple question, this was in the nature of a knightly quest on my part, and yet I was committed to it, as I was committed to scrutinising her, and myself in relation to her, once more.

Whatever love I had had for her I was now able to decipher as that primeval anxiety that I had always known, as if her very presence could invoke this feeling of loss. To gain her would be to lose the world I knew; to lose her might threaten a loss of which I so far had no knowledge. I stood on the corner of Paddington Street, taking deep breaths in order to lighten the oppression round my heart. Behind me was my flat, its silence, its memories. I knew that if I married Sarah I could no longer live there, for that would be a violation of which I could not be guilty. I saw us as a couple without real definition, moodily attached, unreal by daylight, inventive by night. But did even that attraction last? Did the desire to exorcise it signify that it had come to an end? Would the waxy smell of Sarah's abundant hair (no longer so abundant, I reminded myself) be sufficient to obliterate the memory of my dead wife, or even of my living wife, with all her innocent fantasies, her gentility, her legacy to me?

Perhaps, if we had grown old together, we would have learned to make the necessary concessions. Paradoxically, at that moment, standing outside a shuttered betting shop, I longed to be old, to be measured, to have vanquished my doubts, along with the visceral memory of the boy I had been. I did not see myself ageing well with Sarah, who had already struck me as older in that first uncertain glimpse. I realised that all along my love had coexisted with dread, of her indifference, her negligence, the disorder in which she lived, her refusal of the friendship which should be natural between a man and a woman. None of this made her insignificant, unfortunately; for a woman without defining characteristics she was able to exert enormous power. She did so even now, as I stood outside the betting shop. I heaved one last sigh, acknowledged as my intimate enemy, now almost a warning, my feeling of loss, passed a hand through my hair, and made my way to Sarah's front door.

This altered state was my accompaniment up to the moment of our encounter, to be replaced by a prolonged stare. For several seconds we gazed at each other thoughtfully, as if words could be postponed until we could find a use for them. We were thus equals once more, but equals in disaffection. I saw no friendship in her face, which seemed armed against disclosure; nor did the normal courtesies and pleasantries of welcome seem in order. Eventually she raised a black-sleeved arm to her hair in a vain attempt to smooth it down. The gesture was evocative of the bedroom, of waking, but all she said was, 'You'd better come in. But I warn you, I've got to go out soon.'

'There are a couple of things I have to say,' I began, following her into the flat, which seemed markedly more dilapidated than when I had last seen it. The usual furnishings of old newspapers and the mirror, not yet hung, were in place, but most of the floor space was occupied by a large grimy white armchair, a new addition, or an old one, in which I was not invited to sit.

'You don't know anyone who'd like to buy this chair, do you?'

'It's very dirty.'

'Well, they could have it cleaned, couldn't they? Or you could, if you bought it.'

'But I don't want it. And anyway I didn't come here to talk about . . .'

'Only I'm thinking of putting this place on the market.'

'You're leaving London?'

'I've left, you might say. I've been living in Paris.'

'With the Rigauds?'

'God, no. I'm with someone else.'

'I know. De Leuze, who seems to be permanently in reserve. Sarah, why didn't you meet me in Paris?'

'You weren't serious, were you?'

I stared at her. 'I was never more serious about anything in my life.'

'I thought it was a joke. I mean, the George V. The assignation. It seemed hilarious.'

'I wasn't at the George V. Didn't you get my note?'

'What note?'

'I put a note under the Rigauds' door.'

'But I wasn't there, was I? What did it say, the note?'

'It told you where to meet me. Sarah, were you deliberately avoiding me?'

'Why should I bother to do that?'

'Why can't you ever answer a simple question?'

'If you're going to be unpleasant you can go. I don't have to account to you for my actions.'

'Nor I to you for mine, I suppose.'

'Well, you didn't, did you?'

'Didn't what?'

'Tell me that you were going to marry Angela.'

I flung my hands up in exasperation. 'But you were nowhere to be found. You vanished, always without an explanation. Could you not at least have got in touch, telephoned? I walked past this flat night after night, hoping to see a light on.'

'You could have rung the bell. I came back from time to time.'

'But how was I to know? And anyway, I was ill.'

The memory of that illness, which had not in reality been threatening, had in fact been banal, overwhelmed me once again, together with that more primeval feeling of desolation that now seemed to have foreshadowed this entire interview. We stood in the centre of the room and once more gazed at each other. I recognised an ending, and understood that I had been prepared for this.

'There's one more thing,' I said stiffly. 'Your uncle's will.'

'Relax, Alan. You're not in the office now. Anyway, what about the will?'

'He's left you a considerable sum of money, enough to enable you to live your own life, without benefit of protectors. He's also left you the flat, for which I'm sure you've no use, determined as you are to live with this friend of yours . . .'

'That's my business.'

'As I've said, you have no need of the flat . . .'

'I've really got under your skin, haven't I?'

'You might say that. I want you to make the flat over to Jenny.'

I was exhausted. I had said what I had come to say and felt that I could make no further effort. I sat down heavily in the white chair, which revealed itself to be remarkably comfortable. I leaned my head back; for a moment or two it seemed almost possible that I might take a short nap.

Sarah's answer was to remove the accumulated piles of the *Financial Times* from another chair and to sit down, her knees almost touching mine. In contrast to my extreme lethargy she seemed tense. There was even a little colour in her face.

'You are joking, aren't you? Why on earth should I give that old bat a property which I own, which was left to me . . . ?'

'Which you don't need.'

'I might.'

'You've got this place.'

'I told you, I'm thinking of putting it on the market. I thought you might do it for me. That's why I agreed to meet you this evening, for a business discussion.'

'We are having a business discussion.'

'You're mad, Alan. You're a fantasist. First Paris, then this. I suppose you think I'm a complete fool.'

'I think you're the fantasist,' I said. 'Fantasists avoid action; they scarcely have time for it.' I wanted to tell her of my regard, still persistent, but the moment hardly seemed propitious. Besides, I was too relaxed. With an effort I sat up straight and looked at her, face to face, confronting her in a willed union that in the event had proved to be illusory. Now that I was about to lose her (but had it ever been otherwise?)

I was full of tenderness for the pouting face, which looked tired, its colour now drained away.

'I want you to make the flat over to Jenny,' I repeated.

'Why should I?'

'Because it's the decent thing to do. Because you don't need it. Because she's a tired old woman, with nowhere else to go. Because it's time you made a start on your own life.'

'You say I don't need it. Well, I might, mightn't I?'

'You're on your own now. Time for you to find out what it's like.'

That was my one moment of bitterness. I had tried to be impartial, and on the whole I thought I had succeeded. I could not judge the effect this had had on her. I was only grateful that I had managed not to say more, while at the same time conscious that I would never have another chance to do so. I took her hand in mine and held it. I was left with a residue of sadness, both on my account and on hers.

The hand was withdrawn. She had evidently sensed my mood. Yet she was not one to take a reprimand lightly. Colour seeped back into her face, darkened.

'Thank you very much. You've just made up my mind for me. You've just decided me to marry Pierre.'

'I rather thought you might marry me.'

'And follow in Angela's footsteps? No thanks.'

'Please, don't say any more. Just do this one good thing.'

'For your sake, I suppose.'

'Hardly.'

'I thought you were on my side.'

'So did I, oddly enough. It's too late, isn't it?'

'It was always too late. You were too slow, too innocent.'

'And it's the fate of innocents to be massacred, or so we're told.'

'Just leave me alone, will you?'

No word of love had been offered, but these were as little in order as they had ever been. Our conversation was, as ever, quite unsatisfactory. Yet even now a mysterious feeling of kinship, of recognition, had managed to surface. We both felt it. She smiled unwillingly, and at last I felt able to take her in my arms. But it was a valedictory moment. We both felt that too.

'I'll want to see you in the office first thing in the morning,' I said. 'I'll prepare a document; you'll sign it, and it can be witnessed. And no, I don't know why I'm doing this, either. It's just that I want to be fair, and I want you to be fair.'

'Alan Sherwood, the last of the innocents.'

'Oh, no, Sarah. I lost my innocence the day I met you.'

She turned on her heel and made her way through the discarded newspapers to the door, which she held open for me. 'Any time you're in Paris,' she said, with a brilliant and unforgiving smile.

'I'll need your current address,' I told her. 'And anyway I thought there was some talk of your moving to Geneva.'

'I shall certainly not expect to see you there,' she said, with the same public smile.

'I look forward to seeing you at nine-thirty tomorrow morning, in my office,' I told her, looking round for my briefcase.

'Goodbye, Alan. We made fools of each other, didn't we?'

'Not entirely.'

I tried to think of some last word, some tribute to her, but nothing came. It was not a moment for easy graceful words. I shook her hand, quite formally, before the door was shut in my face.

As a young man in Paris, free and unworried, I had had no visitations from my former enemy, and, with no ordeals or obligations that I could possibly foresee, had felt encouraged to look forward to an innocent and hedonistic life in which I should play my part by being orderly and law-abiding after this permitted period of licence. I had once looked forward, but vaguely, to a time when I should be accounted a man of good character. Perhaps it was natural for me then to have little idea that life should develop in complexity, since I had supposed myself to have grown up and learned the rules of the game. I had no idea, perhaps fortunately for my peace of mind, that middle age, the age I was now, could muddy the waters all over again, and that my intimate fears could once again rise to the surface. Walking back down Baker Street I discovered that my original conceptions of vice and virtue were confused, that I no longer knew how to apportion praise and blame, and, more important, that I was in no position to do either. I had become a law-abiding citizen by default, though originally with good if not exactly heartfelt intentions, and to the outside world, with one unfortunate interruption, had remained so. Yet if I had performed a good deed in the course of the evening I had no conscience of having done so. That was my discovery: that there are no rewards, and few consolations, so that what are described as good deeds in children's primers and the boy scouts' manual, are, by the age of maturity, clouded over by knowledge of one's own mixed motives. I had acted for Jenny, but I had thought of Sarah. Had there been no possibility of seeing her I should have undoubtedly been more lax in the matter of Humphrey's will. I should not exactly have left Jenny to her fate, but neither should I have seized the first opportunity to transact business on her behalf. And though, from Jenny's point of view, the evening had been successful, from mine it had been something of a failure, or perhaps would have been had Sarah and I not met, or rather parted, on a more honest basis than we had ever managed before. We had lost each other, but had done so knowingly: we had not been evasive.

That was the only indemnity I could offer myself, and little as it was it would have to do.

It occurred to me, as I put my key into the door of the flat, that Sarah might not turn up on the following morning, but I dismissed this as unlikely: for the first time in my life I was inclined to trust her. I was by now exceedingly tired and even hungry. I ate an apple and a banana, and left everything to be taken care of by my new cleaner, Mrs Simpson. 'Call me Wallis,' she had said at our first interview, which indicates her age at seventy or more. She is a spry sparrow-thin widow who lives on the far side of Victoria Station and who is delighted to come into the West End every day and to be left the money to go home in a taxi. She is intrigued by the clothes in the cupboard of the spare room, but her curiosity is so far unsatisfied: this particular story is not for indiscriminate consumption. I made my plans for an early start, went to bed, and slept deeply and efficiently, as usual. On waking my brain seemed inordinately clear and devoid of anxiety. I dressed, drank a cup of coffee, and left the house at seven-thirty.

In the empty office I drafted the short document, in which I stated that the property of the late Humphrey Miller, willed to his niece Sarah Miller, was henceforth, by the wish of Sarah Miller, to pass to Jadwiga, known as Jenny Miller, to revert to Sarah Miller on the death of the said Jadwiga Miller. This took care of what had seemed to me, on the previous evening, the smallest indictment of unfairness to Sarah's interests. All doubts and uncertainties had now to be dismissed. I sat with my hands flat on my desk, apparently unoccupied, in fact waiting for Debbie, the temp, to arrive, but grateful for this interval of uninterrupted quiet. My mood, at this particular hour, was perhaps a little more vulnerable, for once again I was waiting for Sarah, and I was not entirely reconciled to the possibility of disappointment. But when the girls in the outer office made their gossiping entrance, and one of them brought my coffee, it seemed as if an ordinary day were under way, and my misgivings gradually subsided. At nine-fifteen I resigned myself to waiting; indeed I prepared myself by waiting, as if the ceremony demanded due observance. At ten o'clock Sarah arrived, signed the paper, which was witnessed by Mrs Roche and Telfer, observed that I was doing well out of this (fair comment in the circumstances), and was gone. Within minutes nothing remained of her but the smell of her scent, and when I opened the window even that dispersed, evaporated, and was soon gone.

I was able to give a reasonable impression of getting on with my work, but was interrupted by Brian, who sat down in one of the chairs reserved for clients, stretched out his long legs, and said nothing. I knew him in this mood; it meant that he had access to a number of well-meaning observations but that he judged it delicate to impart them cautiously and without undue weight. I knew what he wanted to say, but I went on writing steadily: this was as much part of the exchange as his apparently inconsequential silence. After a few minutes of this I put down my pen with a sigh and indicated that I was listening.

'I thought you might have married her,' he said finally.

'No.'

'Any particular reason?'

'I shan't marry again,' I said, and knowing these words to be true I felt the onset of my old, my original anguish, as if it had been biding its time until this truth had made itself known to me. Once again the energy, the charm, disappeared from the world, and I was left alone, observing their eclipse.

'You could,' said Brian slowly. 'You're not disqualified. Or no more disqualified than the next man.'

'I lack the talent,' I told him. 'Whatever it takes. I lack the conviction. I think I was meant to live alone and stay out of harm's way.'

'The harm was not yours,' he said, and I was grateful to him for saying so little. 'Felicity told me to ask you for dinner,' he went on. 'Any evening. Although I think she wants to introduce you to a friend of hers.' He looked unhappy. 'You don't want that, do you?'

'No. No, I don't.'

'Unfortunately, as an unmarried man, you're likely to be commandeered for everyone's dinner parties. Are you sure you can put up with that?'

'I'll have to, if that's the deal. But I'll go home alone afterwards.'

'Alan . . .'

I got up. 'It's too soon, Brian. There's still too much to think about.'

'Not too unhappy?' he said, getting to his feet.

'Of course I'm unhappy. But it's quite bearable. Even interesting. I'd like to work it out on my own, for however long that takes. How's my god-daughter?'

His expression brightened. 'That toy rabbit you gave her never leaves her,' he said. 'I dare say she'd appreciate another visit. She seems to have taken to you.'

'People do take to me on short acquaintance,' I said. 'Though in her case I hope she'll condescend to put up with me for quite a long time. Now I am going to take you to lunch.' Our confidences were at an end. 'Where would you like to go?'

'Fish, I think, don't you?'

'Fish it is. And do you know,' I said with some surprise, 'I am exceedingly hungry.'

16

Jenny's smile was enraptured, seraphic, the sort of smile that only a man can evoke, although I was now the only man in her life and unlikely to bring her further joy. In my honour she had made up her face and cooked a meal, my main memory of which was a salad soused in vinegar. I thought it might be not too long before she resumed her visits to Selfridges, if she could find a companion to go with her, a condition which might no longer be taken for granted.

'I knew Sarah was fond of me,' she said. 'It was Humphrey who came between us. He was jealous! You've no idea how difficult he was, Alan.'

There followed a catalogue of Humphrey's faults, which I did not want to hear. I thought it sad that this marriage, which had seemed a happy resolution for two lonely people, should have become the object of so much acrimony. Marriage should be a haven, I further thought, not an avowal of unseen complications. My own marriage had been unsatisfactory, yet now I strove to find in it lost harmonies, aware as I was of my neutered state.

'And Mr Taylor?' I asked, anxious to change the subject.

'He promised me a very good price. He took everything, the watches, the lot. He said I should be quite well off. You'll look after the money for me, won't you, Alan?'

With a sigh I promised her that I would, and suggested a weekly allowance, at which she looked shocked.

'I'd rather have a lump sum,' she said. 'Then I can do what I like. I can go away! I can go and stay with Alice!'

I did not think this an entirely good idea, though it was hardly my place to say so. Mother and Aubrey had a wide circle of friends, with whom they played bridge and went to the races. Insipid as I found these pastimes they seemed to provide my mother with a pleasant and agreeable life, for which I was thankful. A visit from Jenny, talkative and insistent as she now was, would be unwelcome as well as untimely. If she had visions of herself accompanying my mother on her excursions, these would hardly accord with what Aubrey had in mind. He had proved mildly autocratic in his love for my mother, would fidget if she were out of his sight for any length of time. Besides, he had had enough of Jenny at the funeral, when she had been relatively wordless; I did not think he would be better disposed now that she had recovered her previous high spirits. And confessions of marital discord would be as little to his taste as they were to mine.

'You know they're coming home for Christmas?'

'Oh, I shall go before then.'

'Wouldn't it be better to wait until the spring? The weather . . .'

'But I can go again in the spring. It will be nice for Alice to see her old friends. It must be lonely for her, cut off like that. I know what it's like.'

This insensitivity, I reflected, was the voice of true innocence, the innocence of the child who sees the world exclusively from its own point of view. There was no way in which I could disabuse her of this innocence, and the assumptions it engendered, although these seemed to be disastrous, as did her happy confidence that I would look after her financial affairs. There was equally no way in which I could delegate this task to someone else. Quite simply, there was no one else. My mother and I had been reduced to players in Jenny's drama, or psychodrama, willing to do her bidding or to fit in with her plans. I have noticed this characteristic before in those whom life has initially deprived of pleasure, either through poverty, or deprivation, or simply through lack of moral dignity. One hesitates to urge on them the same degree of cynicism that one employs on one's own behalf. One is uncomfortably aware of their losses, in painful contrast to what one perceives as one's own gains. Throughout this conversation over Jenny's dinner-table there had not been one enquiry into my own or indeed my mother's health or well-being. I found this disheartening. Jenny, in autobiographical mode, as an entertaining foreigner who had introduced a welcome note of strangeness into our reduced family circle, had been wholly welcome. As a dependent widow, her original neediness brought into new prominence, she would once more be alert to one's own entirely natural indifference. I remembered, with a twinge of discomfort, the time when I had virtually dismissed her from my flat, and hoped that Mother, or rather Aubrey, would have the grace to spare her a second dismissal.

'You know that Mother's selling Cadogan Gate?' I said, in a desire to change the subject, although I did not really want to discuss this, let alone with Jenny. Mother's decision had saddened me, although it was perfectly sensible for her to move into Aubrey's flat on the floor above. Even this they would only use as a *pied-à-terre*, since they spent most of the year in France. Even more uncomfortable, from my point of view, was the fact that Mother intended to settle the money from the sale on me, with Aubrey's total and rather surprising approval. He was a wealthy man, I reasoned, and my mother's needs had always been taken care of, but I did not see what I should do with the considerable sum of money that would accrue to me, apart from setting up a trust fund for Brian's children, which I should have done in any case, though with slightly more modest resources.

'Why not keep the money?' I had said, in the course of one of our weekly telephone calls. 'Buy Aubrey a race horse, or something.'

'It was your home, darling. I remember you going up the road to Hill House when you were a little boy. It's only right that you should have it.'

'I don't know what to say.'

'Then say nothing. It's all decided. Aubrey sends love.'

'Any other news?' I asked hastily, unwilling to let her go.

'Well, yes, I had a letter from Sybil. It seems that Marjorie is on the way out, poor soul. Sybil promised to let me know.' She sighed. 'That means another funeral. It's so hard to think of death here in the sun.' From which I inferred that there would be no visit of condolence, merely an exchange of letters. No blame would attach to this. Sybil, for all her eccentricity, had a tacit understanding of the difficult fact that age dissolves certain friendships, even the curious relationship that had brought our two families together. Both acknowledged that little now remained of that original connection apart from a memory that had softened but also grown tenuous with time. Whereas Jenny, who was now raggedly peeling a tangerine, was watching me avidly to see if my attention were in danger of wandering.

'Of course Alice will be very well off,' she said. 'But then she always was, wasn't she?'

I glanced at my watch, gave an ostentatious start, and said, 'Good heavens! I had no idea . . . You must excuse me, Jenny. I've a briefcase full of papers to be gone through before tomorrow.'

I find that this excuse is usually accepted by women, rather less so by men. In fact I had promised to look in on a woman I had come to know, a rather charming divorcée named Cecily Barclay. We had no designs on each other, but often found it comforting to exchange news at the end of the day, or even simply to watch television. She was an agreeable woman, attractive, quietly spoken, deliberately calm. She worked as a psychotherapist, and although I had no need of her professional skills, it was comforting to know that if needed they could be easily obtained. In fact that day was a long way off: I judged it a point of good manners to keep my sadnesses to myself. Besides, I was not ill, nor was I in a state of conflict; I merely had a memory, even a long memory, and I found its contents so intriguing that I viewed with distaste any invitation to present them for examination. I preferred to view Cecily merely as a companion, even if that meant keeping her at arm's length. I planned to take her down to the cottage at the weekend. She was an excellent walker, and we both needed exercise. My tactic was not unknown to her, but she respected it. As for her, she found it useful to have a man as escort and occasional protector. We both knew that any intensification of our relationship would be fiercely resisted.

'You'll come back, Alan? Or will you want me to come to the office?'

'No, no, that won't be necessary. I'll be in touch. Good-night, Jenny.'

'You've been a good son,' she said, in a new appraising tone. 'Why couldn't I have had a son? Or a daughter?'

That this observation might be painful to me was clearly not to be taken into consideration, nor, I think, was she remotely aware that she was being disobliging. I gave her a rather stiff kiss, and left the flat with relief, my footsteps increasing in impatience as I negotiated the endless corridors, as if trapped in an ante-room to old age, and trapped under false pretences. I was too ruffled to visit Cecily, whom I would telephone in the morning: I wanted no invitation to unburden myself, which would have been natural in the circumstances. I had learned to be patient with these surges of irritation which overcame me from time to time. This was easy enough in the office, where my taciturn manner was taken for granted, infinitely less easy with those who encroached on my attention when my attention was not available. I had my own technique for dealing with this: the closed face, the glance at the watch, the affectation of busyness, and, once free, the long walk. Thus no one was harmed or hurt, or so I assured myself. In fact I myself was hurt that I had contrived to banish comfort from my life, that I could not simply ask for a measure of solicitude. But that would mean exaggerating my condition, which, less than ever now that I was older, was visible to the average indifferent observer. The truth of it was that I was not merely older: I had become set in my ways, the fierce guardian of my own peace of mind, brooking no interference. I wanted no one's help, yet at the same time I was aware that never to ask for help frequently means to forfeit sympathy.

Three weeks later Mother telephoned, ostensibly to tell me that Marjorie had died, but also to report on Jenny's visit, which, I gathered, had been something of a trial. She had arrived for a long stay with a heavy suitcase containing a full trousseau of resort wear, and Mother could only offer the mildest of excuses that the spare room was not available for longer. 'People do love to descend on one for Christmas,' she had said, to which Jenny had sharply observed that she had been told (by me, unfortunately) that Christmas was to be spent in London. 'Boxing Day only,' replied my hapless Mother, though this was the truth. 'We shall give our usual little party, at which of course we shall hope to see you.' This news was taken rather badly. 'Then I shall be on my own at Christmas,' Jenny had said, to which my mother was forced to issue another invitation, this time to visit Cagnes in the spring.

'Quite honestly, Alan, it was very difficult. She was always a chatterbox, but now she's worse. And there seems to be a certain animus behind her chatter that wasn't there before. Am I being uncharitable?'

'No. I've noticed it.'

'I thought the best thing to do was to keep her out of Aubrey's way. That meant we had to go out all the time: shops and cafés, and more cafés, and then more shops. And she's developed a habit of clinging on to my arm, which I'm simply not used to. Of course she's getting old: we both are. It's just unfortunate that I've grown to love my quiet life here with Aubrey. We're very selfish, I know. I used to think that Aubrey was selfish before I knew him better. Now I see the point of a well-ordered life, and if that means a circum-scribed life—and it does—I can't see that as a failing. Old people should learn to keep to themselves.'

'Actually I feel the same way.'

'But you're young, darling.' There was a pause, in which neither of us referred to events in my life. 'We're so looking forward to seeing you. We're driving dear, so there's no need to meet us, although Aubrey appreciated the offer. You'll write to Sybil, won't you?'

In fact my letter to Sybil crossed with one from her, which was surprisingly brave and sensible. She had been with Marjorie when she died, which she said was a great comfort to them both. 'But now I am alone, and you of all people, Alan, will know what that means.' I was touched by that, though by this time I was no more alone than most people. What she meant was that we were both bereaved, but was too dignified to say so. She reverted to her usual style in the following paragraph: Marjorie had been given a humanist funeral but Sybil intended to get in touch with her on the other side, through the agency of a medium with whom they had both been friendly. 'Of course this is forbidden in the Bible, as you know, but I am not of a superstitious turn of mind. My sister and I were very close, closer than I have ever been to my daughter, from whom I have not even had the courtesy of a letter.'

Neither had I, and her memory was beginning to fade. If I imagined her (but this was difficult) I imagined her resentful at my act of appropriation. Perhaps it was Sybil's letter that brought to mind the fact of Sarah's wilfulness, although I had always found her frighteningly self-possessed. Her present silence, now more than several weeks old, signified that she had nothing more to say to me, and although I knew her address from the will, an address which Humphrey had jealously kept to himself, I did not write. What could I say? I could hardly tell her that her inheritance looked more dingy every time I saw it, that the dead bulbs in the chandelier had not been replaced, that Jenny tended to live in her bedroom, perhaps in memory of the way she had lived in the Hôtel de Départ, and that this bedroom now emitted a musty odour which permeated the rest of the flat. I did not tell her this: I could imagine her shrug of contempt, which was very nearly mine. If I visited Jenny it was to prevent her from coming to the office, yet these visits were an ordeal. She had got it into her head that my mother was unhappy with Aubrey, that Aubrey was a monster who had destroyed the friendship she had always had with my mother, and that she owed it to my mother to compensate her for this unfortunate relationship by visiting her as often as possible. Fortunately she was also absent-minded, and was not clever enough to check my excuses, some of them not even excuses, that my mother and Aubrey had friends to stay, or were planning a cruise to the Greek Islands with yet other friends. She would grow sharp-featured on hearing of these alternative attractions to which my mother had succumbed, but then her face would relax into melancholy, as if yet another door were closed to her.

As time went on Jenny began to complain of indigence. As far as I could judge this was not justified, although she had spent freely on new clothes, for which no one could blame her. She had been under the initial impression that her money was inexhaustible, as if it were Danaë's golden shower. That had now come to an end, and she affected extreme poverty, creeping about the flat with her shawl round her shoulders. Her face would brighten when I told her that her funds, supplemented as a matter of course by my own, were sufficient to enable her to live comfortably, and she would respond by planning another trip to my mother. This had now become something of a problem, but one which my mother, out of the goodness of her heart, did not see fit to avoid. Twice a year Jenny would arrive in Cagnes, and spend most of the week or the fortnight unpacking and packing her clothes, only too ready to take offence at Aubrey's restrained welcome. Since these visits taxed my mother inordinately, to say nothing of Aubrey, I took my own holidays not at Cagnes but at Vif, to whose slumbrous peace I returned with something like affection. The place had been good to me, and Monsieur Pach offered me the sort of unsurprised welcome which I found acceptable. These visits soon became habitual, so that my presence there was taken for granted. I did a certain amount of business for clients in Hong Kong, so that visits to the Far East also became habitual. All in all my time was well occupied. I knew a calm in Vif which I did not know anywhere else except at the cottage, and if this calm verged on melancholy, I accepted that as well. As my mother had observed, all those years ago, I had never been afraid of my own company.

It was on my return from one of these visits that Mother telephoned to say that Jenny, who had been staying with them, had suffered a slight stroke. She had recovered well, but they were driving her back to London, where she would presumably stay for the foreseeable future. They hoped I would join them as soon as possible. On the appointed day I picked up my briefcase once again and left for the Edgware Road. There were three people in the flat when I arrived: Mother, Aubrey, and a neighbour, presumably the neighbour who had come to Jenny's assistance on the morning of Humphrey's death. Jenny herself was lying on the sofa with her eyes closed. I have never seen anyone so obstinately waiting to be waited upon. Aubrey took me on one side. 'She's perfectly all right. Ate like a horse on the way over. I don't want your mother involved any further. Leave that, Alice,' he said sharply, as my mother began to gather up teacups. 'Perhaps Mrs . . .' he paused.

'North,' supplied the neighbour. 'Beatrice North.'

'Perhaps Mrs North could suggest some sort of help. On a daily basis, preferably.'

Mrs North looked doubtful. 'I could ask my cleaner to look in,' she said. 'She's usually with me until about twelve.'

'Excellent,' said Aubrey. 'There you are, Jenny,' he added,

bending over the figure on the sofa. 'Mrs North has very kindly arranged for someone to come in every day.'

'I want Alice to stay.'

'I'm afraid that's not possible. We plan to return to France tomorrow.'

A slight shake of the head from my mother told me that this was not quite true. I had to admire Aubrey's sense of command, though my admiration went into sharp decline when he said, 'Alan will look after things. He's not far away. He'll no doubt look in on you from time to time.' To this Jenny made no acknowledgement; in fact her eyes, which had been briefly open, closed again, as if to repudiate the puny help that had been summoned on her behalf.

At the time I was oddly distracted by a curious dream I had had the previous night, or perhaps in the early morning, when I was close to waking. A young man had come to me, pitifully dirty and unkempt, wearing greasy blackened clothes. He explained that he was a student, and that he lived in a tower block which had no bathrooms. This seemed to me perfectly plausible, as was the fact that he required my help. I took him in, removed his clothes, and ordered him to take a bath and wash his hair. Several times, I added. I then cut his long black finger nails. All this was accomplished without a suggestion of sexual excitement or religious fervour. Nor had I any idea what the dream, which was unfinished, signified. I knew no young men, apart from the exceedingly well dressed and excessively self-assured young crook who was currently consulting me about bringing a charge of entrapment against the police. (I turned him down.) I hesitated to read any warning or portent into this dream. Yet when Mother and Aubrey had left, Jenny sprang into something like life, which indicated that she had suffered no permanent damage.

'You won't leave me, will you, Alan? If you do I shall be all alone. What will happen to me?'

Far more alarming than the dream, which in retrospect was alarming enough, was the prospect of having to coax Jenny from her sofa, as I had once tried to coax Angela from her bed. The memory was so overwhelming that I pleaded an urgent appointment, and with a fervent smile asked the neighbour if she would not mind staying, adding that I should be most grateful for her help.

'You'll be back?' she insisted.

'Not before the weekend,' I said firmly.

Let others work this out, I thought. In the hall I heard Mrs North say, 'What a charming man! Is he a relative?'

'In a way,' said Jenny, in her normal voice. 'I have known him all my life.' This was the only indication I received that something irrevocable had happened to her, and that I must prepare myself for mental as well as physical deterioration.

In fact she made good physical progress, and was able to go out each morning, walking with the aid of a stick, yet whenever I called she was lying on the sofa, with the shawl over her legs. She was well cared for, by Mrs North's cleaner, who came every afternoon, and by a nun from the local convent who visited occasionally. Doing God's work, no doubt. My own visits were held against me. Like many lonely people she complained of solitude the minute she had a visitor, pouring her complaint into complaisant but guilty ears. And one was always guilty, if only for not having been present before the complaint had had time to form.

'You're so hard, Alan,' she would say. 'You don't know what it's like.' At this point two tears would form in her eyes. It was true: she was lonely. No one cared for her. And still she longed for company, for closeness. And no one could trick her out of that longing with false words of encouragement.

One evening I found her slightly more animated than usual, with a dangerous febrility that seemed to promise a further stroke. She grasped my arm as I bent to kiss her, her breath, now clean as a child's, in my nostrils.

'I want Sarah,' she said. 'Sarah will look after me. Sarah always loved me.'

This was so complete a misreading of the situation that it seemed to me that there was nothing more to be said.

'I don't know where she is,' I told her.

'You can find her. You're a lawyer.' Her hand tightened on my arm. 'Find Sarah for me.'

When, on future visits, I repeated that I did not know where Sarah was, she did not believe me. Until the Sunday—and it was always a Sunday—when she triumphantly presented me with a piece of paper on which she had copied two addresses, one in Paris, one in Geneva. 'In Humphrey's diary,' she said, and I noticed that she was becoming short of breath. 'Now you can find her for me.'

I left her with the usual kind vague words one uses on such occasions, put the paper in my pocket, and went home. At the kitchen table, with a cup of tea in front of me, I scrutinised the paper, noting the tumble-down nature of Jenny's handwriting. Dropping, as if exhausted, to the lower right-hand corner, a pencil had inscribed Berthe Rigaud's address in the rue de Rennes, and a number in the rue des Bains in Geneva. Out of conscience, or curiosity, I telephoned the rue de Rennes, to be told by a sharp young voice that Monsieur and Madame Rigaud were now living on their property in the Sologne, and that Berthe Rigaud, whom the speaker had known slightly, had married some years earlier. She believed that her married name was Chapuis, but she had lost touch with her, and could not help me any further.

I thanked her, oddly grateful to her for putting Berthe Rigaud out of reach. I got up, made more tea, and sat down again. My discovery of that moment, but in fact fully formed for some time, was that I would make no attempt to find

Sarah, who was now lost to me, and that Jenny, who had come to rely on me to perform this task, might transfer— would transfer—her final disillusionment from Sarah to myself. This seemed to me as much of a solution as I could achieve.

But it has not been easy, to watch the rage, the obstinacy, dissolve into sadness and a kind of trust. These last few bleak winters have been particularly hard. I do not speak of my own boredom and pity, though both are acute. As Jenny grows weaker she believes more and more hopefully in my quest, which I invent for her every Sunday. So far I have told her of my (fictitious) visit to the rue de Rennes, a story which she followed attentively, longing for the next instalment. From her point of view it is the best kind of saga, for there is—there must be—fulfilment at the end of it: the very form dictates it. I am aware of deceit, dissimulation, all kinds of treachery, not only to Jenny but to myself. But I have reached a stage of life which finds me unwilling to compromise my own peace of mind, and the hours I spend in that dark flat, spinning my tale, amount to the lie I am willing to commit in exchange for that elusive peace.

Soon I shall have to start the story again, but it will not greatly matter. I take her hand, and as I start to talk, her faded eyes look into mine for comfort. 'Not long now,' I tell her, and indeed it has often seemed to me that it will not be long. But she is tough: she does not die. I have also told her that I shall be going away shortly, but the news does not alarm her, for she knows that I will be back, if only to finish the story. I leave the flat disheartened by the ease with which I have brought off this trickery, and with the even more disheartening conviction that at the end I too will be told kindly lies by those who know me well enough to spare me the truth.

17

'Are you eating?' asks my mother wistfully on the telephone, although she is now over eighty, and I am in advancing middle age, have indeed advanced beyond it. I accept the fact that we lead separate lives; I also accept the fact that one day, perhaps not too far off, she will leave me, and that I shall then be alone as I have never been before, albeit in a relatively solitary life. Perhaps I am well qualified for solitude. My discipline rarely lets me down, except perhaps when I am on holiday, as I am now, and find the days long. Even their numbing calm is acceptable; it corresponds to something settled in my nature. In any event I know that no further change can be expected. That too I accept.

It is that difficult hour between five and six, when the light begins to alter and presages a long dusky evening. At home I should be bidding the girls in the office good-night and welcoming as familiars the surge of home-going traffic and the lights of the new supermarket in Baker Street. If I am not going out again I pick up something to eat and am in the flat in time to watch the seven o'clock news. I find it convenient to work in the evenings, now that I am so seldom interrupted; the invitations still arrive, but I rarely accept them. I spend week-ends at the cottage, at least when Brian and Felicity are not using it. Sometimes they drive down for the day, with the children, and I particularly look forward to these occasions, since the children are an object of fascination to me, a fascination quite devoid of covetousness or regret. That is one of the blessings of my becalmed state: I no longer have the capacity for desire or envy, and although I know that this condition has not been arrived at without renunciation (I do not say sacrifice), I find it acceptable, strangely so in view of the ambitions I once had for myself, and the confidence I also had that those ambitions could be satisfied.

Acceptance may well be the only reward I have been able to recognise, but also the price I have had to pay. It is just that at this particular hour, in Vif, it seems a little inadequate, a falling short, although I have heard highly successful men (and women) bemoaning their lot, as if success had endowed them with an almost existential anxiety to examine their achievements and to measure the distance to be travelled— still—before they experience that satisfaction that so eludes them. I have no such illusions. I am what I was always programmed to be, a well-regarded man of some substance, with an uninteresting private life. I am aware that this is an almost anomalous position, well below current norms, but perhaps there is still room for dull people such as myself, if only to throw into higher relief the exploits of those whose lives are more vivid than my own. I read about such people in the newspapers every morning. By the time I leave for the office I am more or less convinced that behind Wigmore Street there stretches a hinterland of scandalous happenings, many of which will come in for my professional scrutiny in the course of my working day.

Here in Vif I am allowed to be as dull as I know myself to be. Dullness is appreciated here, and my days have a dullness I am not able to achieve anywhere else. After breakfast I take my long walk, either to Chelles or down into the town. Coffee is taken at the Grand Café de la Place, or, if in Chelles, at a little bar called Le Papillon. I lunch at one of the two open-air restaurants, for it is still mild enough in October to sit outside. Then there is the walk to the station for the English papers, and sometimes a cup of tea at the English Tea Rooms. This takes up most of the late after-noon, so that I arrive back at the hotel with plenty of time to take my bath and change before dinner. Unfortunately, as on this particular evening, there is rather too much time, and the news from England is not sufficiently interesting to claim all my attention. I get up and walk to my window, which overlooks the terrace, and watch the sky darken. There are few people staying here, although the hotel is open all the year round. I dare say some arrive for Christmas, and I learn from Monsieur Pach that it is getting difficult to book a room in the summer months. October usually sends people to the sun before the winter closes in, and I have the hotel more or less to myself. Indeed I am something of a favoured guest, one who will never make inconvenient demands or disrupt the discreet calm of the dining-room. This suits me well enough. It touches me to be received with deference, as I am here, for I feel myself to have a poor record in those matters which usually attract a good opinion. Certainly I am under no illusion that the deference of Monsieur Pach and his staff is anything other than a profes-sional obligation which they honour, perhaps a little more than usual in my case, since I give them so little trouble and return so faithfully every year.

The accident of that woman at the station, the woman whose highly respectable back I contemplated, disturbed me, although I have got into the way of dealing with disturbing reminiscences, and on the whole manage to master them. There was something so familiar about her stance, her movement from one foot to the other, that I very nearly broke my self-imposed rule and tapped her on the shoulder, if only to see her face. I count my inability to do so part of my new wisdom, although that wisdom is frequently indistinguishable from a kind of willed impotence. If it had been Sarah I should not have known what to say. The story I tell to Jenny on my visits to her treat Sarah as the unattainable goal that we nevertheless pursue. It is the essence of the story that one day she will be found, or rather that she will come to us of her own free will. The woman on the platform was too unremarkable to fulfil such a mythic function. Sarah Miller, or Sarah de Leuze, is now a woman with a domestic history and appointments, having dispensed with her undomestic youth as I have with mine. I could no more follow her now than I could shed the years since I last saw her, in my office, as if she were an ordinary client, and I simply her man of business. That woman's highly polished shoes had no connection with my Sarah, who disdained such conventions. In those days I thought of her as mine, though she continually escaped me. There was no way in which I could lay claim to that matron, with her hat and her handbag, not even to tell her that her memory still held some fascination for me, that I returned to it for further information, as if to understand it better, although any fool, myself excepted, could have made sense of it in the days that I so signally wasted.

That is why I never go to Paddington Street these days. I am sure that the flat has long been sold, but the street, for me, still resonates with a kind of desperation, with that everlasting attempt to take possession. Together with this memory there is the memory of Angela running after me, her white blouse glimmering in the light cast by a street lamp. Attention of another kind was being sought, or was it the same? My wife does not haunt me, except as an image: footsteps behind me, windblown hair, confusion. Strangely, I welcome this image, which seems to me now an emblem of our mutual innocence. My regret is that this innocence was so short-lived, that Angela became wise and knowing after her fashion, and that her knowledge darkened her features and clouded her fragile prettiness. She would not have aged well. I have done rather better, if only because I am more adept at concealment.

Sometimes I measure the time left to me and wonder how I shall fill it. It may of course surprise me by being dramatically circumscribed—by illness, by disability, by accident, by default. I suppose I shall continue as I have begun, for I see no prospect of change. These days in Vif are consoling, inasmuch as they are the outward symbol of contented mediocrity, whereas if I were to return to Paris I should re-awaken every sort of desire, largely for my youth, when desire could be so easily satisfied and so easily renewed. Yet even youth can be overshadowed or compromised. My father, whom I knew so little, had a younger sister to whom he was devoted, and whose early death was surrounded by mystery. What was the cause? A fever disregarded, an illness mismanaged by the family doctor, whose reputation never fully recovered? In any event there had to be a post mortem, something quite shocking in my father's respectable family, and references to 'poor Prue' were always accompanied by pursed lips and sighs of regret. One grows up with such mysteries, and respects them, although a voice in one's head longs for a simple explanation. As one grows older it becomes clear that there are fewer and fewer simple explanations; that is why family piety, which keeps the mysteries intact, is of such value to all who continue to venerate such phenomena. Their transformation into myth is also of some value. To this day I have failed to discover the reason for poor Prue's death. Even my mother's voice is lowered when I question her about it. For Prue is unfinished business, like most of the more disturbing events of our lives. That is how they retain their power, since no conclusion can be drawn. I understand this now that the events of my life come under this heading. If I can take any credit in the matter of my own affairs it is that so far I have managed to look facts in the face. So far, that is, although sometimes I experience a kind of failure of nerve, a weakness which I have done my best to resist.

Occasionally there is a spectacular sunset here, and everyone assembles on the terrace, maids included, to view the sight. There are few distractions in Vif, and this one satisfies a fleeting sense of occasion, noticeable even in those who do not appreciate change. But more often than not the sky is overcast and darkens imperceptibly. For that reason it is as well to be indoors, for there is a melancholy even in this healthy place, even in this hotel. It occurs to me to wonder what I am doing here, out of season, when I could be at home, perhaps sitting in Cecily Barclay's flat sipping a whisky and trying not to pay attention to what she is saying. Her language partakes of that vaguely aspirational order which I take to be common to her profession in these days of raised consciousness and attainable self-esteem. I am too fond of her, and much too lazy, to argue. She believes in easy, or at least reachable, solutions. That is what separates us, a fact that affects her more than it does me. She believes that therapy is the answer to the sort of stalemate at which we have arrived, and I dare not tell her that this stalemate suits me well enough, for I intend to proceed no further. We satisfy each other in a well-meaning sort of way, and we are both too aware that this is something fragile, not to be examined too closely. That is why Cecily is always on the brink of suggesting therapy, and never quite doing anything about it. She knows that we will never marry, but finds it impossible not to believe in happy endings. So one's archaic nature has the last laugh.

In a couple of days I shall return to London. I shall go back to that chaotic flat in the Edgware Road, take Jenny's hand, and tell her that I am now definitely on Sarah's trail, that in fact I caught a glimpse of her, waiting for a train, but as it was getting dark I did not have time to see her face before the train drew in. All I have to do, I shall tell her, is to retrace my steps and repeat the sequence of that particular day's events. Maybe I shall even believe this. Maybe I shall return specifically for this purpose. And when I see Jenny's eyes close and am able to tiptoe to the door I shall tell myself that this particular quest has had some validity even for me, that the transformation of an unremarkable affair into a sort of pilgrimage has a certain nobility which pleases me. It was, after all, so banal, so commonplace. But in that mysterious half-light, with the sound of the approaching train, it did seem possible once again to believe in its force. That is why there will be genuine fervour in my voice when I recount this particular episode, for what Jenny will not know is that for an instant I believed that everything might be restored, that the apotheosis might be waiting for me in some real or imagined twilight, at the end of an ordinary day, and that the rush of the oncoming train will signify not the conclusion of the story but its true beginning.

About the Author

ANITA BROOKNER is the author of sixteen novels, including *Incidents in the Rue Laugier*, *Fraud*, *Dolly*, and *Providence*. She won the Booker Prize for *Hotel du Lac*. An international authority on eighteenth-century painting, she became the first female Slade Professor at Cambridge University. She lives in London.

About the Type

The text of this book was set in Janson, a misnamed type-
face designed in about 1690 by Nicholas Kis, a Hungarian
in Amsterdam. In 1919 the matrices became the property of
the Stempel Foundry in Frankfurt. It is an old-style book
face of excellent clarity and sharpness. Janson serifs are con-
cave and splayed; the contrast between thick and thin
strokes is marked.